GABRIEL PRAED'S CASTLE

BY
ALICE JONES

INTRODUCTION BY
MORA DIANNE O'NEILL

Formac Publishing Company Limited
Halifax

Formac Publishing Company Limited acknowledges the support of the
Culture Division, Nova Scotia Department of Tourism, Culture and
Heritage. We acknowledge the financial support of the Government of
Canada through the Book Publishing Industry Development Program
(BPIDP) for our publishing activities.

We acknowledge the support of the Canada Council for the Arts for our
publishing program.

NOVA SCOTIA
Tourism, Culture and Heritage

The Canada Council | Le Conseil des Arts
for the Arts | du Canada

Library and Archives Canada Cataloguing in Publication

Jones, Alice, 1853-1933
    Gabriel Praed's Castle / by Alice Jones ; introduction by Mora
Dianne O'Neill.

(Formac fiction treasures)
Originally publ.: Boston : H.B. Turner, 1904.
ISBN 978-0-88780-843-2

    I. Title. II. Series: Formac fiction treasures

PS8519.O523G32 2009   C813'.52   C2009-902366-0

Series editor: Gwendolyn Davies

Formac Publishing Company Limited
5502 Atlantic Street
Halifax, Nova Scotia B3H 1G4
www.formac.ca

Printed and bound in Canada

Author photo from Nova Scotia Archives & Records Management,
Notham #50147. Cover painting by Margaret Campbell Macpherson,
Study of Mrs. Cluny Macpherson, Paris, May 1915, private collection.

Presenting Formac Fiction Treasures
Series Editor: Gwendolyn Davies

A taste for reading popular fiction expanded in the nineteenth century with the mass marketing of books and magazines. People read rousing adventure stories aloud at night around the fireside; they bought entertaining romances to read while travelling on trains and curled up with the latest serial novel in their leisure moments. Novelists were important cultural figures, with devotees who eagerly awaited their next work.

Among the many successful popular English language novelists of the late 19th and early 20th centuries were a group of Maritimers who found, in their own education, travel and sense of history, events and characters capable of entertaining readers on both sides of the Atlantic. They emerged from well-established communities that valued education and culture, for women as well as men. Faced with limited publishing opportunities in the Maritimes, successful writers sought magazine and book publishers in the major cultural centres: New York, Boston, Philadelphia, London and sometimes Montreal and Toronto. They often enjoyed much success with readers at home, but the best of these writers found large audiences across Canada and in the United States and Great Britain.

The Formac Fiction Treasures series is aimed at offering contemporary readers access to books that were successful, often huge bestsellers in their time, but which are now little known and often hard to find. The authors and titles selected are chosen first of all as enjoyable to read, and secondly for the light they shine on historical events and on attitudes and views of the culture from which they emerged. These complete original texts reflect values that are sometimes in conflict with those of today: for example, racism is often evident, and bluntly expressed. This collection of novels is offered as a step towards rediscovering a surprisingly diverse and not nearly well enough known popular cultural heritage of the Maritime provinces and of Canada.

Alice Jones

INTRODUCTION

A lice Jones (1853–1933) grew up in Halifax, Nova Scotia, at a time when it enjoyed an established reputation as a military, naval and mercantile centre. Solid fortunes had been made in the import/export trade, and, although the old wooden buildings of the downtown core often seemed weather-worn to international visitors, its prosperous middle class enjoyed living standards comparable with those in any part of the British Empire. The oldest of six surviving children, Alice Jones grew up in "Bloomingdale," a comfortable family estate overlooking the Northwest Arm (the house is now the Waegwoltic Club). Next door in "Bircham" were her cousins, Helen and Susan Morrow, approximately the same age as Alice and her sister, Frances, and the four were to share lifetime interests in art, travel and writing (as well, Susan Morrow was to marry Alice's brother, Dr. Guy Carleton Jones). The successful business and political career of Alice Jones' father, Alfred Gilpin Jones, led to his being appointed Lieutenant Governor between 1900 and 1906, during which period Alice acted as his unofficial chatelaine in Government House. Her mother, Margaret Wiseman Stairs, also came from a prominent Nova Scotian business family and had studied art before her marriage; but it was Alice's sister, Frances Jones, who became a widely respected artist, the first female Associate of the Royal Canadian Academy, the first Canadian to adopt some Impressionist practices and the first artist to exhibit a painting with a

Canadian subject at the Paris Salon.

Although deeply attached to their Nova Scotian heritage, Alice and Frances Jones very early in their lives enjoyed the advantages of international travel and education. During the 1870s and 1880s, Alice and Frances toured widely in Europe, finding subjects for Frances' art and Alice's pen. From 1888 to 1895, Alice contributed travel sketches to the Toronto periodicals, *The Dominion Illustrated Monthly* and *The Week,* producing, in the words of Canadian literary critic Eva-Marie Kroller in *Canadian Travellers in Europe: 1851–1900,* "among the finest in Canadian travel writing." Alice Jones' first novel, *The Night Hawk,* published in New York and London in 1901 under the pseudonym "Alix John" (reprinted Formac, 2001), drew upon her romanticized knowledge of Halifax history during the American Civil War. In her second, *Bubbles We Buy* (Boston and London, 1903; Formac, 2002, as *A Privateer's Fortune),* she expanded her geographical horizons, integrating a gothic story of Nova Scotian treasure with a romance ranging from Paris to London. After the publication of her third novel, *Gabriel Praed's Castle* (Boston and London, 1904), Alice Jones was placed "in the front rank of our Canadian writers" by L.E. Horning in *Acta Victoriana,* and was considered "close to being the leading woman novelist of Canada" by the *Canadian Magazine.* After reviewing *Gabriel Praed's Castle* for *Acta Victoriana* in December 1904, Horning noted simply: "She is one of our best."[1]

An admirer of William Dean Howells' American realism, but at home with literary tastes on both sides of the Atlantic, Jones and her world would have appeared exotic to many of her readers. The Paris Salon had figured prominently in the plot of her previous novel, *Bubbles We Buy;* Jones now found the setting for *Gabriel Praed's Castle* in the artistic milieu of Paris and in the artists' colony of Pont-Aven in Brittany. That world had been her home during the late 1870s and 1880s when she and Frances had gone as students to the City of Light (Paris), Frances to study art and Alice the French language. In this third novel, Jones now drew on her close and sympathetic observation of people and events during those years to create vivid backdrops for the interplay of her Canadian protagonists with the people they meet in France. Actual people, places and events she had encountered during almost three decades in France became the grist for her literary mill and emerge as composite images throughout *Gabriel Praed's Castle* to produce a story whose details are "real," though not replicable.

The novel begins in the studio of American artist Andrew Garvie on the rue-d'Assas overlooking the Jardin du Luxembourg, and opposite the Sorbonne on the far side of the garden. Because she knew both Paris and Finistère intimately, Jones eschews the long passages of detailed description that lesser writers used for "international novels" and employs a few impressionistic strokes to convey all that is needed to install her characters and each situation in her readers' perception. Almost immediately in *Gabriel Praed's Castle*, attention focuses on Garvie's unfinished portrait of Lucrezia Borgia, "that moyen age empress of sin ... her tawny eyes staring out with a cruel, smiling persistence, a manifestation of magnificent evil." Jones may have drawn on a memory of Dante Gabriel Rossetti's portrait of *Lucrezia*, shown in the Royal Academy exhibition in 1883, when creating this image, or on Sarah Bernhardt's performance on stage as Theodora in 1884. That performance would have attracted the Jones sisters since Bernhardt maintained a studio in the same building as Frances' teacher, Auguste Ferrin-Perron. The sultry beauty of either persona contrasts sharply with the sexual repression demanded by the cultural mores of the period. Without explicit references that would distress her general readership,

Jones reveals lust as a driving motive in her subtle descriptions in the novel of the relationship between Madame Marcelle, the *modiste*, and Britski, the art dealer. Sexuality also underlies Britski's conniving effort to control Sylvia Dorr, the hyperkinetic responses of Gabriel Praed to his "Mam'selle," and the angst suffered by Julia and Garvie during their falling-out. However, the women in Jones' novel do not define themselves solely in relation to the male characters, but carve out their own position in society. Although she may have reached into memory to frame most of her characters, Jones conceived her female protagonists, Julia and Sylvia, in her own fertile brain and allowed them to develop throughout the novel. She is conscious of the psychological conflicts that motivate her characters, attuned to the different manners or grades of sophistication that distinguish them, and treats the social inequities that limit their actions with complexity and irony.

On arriving in Paris, the Jones sisters may have resided on the Left Bank in proximity to language teachers based near the university. Frances, certainly, had considered the studio of Jean-Jacques Henner on the Quai Voltaire as a possible school.[2] Regardless, they would have acquired a familiarity with the Luxembourg Garden and the Latin Quarter during their years in Paris. In the first chapter of *Gabriel Praed's Castle*, Jones provides an immersion course for her readers and pens revealing sketches of most of her major characters — Garvie, whose conventional well-born stature masks an inner intensity; Thorpe, whose sensitivity has been mysteriously overlaid with moodiness; Julia Praed, whose Canadian vitality clashes with the posh Paris gowns she has acquired; Julia's father, Gabriel, whose "western backwoods air" belies his considerable mining wealth; and Sylvia Dorr, the struggling "little Boston girl" whose pride has not succumbed to her present poverty. As well, the reader meets the "middle-aged and cynical" David Frye, whose gossip serves to advance the plot when necessary; Mrs Mallock, another expatriate American, whose habitual prey is rich but unsophisticated travellers; and Virginie LaPierre, the artist's model, whose smouldering presence animates the still unfinished painting of Lucrezia on Garvie's easel. For the next three chapters Jones leaves the homogeneous domain of art students in the 6th district or *arrondissement* of Paris and moves across the Seine to the complex world around the American Embassy in the 8th *arrondissement*, where fashionable streets housing travelling millionaires, foreign aristocrats and elegant boutiques hide the newspaper correspondents, artisans and "shabby old women" dependent on their activity, tucked into its dingy attics. With Harriet Oakes, the hard-featured but kind-hearted newspaper woman; Madame Marcelle, the self-made *couturière* with an elegant establishment at the corner of the Boulevards Malherbes and Haussmann; and Monsieur Britski, the unctuous Hungarian dealer in pictures and bric-a-brac, the reader has met the remaining characters whose machinations and interventions will attend the innocent Canadian visitors in their passage from the jaded streets of Paris to the "primrose path of joy" in Brittany. (For Jones, the primroses of Brittany became a personal talisman for renewal. Confined to Government House in Halifax during the winter of 1902–1903, she noted in her diary: "Since New Year we have lived in this grim white world, a world of nature's negation. Can there now be primroses growing in the Breton fields ... shall we ever again see grass sprouting green, and feel the south wind like a benediction?")[3]

Two stereotypes about the artist's life in Paris dominated popular attitudes by the turn of the last century — the penniless bohemian and the self-confident *flâneur*. The *flâneur*, originally described by French poet Charles Baudelaire, was the perfectly turned-out "gentleman stroller of the city streets," the man-about-town who was an impartial observer of contemporary urban life. Jones blends these formulae to produce both Thorpe, the careless Bohemian who nevertheless "can *flaner* most delightfully" in the cafés of the Latin Quarter, and Garvie, "tall, a bit stiff of bearing, with pointed light brown beard, his careful dress telling of a planned afternoon on the other side of the river." Following the example of artists Jean-Léon-Gérôme and Benjamin-Constant, many artists submitted Oriental subjects, such as the Empress Theodora, to the Salons; but Jones may have used the American orientalist Frederick Arthur Bridgman as a model for Garvie, and another expatriate American, Bridgman's friend, the genre painter Charles Sprague Pearce, for David Frye. Like Frances Jones, Bridgman had found a studio in Pont-Aven (Brittany) in the old Manoir de Lezaven in 1883. Thorpe may be modelled on the young artist Dennis Bunker, noted for his mastery of Corot's techniques, who was also in Brittany at that time, before resuming his career in Boston. And Howe, his studiomate, may well be based on the Philadelphian native Clifford Prevost Grayson, whose marine paintings often featured anguished women or children awaiting the return of their fisherfolk. At this time, Pont-Aven played host to 60 or 70 artists for several months each year. Therefore, many others, alone or in combination, could have supplied Alice Jones with original inspiration for the community of artists she describes in *Gabriel Praed's Castle.*

Certainly, Jones has drawn on composite memories to describe the little village in Brittany which she names Tremalo, but which can be no place but "*Pont-Aven, ville de renom, quatorze moulins et quinze maisons.*" In choosing a surrogate name for the village, Jones followed the lead of Blanche Willis Howard, whose 1884 novel, *Guenn: A Wave on the Breton*

Coast, disguised the artists' colony of Concarneau as "Plouvenec." The "triangular Place" in *Gabriel Praed's Castle*, with the highway running along one side down to the old, grey bridge and the "square, white Lion D'Or" on the second, remain features of Pont-Aven today (although the *Hotel du Lion d'Or*, later the Hotel Gloanec, is now *Les Ajoncs d'Or*). On the third side of the triangle sat the *Hotel des Voyageurs*, which later became the *Hotel Julia*, and at the bottom, just before the bridge, nestled the *Pension Gloanec* (*Gloannic* in the novel). Over the years, artists filled the wall panels in the dining rooms of both the *Voyageurs* and the *Gloanec* with paintings (often given in lieu of rent). Marie-Jeanne Gloanec was mistress of the *Pension* near the bridge, Julia Guillou of the *Voyageurs,* and the demoiselles Lintilhac governed the *Lion d'Or.* Alice Jones merges the three establishments in the novel, since the description of the aubergiste, in "the plain black cashmere dress and little white net cap, a costume marking a social grade higher than the peasant woman, and yet not that of the lady," suits Madame Julia at the *Voyageurs*, but is named Marie-Jeanne, and is in charge of the *Lion d'Or.*

On Garvie's arrival in Tremalo, he learns from Marie-Jeanne that a stranger staying at her inn has rented a car in the Breton city of Lorient and often visits the chateau at Rosbraz, the former home of a noble family, the Rostrênans. Here again, Jones drew on a medley of memories. The village of Pont-Aven sits at the site of the first bridge over the Aven, seven kilometres from its mouth on the Bay of Biscay. Near Rosbraz, the harbour that serves Pont Aven, can be found its 14th mill, Le Moulin du Grand Poulguin, sold out of the family by the Marquise des Nétumières in 1883. The Château de Poulguin, an old ruin recommended to travellers in the 1880s for its beautiful mantelpiece in the habitable part, was accessible by ferry from the harbour. The Seigneurie de Rostrenen, in fact, lay in the next *département*. While in Britanny, the Jones sisters may have been among the many visitors who were attracted to the popular *pardon* of Notre Dame de Rostrenen held in August each year (the Breton *pardon* consisted of a religious procession of the villagers dressed in their finest costumes, followed by feasting, dancing and athletic games). Jones has Julia and Garvie visit the actual ruins of Rustefan at Pont-Aven, but she may have had the familiar Manoir de Rozaven in mind when she envisaged a château for her Rostrênans at Rosbraz. Moreover, the mansion in Montreal for which Gabriel Praed needs to purchase Gothic furnishings in Britanny may well have been inspired by "Ardvarna," a house built between 1894 and 1897 for Brenda Meredith, the daughter of shipping magnate Andrew Allan; Jones no doubt visited this house since her father's company was the agent for the Allan Line in Halifax.

Jones's story also reflects the level of anti-Semitism and xenophobia found in rural areas of France, such as Brittany and the Vosges, throughout the late Victorian period. The Jones sisters may well have been conscious of such developing anti-Semitism during their Breton years through their friendship with Henry Rosenberg, who later served as principal of the Victoria School of Art and Design in Halifax. No doubt an informal cohort of the artistic community in Pont-Aven had shielded artists such as Rosenberg and Henry Mosler from the prejudice of the locale populace (Mosler's 1879 painting *Le Retour*, which presented the return of the prodigal son in Breton garb, was the first painting by an American acquired by the French government). After 1889, anti-Semitism in France erupted in the aftermath of the Panama Canal Company Scandal, and, as noted by Hannah Arendt in *The Origins of Totalitarianism,* indirectly paved the road to the Dreyfus Affair of 1894, when a French military officer of

Jewish descent was wrongly convicted of treason. Overall, 800,000 investors lost one billion francs in the financial collapse surrounding the Panama Canal Company, and in the novel this bankruptcy allegedly cost the Rostrênan family its fortune.

The year 1889 witnessed another scandal in Paris, albeit on a much smaller scale. In his *Journal* for March of that year, French literary and art critic Edmond de Goncourt recorded the gossip surrounding the art dealer Étienne Boussod's efforts to sell an unsigned landscape, allegedly by famed artist Jean-François Millet, to a wealthy American for 35,000 thousand francs. When neither Millet's son nor widow recognized the painting, the art-dealer offered the widow 4,000 francs for a selection of the artist's drawings and requested a letter authenticating the painting. A few days later, however, before the painting was sold, the elderly Charles Chaplin (one of American artist Mary Cassatt's teachers) came into the shop and recognized the painting: *"Mais voila un signature qu'il faut effacer. Car ce Millet est de moi!"* ("But there is a signature which must be removed, for this Millet is by me.") Jones undoubtedly had this incident in mind when she developed her sub-plot around Britski's scheme to sell Thorpe's landscapes as the work of well-known landscape artist Camille Corot. The American presence in Paris was considerable and exhibited an insatiable appetite for art. By the 1890s, counts of the unofficial "American Colony" — the artists and the massive influx of tourists — sometimes surpassed 100,000 during the high season. Both Corot and Millet, artists greatly admired in North America, had died in 1875, leading to a posthumous proliferation of work alleged to be theirs. In 1953, *ARTnews* observed that there was a "saying in France that Corot painted 2,000 canvases, 5,000 of which are in America."[4] As fluent French-speakers, Jones and her sister would have followed all the art gossip and known of other unscrupulous schemes to rook uninformed visitors in Paris. *Gabriel Praed's Castle* reflects this kind of insider knowledge.

While Jones appears to have drawn on her experiences during the 1880s as part of the background for *Gabriel Praed's Castle*, she also carried the novel into the twentieth century. When Julia takes her father sight-seeing in Paris, she insists that they forgo the carriage and ride in "one of those nice little yellow cabs with the fat drivers in shiny hats." Paris had been served by gasoline-powered taxicabs since 1899 and Jones' observation of the colour repudiates the myth that Harry N. Allen of New York had been the first to paint taxis yellow. By 1900, Peugeot was producing 500 vehicles annually, but in Brittany they would still have been sufficiently rare to arouse suspicion in Marie-Jeanne. However, to further root her story in the present, Jones has Britski refer to the expulsion of the Sisters from Breton schools as one of the reasons that his "Rostrênans" needed to dispose of their property in secret. To counter royalist and separatist leanings in Brittany and enforce the suppression of the Breton language, the French government had promulgated a law in 1901 that allowed the Minister of Education to close convent schools. Although she was acting as her father's chatelaine at Government House when she was completing the novel, Jones was clearly maintaining her interest in contemporary Brittany as she worked on it. Indeed, in her diary for 3 January 1903, she noted a conversation that she had in Halifax with a young subaltern who had been raised in France: "It was nice to yarn about the peasants and their ways and to hear about the troubles over turning out the nuns. He thinks that there is a revolution in the near distance." But there is no revolution on the horizon in the novel — just "a Breton autumn, when the bracken and the chestnut leaves are golden bronze and the heather is abloom."

Although not writing a "New Woman" novel, Jones admired the independence exemplified by the "New Woman." In *Gabriel Praed's Castle*, Julia resists the blandishments of the morally suspect Mrs. Mallock and finds in Sylvia the guide she seeks: "Was it possible for her to make herself a woman like Sylvia Dorr? A woman who understood about all these wonderful things, which she was just beginning to know were in the world." Under Sylvia's gentle and upright mentorship, Julia loses her gaucheries while retaining her vitality and forgoes conspicuous display in favour of simple elegance. Sylvia herself draws strength from the journalist Harriet Oakes, whose experience of the world precluded being fooled by it. Kit Coleman (Canada) and Nellie Bly (America) may have been obvious journalistic models for the Oakes character, but when Harriet comments after her expedition to the Villa Mariposa with Sylvia — "How I wish I could write a novel. I see so many strange things.... I think I shall try some day." — she is perhaps speaking in the voice of Jones herself. As a woman of the world, Jones knew that the sinful rarely suffered damnation in this life, so, in her novel, the avaricious Mrs. Mallock, exposed but unrepentant, slinks off to London in search of more malleable prey. To Madame Marcelle, on the other hand, whose part in the scheme was motivated by desperate love, Jones grants a prosperous refuge in a South American city. Virginie, Garvie's gypsy model, may be rejected as a failed human being by other characters in the novel, but, from the beginning, Jones the author makes us aware of the societal prejudices that have motivated the model's actions. "The artists don't use me for saints," Virginie says defiantly in Garvie's studio; "I suppose they think Lucrezia Borgia and her kind suit me better. She, it seems, was a lady without prejudices." In the château, before Virginie leaps over the wall, she responds angrily to the artists' claim that she had been always treated fairly: "Was there ever a scoff or *blague* that you failed to sharpen on me?" So, Virginie exits from the novel as a continuing mystery. Gabriel Praed's *naïveté* may have verged on caricature earlier in the story, but in the climax, when he rejects the vengeance demanded by melodrama and the other characters, the Canadian backwoodsman achieves true nobility: "I understand, fast enough. It's none of your business. The stuff's mine, and I paid for it. *Let her go!*"

In their introduction to *New Women: Short Stories by Canadian Women: 1900–1920,* Sandra Campbell and Lorraine McMullen observe that many of the stories by Canadian women writers between 1900 and 1920 "are conventional, uninspired exercises in the popular modes of the era: historical romance or local colour, 'society' love stories, or moralistic melodramas rife with penniless waifs, unexpected bequests, and surprise endings (especially on Christmas Eve)."[5] A surface reading of *Gabriel Praed's Castle* could see it slotted into any of these categories, for the novel is a story of love and money set in the France of an earlier generation, with Gabriel Praed's dialect and the Breton peasants for local colour, Britski as the evil villain, and Rupert and Sylvia as the penniless waifs who benefit from unexpected good fortune. On one level, then, Jones produced a plot that satisfied the popular market, including the American one. The novel received an enthusiastic review from the *New York Times* in October 1904, and by December it had gone into a second printing. But, as a cosmopolitan and progressive citizen of a wider world, Jones had also included in her novel indications of deeper concerns. She lifted it out of a formulaic realm through her exploration of female mentorship, her cognizance of the manners and prejudices of her own social class, and her subtle presentation of the sexual and psychological forces driving her characters. As it had been for Henry James in *The American* (1877), Jones' ostensible theme was the collision between North American innocence and European corruption. But like James in *The Ambassadors* of 1903, she could admire European experience even as she recognized the corruption. At the end of the novel, Sylvia and Thorpe retreat from that corruption to the safety of Boston, but Julia and Garvie have acquired the aesthetic and moral judgment to occupy the dual worlds of Europe and North America — as Alice Jones herself had done. In 1907, three years after the publication of *Gabriel Praed's Castle,* Jones moved to Menton in the French *département* of Alpes-Maritime, near the Italian border, close to her sister Frances in Alassio — and away from winters in Halifax that had made her dream longingly of primroses in Breton fields.

Mora Dianne O'Neill

ENDNOTES

1. For further discussion of the works of Alice Jones, see: Gwendolyn Davies, "Alice C. Jones" in W.H. New, ed., *Dictionary of Literary Biography: Canadian Writers: 1890-1920,* Vol. 92 (Detroit: Gale Research Inc., 1990), 165–8, and Gwendolyn Davies, "Art, Fiction, and Adventure: The Jones Sisters of Halifax," *Journal of the Royal Nova Scotia Historical Society* 5 (2002): 1–22.

2. Frances Jones' letter in Isabelle de Lannoy, *Jean-Jacques Henner, 1829–1905,* thèse de l'École du Louvre, Paris, 1986, cited in Denise Noël, *Les Femmes peintres au Salon, Paris, 1863–1889,* thèse de l'Université de Paris, 1997. For a discussion of the career of Frances Jones Bannerman, see: Mora Dianne O'Neill, *Two Artists Time Forgot* (Halifax: The Art Gallery of Nova Scotia, 2006).

3. Alice Jones' Government House diary is located at Nova Scotia Archives & Records Management, MG 1, Vol. 524–525.

4. Milton Esterow, "The Ten Most Faked Artists," *ARTnews* 104, 6 (June 2005).

5. Sandra Campbell & Lorraine McMullen, eds., *New Women: Short Stories by Canadian Women, 1900-1920,* (Ottawa: University of Ottawa Press, 1997), 2.

I

STUDIO TALK

THREE men sat smoking their after luncheon cigarettes in Andrew Garvie's big studio in the Rue d'Assas, overlooking the green stretch of tree tops in the Luxembourg garden.

While well furnished, as suited the abode of the rich Michigan lumberman's son and the successful artist, it was lacking in the frippery of bric-a-brac with which many younger men surround themselves.

For Andrew Garvie had been working nearly ten years in Paris, strenuous years of toil that had brought him recognition from his peers and from those to whom he looked as his masters.

He had already had a mention at the Salon, and this year the betting was strong in the studios and cafés of the Quarter that his *Theodora* would win him a second medal at the coming Salon.

Some people called him a neutral-tinted man, but they were those who failed to understand how much of the more intense side of his nature went into his painting, leaving a surface that seemed to belong to the mere society man such people thought him.

The other two smokers were David Frye, middle-aged and cynical, who made a settled income out of neat pictures of peasant family life, and Rupert Thorpe, the latent power in whose clear-cut, sensitive face was veiled by a moodiness which did not seem natural to it but which was somehow in keeping with the carelessness of his dress.

On an easel stood an unfinished picture representing the half length of a ruddy-haired woman in medieval attire, holding a jewelled cup, her tawny eyes staring out with a cruel, smiling persistence, a manifestation of magnificent evil.

"It's for that Bond-street show," Garvie said, as though the picture had already been under discussion.

"She'll make the beef-fed islanders sit up," said Thorpe enthusiastically. "Jove, to have seen and known that moyen age empress of sin, the imperial Lucrezia, might almost have been worth being poisoned by her. And how curiously characteristic you've got it of Virginie. There's the sleeping tigress all right."

"Yes, Virginie is distinctly feline. But she's the best of models," Garvie agreed. "I could hardly do without her." .

"Don't let her know it then," Frye put in oracularly.

"Heard anything from the Salon yet, Frye? You're high up on the list," Thorpe asked. The question seemed casual but the other two were conscious of the underlying nervousness. The carelessness of Frye's answer was genuine.

"No. Boutillier only got his acceptance yesterday, so they won't come to the Fs for a day or so. But it's best not to worry about it. If one is hung with a number, it's fate; if one is kicked out, it's equally so. In either case, we live through it."

"Yes, it's wonderful the lot of killing we do take. Cats are nothing to it," Thorpe scoffed bitterly. Then, with a determined effort to drop the too-important subject, "What a swell you were yesterday, Garvie, when I saw you driving with that black-haired, gorgeously attired girl. It was only the western backwoods air of the old gentleman that gave me courage to raise my hat. Who are they?"

Garvie laughed. "Yes, the girl would be splendid but for that same gorgeousness of attire. Perhaps her tastes may tone down. They are western, all right, but the Canadian forests have the credit of her superb vitality and his broad shoulders. The father is Gabriel Praed, a mining Crœsus from British Columbia; and the joke is that he has regularly adopted me."

"To him that hath shall be given," quoted Thorpe. "But why the honour?"

"It seems he went, when a mere lad, from the Ontario backwoods to one of my father's lumber-camps in Michigan. He got on well, married a French girl, who died young, leaving Mademoiselle that legacy of black hair and grey eyes. Her death made him restless, and, giving up his job as foreman, he went off to British Columbia where he got interested in mines. Everything prospered with him, but it is only within the last few years that he has blossomed into a million-aire. Now he has left his sons in charge and come abroad to see the world. The father is as simple socially as I suppose he is shrewd financially."

"Not an uncommon combination," put in Frye.

"And he seems to feel that for the sake of 'old man Garvie' as he calls him, we're bound to be friends. It's rather a nuisance, though I like the old fellow, too."

"And the daughter?"

"Well, she is a bit crude and emphatic, some-thing like her costumes. And yet there is an ap-pealing touch about her, an occasional wistful way, as though she understood they weren't quite up to the social mark, and were feeling astray."

"A dangerous pose," Frye commented.

"You old cynic! I've half a mind to introduce you to her. But, seriously, I feel bound to keep a friendly eye on them. There's a Mrs. Mallock who has fastened on to them whom I don't much fancy. I've heard of her before as exploiting newcomers."

"A picker up of crumbs from rich men's tables?" Frye asked. "Well, I suppose Crœsus can spare the crumbs."

Garvie had an emphatic air of disagreeing with

him as he said: "It's all right if it's only a few crumbs, but there's been a lot of harm done by that kind of people. They settle themselves in some boarding-house where they lie in wait for the richest, most unsophisticated travellers, onto whom they fasten. I have heard of more than one wretched foreign marriage into which they have drawn American girls."

Thorpe laughed as he unfolded his lazy length and rose. "Well, it's up to you to stop her little game," he said. "I must get back to my studio now."

Garvie was watching him keenly. "Look here," he said, "You know I'm going to take a run down to the old quarters in Brittany as soon as that thing is done," nodding towards the Lucrezia. "Why don't you come with me? You're not looking very fit."

Something in the kindness of the words brought a tremor of suppressed feeling over Thorpe's face, then, in an almost brusque tone, he said: "Thank you, I wish I could, but I've got to keep at work. It's good in you though. Ta-ta."

"What's the matter with that boy?" Frye asked, after they had smoked for a bit in silence.

"Don't know. Wish I did."

"He used to be the most sociable youngster in the Quarter, and now he'll hardly speak to a soul."

"I suppose waiting for the Salon news has got

on his nerves. He was hardly used last year, you know," Garvie hazarded.

Frye shook his head. "It's more than that. He must have managed to get into some real scrape to be so altered," he said.

"What do you think it is?"

"The old disturbing force—women. Perhaps some model has got hold of him."

Garvie laughed shortly. "Those eternal bugaboos of yours, you old woman hater. But I fancy he is under the rule of Miss Dorr—that dainty little Boston girl who designs fine clothes for Vanity Fair. You know her?"

"I've met her sometimes. She works hard, doesn't she?"

"Yes, and I remember in my Harvard days going to a dance at her home, when she was like a little queen to me. I got her to design my Theodora dress, but she is proud, and on the alert not to be helped."

"And Thorpe is a friend of hers?"

"He was, though his gloom may mean some break between them. Anyway, I shall keep a lookout for a chance to help him. He's got too good stuff in him to be let go under, as you and I have seen so many do since we've been here in the Quarter."

"It's Kismet, I suppose," Frye said, rising. "Well, I must be off."

Opening the door, he revealed a girl standing outside as though about to knock.

"Jove! Here's Virginie looking more delightfully medieval than ever. Which saint have you been posing for today, cherie?"

The girl stood facing him with a defiant air. Her thin figure was clad in dark green, and her pale face was framed in loose masses of red hair.

"None, as it happens," she answered without a smile. "The artists don't use me for saints, you see. I suppose they think Lucrezia Borgia and her kind suit me better. She, it seems, was a lady without prejudices."

Garvie listened in silence, while Frye spoke: "You malign yourself, my dear, though I am glad to find you so well up in your historical studies. Well, I leave Garvie to smooth your ruffled brow. *Au revoir.*"

As he went, the girl came forward to stand before the picture on the easel. "It is strong, that," she murmured. "It would be a thousand pities not to finish it."

Garvie sprang up dismayed.

"Not to finish it? I should rather think so. What do you mean by that?" he demanded.

"It will take many more sittings?" she asked, watching him closely from under heavy white lids.

"There is a good fortnight's work in it. But can't you say what you are up to?"

"You couldn't finish in a week?" she persisted.

"Certainly not. Why should I scamp my work for anyone's freaks?" Then trying persuasion,

15

he added, "Look here Virginie, tell me what all this means?"

She only shrugged her shoulders evasively. "*Ciel!*. What do I know? But if I should go away suddenly could you get someone else?"

Garvie's voice now shewed that he was really angry. "Someone else? Do Lucrezias grow on every bush, pray?"

Virginie laughed harshly. "Come then, do not enrage yourself. It will make your hand shake. I wanted to find out if you really need me as much as you say you do. See, the light is still good and I can pose till four, if you like."

"All right," Garvie said, watching her dubiously as she crossed the room and proceeded to rummage out her costume from a big chest.

This unexplained rousing of the dormant feline nature was distinctly unsatisfactory to him.

II

HOTEL CLEVELAND

THE Hotel Cleveland was a small, smart house in one of those bright Paris streets near the American embassy. Like so many other Paris buildings, it formed a diminishing social scale as it went upwards.

The first and second floors were devoted to travelling millionaires, or English or Russian aristocracy; above these was a medium strata of comfort, while the shabby attic rooms, refuge of discarded furniture, were the abode of newspaper correspondents, artists, or those shabby old women who pass sordid lives in foreign pensions.

When Sylvia Dorr had made her first visit to Paris, a brightly interested American girl, she had taken her pleasant third-floor room as a matter of course. Now, working for her daily bread, she was thankful to be able to pay for the dingy attic where she drew her clever designs for fashion papers. There had been winter days when, weakened by influenza, it had not seemed at all certain that she might not have to seek cheaper and even less attractive quarters.

It had never occurred to her that she might

ask forbearance from Madame Comerie, the plump and urbane landlady. Instinctively she realized the inflexibility that underlay her unctuous smiles. It was the hard-featured middle aged newspaper correspondent, Harriett Oakes, whose room was next to hers, who had been her tower of strength in those dark days, days now past.

On this bright March morning when Sylvia stood before her cracked looking-glass pinning on her hat, she had, for all the plainness of her dress, a certain air of distinction. True, her thin face had lost its first girlish freshness in the late years of toil, but what it had lost in freshness it had gained in character, revealing a serene depth of purpose that made its fragility that of tempered steel. Her figure was graceful, for all its thinness, and her masses of light yellow hair kept their first radiance.

As she finished the arrangement of her veil and turned away, her eyes lingered on a spirited sketch in pastels that was pinned on the wall.

It represented a twilit slope of meadow, crowned by a wood of birch trees in their first glory of young leafage, against which hovered vague shapes that seemed to be gazing wistfully down at the red flare of a bonfire half-hidden by black silhouetted groups. Across the bare paper at the top ran the legend in red chalk—"St. John's Eve—Brittany. Rupert Thorpe."

Gazing at it, the sensitive corners of her mouth drooped, and she caught her breath in a little sigh. "And to think that after all our talking it over, I never saw it when it was finished. It's two months since I've even seen him. I wonder why—I wonder why."

A knock at the door, and her friend Miss Oakes appeared in street dress. "Why, you are going out early?" she said, surprised.

"Yes, Madame Marcelle sent for me. It is unusual, after we have settled the week's orders."

"Some daughter of vanity wants a bit of finery designed in a hurry, I suppose. Well, they won't ruffle the fair Marcelle's equanimity. Have you ever seen her gracious calm disturbed?"

"Never," Sylvia said eagerly. "She really is very pleasant to work with, you know."

"Yes, she's wonderfully angelic for a fashionable dressmaker," Miss Oakes acknowledged. "If she ever gets the best of her customers I'm sure it's as a mere matter of business. For all that, she and her worthy mama, our dear landlady, are true Normans in their eye to the main chance."

"I suppose that they never would have got on if they hadn't been," Sylvia pleaded.

"Comerie has raised the rent of my room," her friend remarked casually.

Her casualness did not prevent Sylvia from looking troubled. "How queer. My week's bill is just the same," she said thoughtfully.

"Oh, I suppose she has orders from Marcelle to keep you. I have an idea that she is under her daughter's thumb."

19

"If you leave, I shall go too," Sylvia insisted.

"Oh, I think I'll hold out here until June, when I shall take a country holiday. Cheap village inns, and places I can write up. You'd better come too."

"I'd love to," and Sylvia looked wistful. "But we must hurry or I'll be late."

As they were going out they passed in the hall a well dressed woman, whose trim figure and elaborately arranged hair gave her a spurious air of youthfulness that failed on closer inspection.

Her greeting was patronizing, though more directed to Sylvia than to her friend.

"Mrs. Mallock radiates prosperity since her last American trip. She must have made a good thing of it," Miss Oakes commented.

"How?"

"Oh, well, she is said to have different little ways of bringing fish into the net. First of all, I think she takes out clothes for some of the dressmakers here—a good medium figure, you know—and she may get a diamond ring or some lace trimming through the customs as well. Then, coming back, the voyage gives her a chance to pick up some green travellers, whom she brings to the Cleveland and takes to Marcelle for dresses, and goes shopping with at odd times. It all helps the widow's mite, you see. I rather fancy though, that she's got some bigger game than usual on hand just now."

"Why?"

"I think she picked up some people on her last trip across whom she didn't bring here. I overheard Madame Comerie accusing her of bad faith, and she, who used to crawl on all fours to the 'patronne,' said quiet skittishly; *'Chere,* this is a wholesale not a retail affair. Before you excite yourself, just wait to hear what the others think about it.'"

"Who were the others?" Sylvia asked eagerly.

A glance at her troubled face caused Miss Oakes to make a hasty answer. "How can I tell? Anyway, it's none of our business. We neither of us have leisure to reform the world. Here you are. So long."

Madame Marcelle's rooms, on a Boulevard Haussman *entresol,* were considered by her customers to be something worth gushing over. Their decorations were in the light colouring and delicate outlines of the best Louis XV period. Panels of Aubusson tapestry were let into the walls, suggesting in their harmonious dimness dreams of cool green forests and wandering nymphs.

Amongst these beautiful relics of the past, girls in rustling black silk were laying out as beautiful modern finery. Gowns that were revelations of luxury were thrown carelessly over chairs, silks and laces lay on tables, just enough unfolded to tempt further inspection.

Amid these splendours Madame Marcelle moved serenely, herself a splendid type of mature womanhood, with the opulent lines of her figure outlined by her handsome black dress, and her blonde hair crowning her fresh Norman face.

"Ah, how good in you to come so promptly, my child," she said in smiling greeting. "Come and let us talk business," and she led the way to a recess containing two arm chairs. "I want you to design an historical dress for a pretty girl who has a fancy to look like a court lady. I believe she means to have her portrait painted in it, though that is not our affair."

"And what period does she want?" Sylvia asked.

"Heavens! She knows nothing about periods. Something with beautiful brocades and laces, she says, that is all. So you can do much as you like. But see here," turning to a table beside her. "I happened to know of this uncut bit of old brocade at a dealer's, and this unique set of paste buckles and buttons. They are costly things, but she does not seem to think of the price. You could design a good costume for them, could you not?"

Sylvia realized the beauty of the cream-coloured, flower-strewn brocade, but, handling it, she doubted its age. However it was not for her to express such a thought.

"It is a superb design," she said. "What do you say to an Anne of Austria dress? Shall I do you a little sketch now?"

"Do, like an angel. Sit here at my desk, while I go out for a few minutes. I have forgotten the lace, a wonderful *pointe d' Alençon* collar and cuffs, which I should like you to use."

"It should just go with the dress," Sylvia, who was quick to see that this was an order, agreed.

With Madame's departure quiet fell upon the room, and Sylvia worked away, absorbed in her sketch.

Presently she vaguely heard a stir of entrance, and a clear young voice asking in the most atrocious American French for Madame Marcelle.

Glancing up she saw a tall girl, with blue-black hair and bright colour, clad in a big fur-trimmed wrap. The shopwoman's protests that Madame would return in one little moment, that she had not expected Madame so early, received little attention, and, catching Sylvia's eye, the newcomer came towards her, saying in a breezy fashion, "Oh, what lovely brocade. Is that for my dress?"

The shopwoman seemed to think it was now Sylvia's affair, and the latter spoke in English.

"Madame Marcelle said it was for a fancy dress —an American young lady's."

"That's mine, all right," came the vigorous interruption. "But are you English?" And a pair of frank grey eyes studied Sylvia, from under long black lashes.

"I am American," was the smiling answer. The older girl felt that she could have a great liking for this bright young creature.

"Oh, are you? I'm a Canadian myself, but anyway, that's next door to it. I always feel most at home with Americans over here," and she gave a short sigh as at a recalled sense of strangeness. Then going on: "But you don't belong here, do you? I have never seen you before."

Sylvia flushed as she answered the question frankly. "I often draw designs for Madame Marcelle. She asked me to sketch something for you. Will you look at this, and tell me if you like it?"

The stranger took the drawing, but after a passing glance at it turned her puzzled eyes back to Sylvia.

"But do you have to *work* at this kind of thing? You are not like these other people here, I know. Oh, please don't think me rude, but you see, I felt sure you are a lady."

Her heightened colour and the drooping curves of her lips gave her the air of a child caught in an indiscretion. Sylvia's amused laugh reassured her as she answered, "Oh, you are not rude. Yes, when I was your age I could order a pretty dress without counting the cost too closely, if that's what you mean. I had a good time, and now I'm glad to have such pleasant work to do. Come, will you tell me what you think of my design? Now that I have seen you I know how splendid you would look in it."

The other girl scanned the sketch with admiring interest. It showed the picturesque stateliness that Vandyke gave to his portraits of the ladies of Charles the First's court.

"My! How clever you must be to draw like that!" was the delighted exclamation. "Yes, of course it's lovely. And do you think I'll look what novelists call 'queenly' in that?" the girl asked wistfully.

The quaintness of this appeal from the magnificent young woman struck Sylvia's fancy, and her answer was cordial. "Of course you will. Nothing could suit your style better."

At this the girl beamed, saying gratefully, "How nice you are! But look here, you'll tell me your name, won't you? Mine is Julia Praed, and father and I live at 62, Avenue Friedland."

"I am Sylvia Dorr, once of Boston, now of the Hotel Cleveland."

"Why that's where Mrs. Mallock lives. Do you know her?" was the surprised query.

Some fancy brought to Sylvia's mind the overheard words, *"Chere,* this is a wholesale not a retail affair."

"Yes, I know her slightly," she answered.

"She crossed with us, and father has found her very useful in helping us to find our flat, and all that," said Miss Praed with a half-questioning glance.

"She crossed with us." That settled the question. This girl and her father were Mrs. Mallock's treasure-trove.

25

With a soft little swish of drapery, Madame Marcelle appeared, and Sylvia fancied she was not overpleased at sight of the two girls in familiar converse. Her apologies in prettily foreign English were interrupted by Julia.

"Oh, it didn't matter one bit. Miss Dorr and I have been having a real good talk. But say, Madame Marcelle, this dress she has drawn is too lovely for anything. You'll go right on with it, won't you?"

The dressmaker protested that she must have a more finished sketch, which sketch Sylvia promised for the next day.

"Then I will meet you here on Friday, about the same time," Miss Praed said to Sylvia, but Madame had various soft-spoken reasons why the designs should be sent to Avenue Friedland.

Sylvia silently yielded to a cynical sense of amusement. She would show her employer that she had no wish to tamper with the captive of her bow and spear.

But the heiress stuck to her point, that Sylvia must herself explain the costume to her, and Madame Marcelle yielded, with a honied smile.

"An attack of influenza would just suit my dear employer," Sylvia said to herself as she walked home, with a certain dreariness at heart. She loved to believe in people, and she had felt very grateful for Madame's kindness to her.

III

THE CANADIANS

THAT evening Garvie dined with the Praeds, in the showy rooms where they seemed to have camped down in much the fashion they would have in the hotel of a western mining town.

Mrs. Mallock formed a fourth in the little group, and her stream of babbled flattery, turned now on one now on the other, veiled the young hostess' little fits of brusque shyness that alternated with her impulsive candour.

It really did Mrs. Mallock credit, Garvie reflected, how well she veiled her annoyance when she found him on the premises.

Happy in entertaining "old man Garvie's" son and the lady whom he looked upon as his social finger-post in Paris, Mr. Praed beamed upon the table from under his beetling grey brows, while he asked Garvie questions about his profession. "That show now, that's to have your picture in, when's it going to be open?" he asked.

"The Salon? Oh, in six weeks or so," Garvie answered.

"I'm so impatient to see your Theodora," Mrs. Mallock put in. "She is that snaky, wicked

Italian queen whom we used to go to see Sarah
Bernhardt play, isn't she? Do you remember
when she takes the cagger from her hair to stab
the soldier? The litt e cry she gave always made
me quite faint. M·s. Van Kempt was good
enough to offer to take me to your studio the
Sunday afternoon you let society have a peep at
the picture, Mr. Garvie. She said you wouldn't
mind any friend of hers coming—but my unfor-
tunate neuralgia. Mr. Garvie's reception was a
fashionable event, I assure you, Mr. Praed. We
Americans were quite proud. I remember that
evening at Mrs. Courtland's the gossips were
speculating about the red-haired model you are so
constant to—in your pictures, I mean. They said
she was your Fredegonde last year."

"She was, and is likely to be something else
next year," was the uncompromising answer.

Julia, marking Garvie's annoyance, asked simply, "Do you always have a model, Mr. Garvie?"

"Generally, unless I am working from a study."

"It makes it easier?"

"Much easier."

Here Mrs. Mallock broke in with a giggle,
meant to be arch: "And more interesting too?
Really, dear, I wouldn't ask so many questions
about models."

Julia flushed, but held her ground. "Perhaps
I'm stupid, but I've never known any artists before."

Garvie looked kindly at the girl's appealing face,

saying, "Ask me any questions you like, Miss Praed, and I'll answer as well as I can. I'm sorry that Mrs. Mallock should consider my conscience so tender," he added stiffly.

That lady gave ground at once before the attack, protesting in flustered tones, and showing signs of embarrassed pique:

"Oh, I assure you I really meant nothing more than a little joke on general principles."

She looked none the better pleased when Garvie, turning to Mr. Praed, asked:

"And how is the search for old furniture getting on?"

Here Mr. Praed looked up from his apple-pie, glorified by French genius. A new light came into his keen grey eyes as he answered:

"Fair and softly, sir. An old business man likes to go slowly. I've found a most intelligent man, or rather Mrs. Mallock has helped me to find him; a Mr. Britski that keeps that big shop for pictures and old stuff in the Avenue de l'Opera. Ever heard of him?"

A quick glance at Mrs. Mallock shewed her innocently absorbed in her plate of forced strawberries, and trying to appear oblivious to the turn the talk was taking.

"Britski? Oh, yes, every artist in Paris knows him. A very intelligent man, as you say. What he doesn't know about pictures and bric-a-brac isn't worth knowing." Garvie agreed.

"Oh, that's satisfactory. I always like to get

hold of the best man in the trade, and I saw he knew what he was talking about. Not to say that at first he understood just what I was driving at—thought it the ordinary small affair of a few pictures and bits of old furniture picked up round his shop, or galleries as he calls them. How could I tell that stuff was genuine or that he wasn't taken in himself by it. I shews him a photograph—the same as I shewed you, sir—of that Gothic edifice as the architect's a putting up for me in Montreal, and 'find me,' says I to him, 'a real old castle with real old fittings, furniture and drawing room ornaments and all, round just as the real old family had them arranged. Then, I'll buy the whole lot out and out, and take them home and shew that architect that Gabriel Praed does know how to furnish his house for himself, Eh, Miss Julia?"

This was his name for his daughter when in a high good humour.

That young woman retorted doubtfully. "Well, I hope when you get the things, they'll be pretty and *clean*. There are such lovely *new* things in the shops here, father."

The old man chuckled, saying: "Well, you do the house at the mines your way, and I'll do the town one mine, antique fashion, and so we'll both be suited. If it weren't for that architect's Gothic plan I can't say as I mightn't have liked modern things myself. But if you've once chosen to be

Gothic, well then you must be it. Eh, Mr. Garvie?"

"Certainly. It's best to be consistent. But I suppose Monsieur Britski told you that such a chance doesn't turn up every day?"

Mrs. Mallock's eyes met Garvie's in a momentarily keen glance before they returned to the strawberries.

Settling himself comfortably back in his chair, Mr. Praed began:

"Well, he did say as how that might be the way in general. Said his best things often come from ignorant country auctioneers, who have picked them up cheap. Still, he seems to have heard talk of a family away down in the most outlandish parts of the country, who lost most of their stocks and bonds in that Panama canal business. Until then they were as rich as they had been in the days when a gentleman's dress suit was made of tin—I'm glad that fashion has gone out, anyway—and those dress suits and other such fancy articles, they've always kept round, the same as people hang up Japanese fans nowadays. Britski says that they've been selling the things for the last year or two in small lots, enough to keep them going. Now he has heard that the father is dead and the daughter, who's the only one left, has to let it all go. He's making inquiries about it for me."

Julia had been listening as though this were news to her.

"But father, whatever are you going to do with a lot of tin armour, unless you're going to found a museum in Vancouver?"

"No, my dear, I'm not," was the cheerful answer. "That's just a figure of speech, though it's iron and not tin. What it amounts to is, that if this story's correct, there's the whole furnishing and drawing room ornaments of a first class, middle-age dwelling-house going cheap, and G. P. is the man what's going to get it."

So this was the scheme that Mrs. Mallock and Britski were working. Well, at any rate it was better than trying to entangle the girl into an undesirable marriage, Garvie said to himself. Still, he would shew the woman that he was keeping an eye on her.

"Then you mean to take the stuff on chance, from a catalogue?" he asked casually.

"Now, Mr. Garvie, do you suppose that a man as your father taught business ways to, is the one to make bargains blindfold?" came the pathetic remonstrance. "And then, ain't it the point of the whole thing to see how that furniture looks in its own natural place, so as to give it the same aspect when I get it landed out in Canada. Lord, there'll be a nice duty to pay first, and not even the preferential tariff to help! No, sir, when Mr. Britski is able to tell me that I can have the refusal of the things, off I go to have a look at them, no matter how queer and outlandish a kind of place it is."

Mr. Praed spoke as though announcing a journey to the North Pole, and Julia seemed to share his feelings as she asked: "But father, how ever would you get along in those country places without understanding a word of French?"

"Well, my dear, I've been on my own hook among the Dagoes in Mexico, and camped with the northern Indians at home, and I guess it will take more than a Frenchman to put Gabriel Praed off the tracks. What do you say, Mr. Garvie?"

"I daresay you will find it simple enough," the latter agreed, then turning to Julia, asked: "And how will you amuse yourself while your father is in the wilds, Miss Praed?"

"What does a woman want better than shopping in Paris?" put in Mrs. Mallock. "Especially when they have at hand such a creator of beauty as Madame Marcelle?"

"Oh, but I've found out the real creator behind Madame Marcelle! Fancy, Mr. Garvie, she's an American girl. Just perfectly sweet too, and a lady, though she has to draw these fashion-book things for her living. I found her at Madame Marcelle's, and we had such a nice long talk before Madame came in and stopped it. Her name is Sylvia Dorr. Isn't it a pretty one?" Julia said, her soft grey eyes turned eagerly towards Garvie, the clear tinting of her face all aglow with girlish interest.

"It certainly suits her daintiness very well," he

said quietly. "I know Miss Dorr—knew her years ago in my Harvard days when she had a pleasant home in Boston. Of late, she has once or twice designed an historical costume for my models. Her knowledge of detail in such matters is marvellous. She has given years of study to it, and would long ago have brought out a book on the subject but for the loss of the family means, which forced her into more money making work."

What was there in his words to make Julia fancy them a well-bred rebuke to the over-eagerness of her vulgar monied patronage of one of his own class; that he was emphasizing her own ignorance in comparison to the other girl's knowledge. To his amazement Garvie saw that she flushed and paled, and even fancied that he caught the gleam of tears in her eyes, though they were winked away as she said in more subdued tones:

"She was as sweet as she could be about drawing an old times dress for me that I fancied I'd like, and I'm to see her about it at Madame Marcelle's tomorrow morning. What do you think, father, of my having my picture painted in a fancy dress to seem more like hanging up in that Gothic house of yours?"

Her father banged his hand down on the table emphatically enough to make Mrs. Mallock jump.

"That's a real smart idea of yours, Miss Julia. Now if only you could persuade Mr. Garvie to do us the honour and pleasure of painting it—"

he paused dubiously, and Julia with flaming face sat staring down at her plate.

One glance revealed her distress to Garvie and caused him to break the pause with ready goodwill.

"There is nothing I should like better, Mr. Praed, I assure you. If you saw some of the parchment coloured, or worse, painted old women, who want one to do their portraits, you would understand what a welcome change your daughter would be, as a sitter. But I am hurrying to finish my winter's work so that I can get away to the country for a few weeks' fishing. If you like to trust it to me, though, I know a clever young fellow, named Thorpe, who is I feel sure, equal to doing justice to his subject. I can look him up and arrange about it tomorrow. Will that suit, Miss Praed?"

"Oh, yes, thank you, if it's not too much trouble," Julia said with nervous politeness, and her father, though he looked disappointed, agreed.

"My dear Julia, how you and your good father can put up with that man's supercilious patronage in the way you do, I *cannot* understand," Mrs. Mallock said afterwards, while the men were smoking.

"Oh, I think he means to be kind to us, only I suppose we *do* seem stupid sometimes," the girl answered wearily, seeming uninterested in the subsequent flatteries lavished upon her by that lady.

That night there were a few tears dropped on her pillow as she settled the black masses of her hair into it, saying disconsolately to herself, "How different it would be if I had a sister or any woman folk of my own. Father's just as good as ever he can be, but—somehow I seem lonely."

It was a new mood for the girl who had hitherto been looking on life as a fairy tale unrolled for her benefit.

IV

MAKING FRIENDS

SYLVIA'S thought of influenza must have been unlucky, for on the morning of her appointment with Miss Praed she awoke with a feverish cold. The dismayed dread of illness, that is such a torment to a wage-earner, kept her from running any risks; and, sending a note to Madame Marcelle, she settled down for an indoors day.

The March wind whistled at every crack of the ill-fitting windows, and with a fur cape over her shoulders and her table drawn up close to the stove, she still shivered. It was no use. She was too stupid to go on with her day's work, and so she sought for comfort in spreading out on the table the contents of a portfolio which held the illustrations for her long-planned book on the history of costume. Resolutely as she had put aside her ideal for more practical work, she had found as soon as she was well started, that she could every now and then do some illustrated magazine article that might be used to complete the book. It was not often that she allowed herself the indulgence of looking over this portfolio; but now, depressed and ill, she turned to it as she might have turned to a friend's face, or to the cheer of firelight. The spell worked, and she forgot draughts and headaches, as she added an occasional note or outline.

"It is good work," she murmured, "and some day, perhaps ─"

At a knock at the door she looked up absently, expecting to see the porter with fuel. Instead, there was the radiant vision of Julia Praed, clad in deep shades of purple cloth, soft grey fur around her face, her hair crowned with a wonderful arrangement of deep-tinted pansies.

"Miss Praed," she said rising, "Oh, I hope there is nothing wrong with the design of the dress?"

"Oh, that's all right. Don't bother about the dress. They said you were ill, and I came to see you. And look here, I've brought you these," and she held out a great sheaf of long stalked tulips that seemed to have absorbed the sunshine in their golden globes.

The wistful look that so often greets flowers in cities came into Sylvia's eyes. "Oh, how nice in you," she breathed fervently. Then, "I'm afraid the room is chilly. Nothing keeps the draughts out today," and she shivered, drawing her wrap closer.

"And you've got a cold? My, your hand's burning," Julia said taking it in hers. "Here, let me shut the door, and you come back close to the fire. Can't I fix up that stove?"

Sylvia checked her as she knelt to investigate it.

"Oh don't, you'll only spoil your things. It's a spiteful little wretch, and smokes if one puts more than one briquette in. Somehow, everything seemed wrong today—except your visit, that breaks the bad luck," she added with a smile.

"Does it? I'm so glad I came," Julia beamed from her seat in the rickety arm chair.

"I've been to Marcelle's this morning," she went on. Then, "Look here, is she really nice to you?"

Sylvia glanced up startled, "Oh, yes, she has always been good to me. Indeed, but for her, I could never have got on as I have; but why do you ask?"

"Oh, well, I never trust these smiling French people much, and I wanted to know. If she's good to you I don't mind how many little tricks she has—if she weren't, it would be different."

Sylvia, with remembrance of Harriett Oakes's talk of Mrs. Mallock and her associates, felt uneasy at being made a guarantee for the dressmaker, whom she guessed was making large profits out of Miss Praed. However, she could say nothing.

Her visitor created a diversion by saying, "Oh, what lovely pictures those are! May I look at them?"

She leant forward to the table, where lay three or four water-colour drawings from the portfolio.

They might well have attracted more experienced eyes, for their workmanship was charming, in the light style of Louis Leloir.

They shewed Marie Antoinette and two or three of her court ladies, in those halycon days when that court was a fairy tale of life. Details of faces and costumes had been studied from old prints, and Sylvia had added backgrounds from the Trianons gardens. Julia's eyes opened like those of a pleased child.

"How beautiful they are!" she breathed softly. "And you did them? But are they real people, or did you just invent them?"

"They are Marie Antoinette and her court ladies, when they were young and used to play at being farmer's wives at the Trianons. I suppose you've been out to Versailles?"

"No, I never thought of it. Can I go there any time? What a goose I was not to think of it sooner. Why, at school, I used to love to read about the queen, and used to cry at the part where she hadn't the stuff to mend her clothes in prison. And these other ladies are real people too, are they?"

"Yes, there is the Princesse de Lamballe, and the Contesse de Polignac, and the Princesse Elizabeth. I copied them from old prints in the Bibliothèque Nationale."

"But," Julia flushed and hesitated before she brought out—"don't think me rude or stupid, please—but won't you sell these, and get some money to be more comfortable?"

Sylvia hastened to reassure her. "A very wise question, but, you see, I make money more surely and easily with my fashion sketches. That is why I have not finished the book these belong to. Don't look so astonished," she said, laughing. "Yes, I really was writing a book all about the little scraps of the history of dress I had picked up, when"—a sudden shadow of past trouble sobered her face—"when everything went to pieces around me, and I found that I must turn to and work, as other women have had to do before."

"Oh, how dreadful!" came from Julia.

"No, I don't think now that it was dreadful," the other persisted. "What right had I to suppose that the world was always going on as a down cushion for me? And I was more lucky than most girls brought up as I was, for there was one thing that I could do—draw those fashions—and I did it," she ended with a touch of pride.

Julia's face was aglow with admiring curiosity, as she asked, "Well, but wasn't it very hard to come off here all by yourself to work among these French people?"

Sylvia was not of the type that confides easily. It usually took a long probation to break down her delicate reserve. But now there was something in the simple girlish friendliness that warmed her heart and she answered frankly; "It wasn't easy, but nothing worth the doing ever is, I think. And then my heart was so set on my work. I'm an obstinate creature, and all my friends had made such a fuss that I was determined to shew them I could do it. Only, I was sorry to put my book aside. It was so nearly finished," she added.

"But why can't you finish it now," came the eager question.

"Well, it really is practically finished," Sylvia admitted. "You see, every now and then I earn some money with magazine articles, little chatty sketches of historical great ladies, illustrated with drawings from old pictures. I found I could really use these as part of my book, at least bits of them, so that my work in the libraries and galleries helped it along. Yes, I think it really is finished now," she added with a little sigh of achievement, "and perhaps some day I may be able to get it published."

"But why can't you do it now?"

The quiet, firm glance of the blue eyes met the impulsive questioning of the brown ones, and denied their plea. "Because it is not easy, all at once, to find a publisher who will undertake as expensive a work as this would be, with so many illustrations, and because I do not choose to let certain kind rich friends at home advance the money, as they have offered to do. And so it must just wait until some publisher thinks it worth the printing. May that day come soon! And meanwhile, these ladies must be content to remain tucked away in the portfolio," and she bent over the loose sheets to arrange them.

"It seems a shame," Julia said regretfully.

Then with apparent irrelevancy, "I do believe you're proud after all."

Somewhat nervous as to whether this impulsive young woman might not, even now, insist upon offering to pay for the publication, Sylvia hastened to turn her off with a laugh. "Well, if so, let us hope it is the right kind of pride, which is not a bad thing in its way. And now tell me about the dress. Is it going all right?"

"Oh, yes," was the somewhat listless answer. "I'm going to have my portrait painted in it, if I can get any one to do it."

At this Sylvia laughed out. "Get anyone to do it! It's plain to be seen, you don't know much of artists. Why, they will all be struggling for the chance."

Julia responded with a forlorn little laugh. "Mr. Garvie isn't struggling to, at any rate. Poor father didn't understand how grand he is, and asked him to paint me. But no, he just made a lot of excuses. He was going away as soon as he had finished some work, he said. He has promised to find someone else though, a Mr. Rupert Thorpe. Do you know him?"

A soft colour came into Sylvia's pale cheeks as she answered; "Oh yes, I have known him a long time. I do hope you will arrange it with him, for he is clever, and should do you a charming portrait."

Where were Julia's thoughts that she did not mark the change worked by Thorpe's name? Her gaze was fixed on the stupid little stove, and she spoke somewhat absently. "That's all right then. And if that dress doesn't seem to suit for the picture, you'll design me another, won't you?"

Sylvia laughed. "You extravagant creature! Why, that dress will cost a fortune by itself. Anyway, I mustn't take any orders from you save through Madame Marcelle. It wouldn't be fair to her."

"Oh well, it's all the same," Julia answered, in blissful unconsciousness of the difference between the sum paid to Sylvia and that charged in her own bill for the design.

Just then there came a light, sharp knock at the door, and it opened to disclose Mrs. Mallock, very smart in visiting attire, with the flush of rapid movement shewing through the powder-coating on her cheeks.

"Oh here you are, my naughty little truant!" she began, in her high-pitched voice, vibrant with the false note of affectation. "I assure you, I was quite flustered when Constantine told me that you had come all the way up here to wait for me."

She had taken no notice whatever of the owner of the room, and Sylvia, without rising from her fireside seat, looked on with a tremour of amusement around her mouth, thinking how unlike a "naughty little truant" was the big, handsome girl, in her sumptuous purples, who lounged back so negligently in the decrepit arm chair.

Julia greeted the newcomer with the nonchalance which even the least self-assertive learn to bestow upon those who flatter them.

"Constantine was mistaken," she said brusquely "I came up here to see Miss Dorr."

Mrs. Mallock took the check well.

"Oh, I see. Something about the dress Madame Marcelle is making you. Well, my dear, if you've finished your business here, I'm quite ready for a drive in the Bois, or—let me see—it is dear Madame de Touraine's day, and I promised your father to take you to see her, you know. You will find it such an advantage to meet some of the old aristocracy, and there are so few Americans who are able to introduce you among them. Shall we be off, then?"

"Oh I guess I won't bother about the French aristocracy just yet awhile, thank you, Mrs. Mallock. I think I'll stay on a bit with Miss Dorr, if she'll have me. And as she's got a cold, and there's a kind of northwest blizzard coming up the stairs—" She paused and looked suggestively at the door that Mrs. Mallock was holding open.

There was a vicious spark of fire in that lady's light eyes, but she laughed with apparent zest, saying, "You dear, droll creature, how shall I ever break you in to society! Well, perhaps when Miss Dorr wants to get back to her work, you'll come down to my little snuggery, and have a cup of afternoon tea. I don't suppose you indulge in tea, Miss Dorr."

Whether this were a semi-invitation, or a hint that Julia would get no tea in her present quarters, Sylvia did not understand, but she took the latter view in her answer. "No, but I am going to make myself a cup of chocolate presently, and, if Miss Praed cares to stay, she shall have our company cup. I expect Miss Oakes in soon," she went on to Julia, "and I promised her some buttered toast."

"Oh, do let me make it. Let me do everything," the latter cried joyfully. "I haven't had a chance to do a thing for myself for ages, and you'd never guess how smart I was about the kitchen at home."

"All right. You shall play house as much as ever you like," Sylvia agreed.

Mrs. Mallock saw that the comradeship of youth was too strong for her. "I'm afraid I cannot offer you the temptations of cooking, and so I'll be off," she said acidly. "*Au revoir*, my dear. I hope your cold won't come to much, Miss Dorr." And, with a protesting rustle, she was gone and the door was shut.

"Break *me* in to society," Julia commented, as she took a general view of her friend's preparations. "I rather fancy it will be somebody else but me that gets broken in before we're done."

V

IN THE QUARTER

IT was after the *déjeuner* hour on the Boulevard St. Michel, and, as the March sun was bright, the seats around the little tin tables outside the cafés were full.

Here were the men of the future, French, English and American students, medical, literary and artistic. Youth and its effervescence was in the air, and that one square acre of ground covered enough theories and ideas to furnish half a new continent.

At the Taverne du Panthéon, opposite the Luxembourg gate, the groups were the most varied. Actresses, models, and such, supplied bits of brilliant plumage amongst the sombreness of masculine garb. Flower-girls with baskets of violets were making their way between the seats. Two well-known artists were arguing so vigourously over a much-discussed picture of the year that a little group of listeners had formed around them. At the end of the terrace, just beyond a bright-coloured cluster of young ladies of the Quarter, Rupert Thorpe sat alone.

He had left half-finished his coffee and *petit*

verre, he had even neglected to light a fresh cigarette. Among the crowd were many models and artists with whom he was habitually in the friendly intercourse of everyday life.

With men and women alike he was a favourite. "He can *flâner* most delightfully, *ce petit Thorpe,*" the girls said, and "it's worth while to get Thorpe started on his art theories," the men acknowledged. But to-day he neither *flânéd* nor talked out his art views, only sat and stared past the crowd at the budding chestnut trees around the Palace opposite, with the pained isolation of the wounded animal in his eyes. Whatever his thoughts might be, they had him so in their grasp that he never noticed the familiar figure of Andrew Garvie as he threaded his way between the tables, with here and there a friendly greeting or bandied jest. It was only a touch on his shoulder that roused him, and then he started as though his nerves were not in good order.

"Hullo, what's the matter? An evil conscience?" was Garvie's greeting, as he seized on a just vacated chair and seated himself.

There was a strong contrast between the two men. Garvie, tall, a bit stiff of bearing, with pointed, light brown beard, his careful dress telling of a planned afternoon on the other side of the river; Thorpe, of medium height and slight build, his clean-shaven face revealing the mobile, sensitive mouth, to which the moody lines did not seem natural, his careless dress shewing that he had come straight from his morning's studio work, and probably meant to return to it.

Without moving after his first start, he answered Garvie's greeting. "An average one, I believe. Look around and guess if there is such a thing as a good conscience within a hundred yards of here. There is Celestine Rouet, who, six months ago, drove that poor devil of a wine-merchant into shooting himself. She looks quite pleased with herself. Then there is—"

"Shut up, you death's head," Garvie interrupted. "I don't wonder at your gloomy looks if such were your meditations."

"No, I wasn't thinking about Celestine and her ilk. I was just meditating a murder or two on my own account, or a little scientific torturing. It must have been great sport to be an inquisitor, or one of your favorite Borgias."

"The Borgias were much too well bred to torture. They only poisoned."

"Well, I suppose they got some entertaining primary convulsions out of their friends, anyway."

Garvie, seeing that he was talking off a dark mood, humoured him, asking idly, "Who would be your victims?"

"Oh, a varied selection of those who trip up the footsteps of genius."

"Well, it must be a comfort to know yourself a genius. It's a point better men than you or I are doubtful on."

49

"I look like a genius, don't I?" came the scornful retort. "Now you—your very hat and gloves bespeak the man who is *arrivé*, whose portrait a month or so hence will be in the home papers, as the successful artist who won a second, perhaps a first, medal."

"Don't be childish, Thorpe. Genius is no excuse for cowardice," Garvie said more sharply.

"Again that touching word. And why cowardice, pray?" was the cool retort.

"Any man is a coward who blames others instead of himself for his failures."

"Sounds like the wisdom of La Bruyère, or Rochefoucauld. Have you been lecturing at a young ladies studio, perchance, that you have assumed that air of virtue?"

Garvie had been lighting a cigarette, and now leaned forward, his elbows on the table to say earnestly, "Look here, Thorpe, I want to talk to you."

"Well, it seems to me that you have already been indulging in that amusement."

"I want to talk seriously, man, if you'll stop playing the fool. I first went to find you at your studio, and then have been round to half the cafés in the Quarter—"

"What condescension," the other still scoffed, though he had turned and was now watching his friend closely, almost nervously.

Not noticing these last words, Garvie went on. "I've been asked to paint a portrait—a good-looking girl, and money no object—but I don't feel as though I could start in on any fresh work just now. I must vagabondize a bit first, and then I'm really set on some careful work at early spring foregrounds for a subject I have in view. So when I declined the tempting offer, I mentioned you as the most desirable substitute."

For all the elaborate carelessness of the suggestion, it scattered the moody cloud on Thorpe's face, bringing in its place the tremulousness of a hope that had all but died out from exhaustion.

"Thanks, old fellow," he said in a somewhat choky tone. "It was very good in you to think of me. I haven't done a portrait for ages. It will be rather fun. What is the young woman's name?"

"Miss Praed."

"Not the daughter of Gabriel Praed, the Canadian millionaire?" Thorpe asked with a startled air.

"The same. Ever heard of him?"

The other struck a match to light a fresh cigarette before he answered. "Don't you remember telling Frye and me about them the other day? But does the daughter really want me to have the job? That kind of people usually like a big name."

"Oh, they take my word that you are a budding genius. I am to settle it now, so that I can tell her this evening when you will begin."

There was nothing in this to cause Thorpe to

look as undecided and miserable as he did. A glance shewed his friend that he had grown very pale, before he broke out desperately; "Look here what is the hurry about it? I can't give a definite answer until I've seen someone else with whom I have a bit of work half arranged. I really don't know if I'm free to undertake this. Don't think me a fool or an ungrateful brute—there's a good fellow."

Garvie, feeling that firmness was the truest kindness, ignored the appeal, and answered, "You must be a fool if you refuse an offer like this."

He had guessed right, for the other flashed responsive, "No hang it. I'll accept, whatever happens."

Garvie did not shew how puzzled he was beginning to feel. "Well, Miss Praed would like you to go to see her and settle on the dress you prefer. Shall I say to-morrow at two o'clock," he asked in a matter-of-fact fashion.

Thorpe was now all eager alertness. "The sooner the better. What's her colouring?"

"That creamy Irish skin, with the pink coming and going, grey eyes, and blue-black hair. She's a splendidly vigourous bit of young womanhood."

"Not beefy, I hope," Thorpe objected.

"Heavens, no. There is a lot of individuality in her face, latent perhaps, but certainly there. A man might almost find too much of it in a year or two."

Thorpe laughed in the old whole-hearted fashion his friend remembered. "Lord, man, you don't want an Amelia out of *Vanity Fair,* do you?"

"Though the type is out of date, it might still have its merits for domestic life. Reposeful, you know," was the lazy rejoinder.

"Reposeful! That's the very last thing it could ever have been. Those early Victorian ladies of Thackeray's were forever clutching their off-spring to their bosoms and invoking Providence in floods of tears. Fancy the horror of a lively American child at taking part in such a tableau. But it's the meekness that hits your fancy. I always thought you had a touch of the Englishman in you."

Garvie was inwardly chuckling at his success in arousing Thorpe's love for argument, when he saw his interest flag and the preoccupied shadow darken his face. "Look here," he broke off abruptly—"I want to ask you something. Do you think it would seem queer to Miss Praed if you were to ask her not to talk about this portrait—about my painting it, I mean? You might put it to her as a habit with artists."

There could be no mistake about his earnestness now. Garvie saw the fingers that held his cigarette twitching nervously. The unaccountability of all this began to irritate him, and he answered somewhat tersely, "I *might,* of course, and it is just possible that Miss Praed might take my word for it, though she is no fool, but you can hardly

53

expect me to swallow such a whim without some good reason."

Thorpe was intently outlining a pattern in ashes on the tin table as he said in a low voice, "No, but sometimes a friend will make the best of a poor excuse, seeing one is in a tight place—"

He paused, and Garvie noticed the voice of a girl at the next table, humming.

Oh, que la vie est gaie—

"Might'nt it be best to trust a friend?" he suggested quietly.

"I *can't*. Heavens alive, my dear fellow, don't you see that I would if I could? You'd better give up the whole thing, and have nothing more to do with me." As he ended, Thorpe sprang up, shoving back his chair, which grated harshly on the asphalt. There was enough agitation in his voice to cause a few curious glances.

Garvie took it all impassively, saying, under his breath, in a compelling voice: "Sit down, and try to be sensible, See here, the best thing you can do is to go to a doctor. You look like a ghost, and you can't keep still for two seconds. You may be getting a fever. There is a lot of typhoid about over here lately, Briggs was telling me."

Thorpe greeted this theory with a laugh. "No such happy solution to the problem, I am afraid. My dear fellow, I have the health of an ox."

"You don't shew it then. Well, if you are not ill, will you have enough common-sense to promise to go and see Miss Praed, 62 Avenue Friedland, tomorrow? Remember, if you promise I consider you bound to me."

"All right. I promise by all the gods. I will go."

VI

SIGHT-SEEING

DON'T you think, father, that we ought to go and see the real old places in Paris, the places where all the dreadful things happened to the Kings and Queens, and that sort of people? Why, I've been reading about it here," and Julia Praed thumped an open Baedecker on the edge of the table, "and you can see the prison cell where the Queen, Marie Antoinette, slept the night before they cut off her head, and at a church they shew you the bloodstained robes that an Archbishop of Paris wore when they shot him—"

"Hum, I can't say as it sounds exactly cheerful," Mr. Praed put in dubiously. "Still, Julie, I suppose, as you say, it's our duty to improve our minds, and I don't deny as we've been frivolling most of the time we've been over here. Yes, you're right, and I'll speak to Mrs. Mallock about getting someone as knows to shew us around."

At this proposition, Julia shook her pretty head so energetically that a great pin of amber tortoise shell flew out from her hair, letting loose the heavy black waves.

"There now," she said, putting up her hands

to repair damages, "that's because I wouldn't let Jeanne take time to do it properly before breakfast. No, father, that's just what I don't want to do, to go asking Mrs. Mallock how I'm to learn about things. She thinks me enough of a fool as it is."

"Why, Julie!" came the troubled protest.

"Oh, that's all right. I don't blame her for it. But, all the same, I'm not going to stay any more of a fool than I can help. Now, just you listen to what I want," and she sent across the breakfast table a smile that would have made her father go to Kamskatka at her bidding.

"I just want," she went on, emphasizing her words with little nods, "for you and me to go off by ourselves—not with the carriage, but in one of those nice little yellow cabs with the fat drivers in shiny hats. It will make us feel more like real travellers, and I'll put on a plain dress that nobody will notice me in."

"You couldn't do that," said her fond parent. "But how will we know where to go?"

"Why, haven't I been reading this book, and don't it tell one everything? Now you leave it to me, and just see if I can't manage."

Mr. Praed agreeing, they set forth early on foot, to take a cab around the corner, and, in a fashion, elope for a few hours from their new state.

The gloom of the Conciergerie cells depressed Mr. Praed's spirits, but he was presently cheered and excited by the discovery that Notre Dame was Gothic. "Just like our new house, only I must write and tell the architect as I wouldn't like quite so many queer figures crawling over it—might make a visitor as had been enjoying himself think he had the jim-jams."

He immediately bought several books of views from a hawker on the steps, "to send home to John and George, and let them see what Gothic looks like."

The splendours of the Treasury and of Napoleon's coronation robes enabled him to support the sight of Monseigneur d'Affre's bullet-pierced garments, and altogether their morning was a success. Especially so was it, when they ventured into a crowded Duval for *déjeuner,* and her father noted the admiring glances that followed Julia down the room, and listened with pride to her bold attempts to order their meal in French.

"There, I've done it, you see," she said, flushed and laughing, as the waiter rushed off with his order.

True, the *"aloyau"* she had ordered, turned out to be "just little bits of fried beef," instead of the larks she had expected, and her father shook his head decidedly when an uncooked, prickly-leaved artichoke was set before him.

"Take it away, my man," he said. "Whatever you may call it on the paper, it looks to me like first cousin to a raw thistle, and I'm not the kind as eats *that.*"

With a sense of achievement, they drove back to the more familiar streets in one of the first open cabs of the season.

At the Place de l'Opera, Mr. Praed announced his intention of going into Munroe's for letters, and as Julia wanted to walk home, he paid the cab and they parted.

Her theory as to the unobtrusiveness of her own appearance was soon dispelled by various glances of bold approval, while one lounger, more enterprising than the rest, stalked her all the way up the Rue Auber.

She knew that the man, a middle-aged dandy, was there close behind her, but she did not allow such a trifle to interfere with her purpose of sitting awhile in the Parc Monceau, any more than she had allowed the chance of meeting a stray bear to spoil her mountain rambles in her far-off western home among the Rockies.

There, she had carried a smart little revolver; here, she had her purse, her ready tongue and wits for sufficient protection.

Mrs. Mallock had tried to frighten her out of solitary street rambles, but she had answered, "I don't see how a girl with any sense can be really frightened when she has only to hail a cab and drive home;" and on this principle she acted in case of necessity.

Since the age of sixteen her life had been of the kind to develop courage and self-reliance. Before that, she had spent two irksome years of restraint in a convent school in Portland, Oregon, that fair city that lies among its gardens between the sea and the mountains. Her father had then yielded to her entreaties and taken her home to the house on the hillside above the village that clustered around his mines, on the banks of the swift Fraser river.

Here, while her father and brothers were away all day, her life was a solitary one. Chinese servants freed her from the household drudgery of the women settlers on the plains, so that she could roam the mountain paths at will on her stout little pony, learning the lessons of fortitude, which nature gives to those who seek her in her high places.

So now there was no girlish timidity to mar her enjoyment of the puppet show of outdoor Parisian life, as, finding an empty chair, she settled down to share the sunshine with the nurses and babies.

The March afternoon was still bright, and all Paris seemed resolved to enjoy it. The women in the carriages that passed had that Parisian look of wearing a hat fresh from the milliners. The grassy slopes of the little park shone emerald green, and the flowers of the earliest bulbs flaunted bravely in the borders. The gaily-coloured ribbons and streaming cloaks of the stalwart nurses and the white dresses of the children who played around them, all added their share to the universal brightness.

It was not to watch the panorama of foreign

life that Julia had come here, but in the need of thinking out some of the new ideas which had lately been seething in her brain, and of which her morning's activity had been the outcome.

Was it possible for her to make herself a woman like Sylvia Dorr? A woman who understood about all these wonderful things, which she was only just beginning to know were in the world; a woman whom men liked to talk to, and praised for something more than looks or dress? She had been like a child in her delight in her new toys of pretty clothes and jewelry, when all at once these toys lost their value at the discovery of better treasures beyond, treasures on the attainment of which her heart was set. Now she wanted to *be*, as well as to have and enjoy.

No wonder Mrs. Mallock despised her as a dupe, and Mr Garvie treated her like an ignorant child. She *was* ignorant, but she would shew them what she could do when she tried, and at this resolve she drove the ivory point of her sunshade into the ground so sharply that a little child busy among its heaps of gravel ran to its nurse in fear.

This made Julia laugh, and cease from tragedy. After all, she had always accomplished what she wanted, and there was no reason she should not do so now.

She was far from being totally uneducated, having, during her two years of school-life, learnt easily and quickly anything that had enough pic-

turesqueness to take her fancy. But while quick-
witted enough, she was too full of vitality to have
the instinctive craving for books which goes with
a less active nature. So when she had turned her
back on cities, reading formed no part of her solitary hours

She was content to roam the hills in the day, to
join in her father's and brother's talk around the
fire in the evening. In such a life she learnt
much of nature and of men, but the booklore that
had never been an innate part of her being, slipped
away like an outworn garment.

The new riches had brought new activities.
She had travelled with her father on business trips
to Vancouver or Chicago, where she had become
familiar with showy hotels and theatres, but
where nothing among the people she had met had
revealed to her her own deficiencies. She had
gone with him into the wilds to inspect some of
his increasing investments, once even as far north
as Dawson City, winning praises from rough men
for her courage and agility. Never, until they
had started on this European trip, had she been
as far east as Toronto, but the habit of travelling
once acquired, one country is much like another,
and finding herself in the same atmosphere of
admiration east as west she had been until lately
on very good terms with herself and the world.
What it was that had caused this new self-discon-
tent she might have found it hard to express.
She only knew that she wanted to understand

the world around her as she saw that other women understood it; wanted to be able to talk and think as it was natural for Sylvia Dorr to talk and think.

With her usual directness of action, she had seized upon a Baedecker guide-book as the first means of culture at hand, though now, pondering over her energetic morning, she could not but feel that she and her father had been groping somewhat in the dark. "No matter, I'll get at it sooner or later, if I have to take poor father right through the book," and she laughed in rather a cheerless fashion.

She was just planning the purchase of more books on French history, when the knowledge that a man had stopped in front of her caused her to raise her head with an angry flush. The anger changed to a little laugh of pleasure as she recognized Andrew Garvie.

"Oh, it's you?" she greeted him. "How queer it seems to see somebody one knows among all these people."

"The world is small," he said as he held her hand. "I was on my way to call on you, and so am doubly in luck, for I should have missed you there. And now, may I sit down and talk? See, there are two seats over in that side path, a little removed from the nurses and babies. I don't suppose you are enamoured of their society. No? That's right."

Having reached their bourne, Garvie began:

"How is it you are all alone? Has the amiable hanger-on gone on strike, or is she busy with your father?"

He had seen enough in Julia's manner the last night he dined with her, to know that he could speak freely.

She laughed as she said: "Mrs. Mallock? Oh no, she isn't with father. He and I just went off by ourselves this morning to poke round Notre Dame, and see the old things. I've heard her sniff at travellers going about like that, so I knew it wouldn't be grand enough for her. She would only have got neuralgia if I had asked her."

"It strikes me you're getting a little tired of the lady," Garvie said. He was leaning an arm on the back of his chair, watching appreciatively a ray of sunshine against the curve of Julia's neck and the loose bits of black hair. Never had he seen her looking better than to-day, in the costly simplicity of her grey cloth walking-dress and violet-wreathed hat.

"Well, I think she wants to boss us too much," Julia acknowedged. "At first, she went about it as gingerly as a cat walking on hot ashes, but now that she is less careful, she sometimes shews what a fool she thinks me. Once or twice, she got quite scratchy when I wouldn't do just what she wanted."

The complaint was made with whimsical lightness, but Garvie answered it more seriously. "I think your best plan is to get scratchy too."

"I do, but father thinks her an oracle, and I don't want to drive her away and have him miss her. You see, she takes good care never to shew her claws when he is around." With a pretty little air of appeal, she turned to him; "You know Paris, Mr. Garvie. Now, do you think Mrs. Mallock is a nice friend for me to have?"

Rather pleased at the chance, he answered frankly, "No, I don't. I should advise you to try to drop her, gradually and politely, so as to make as little of an enemy of her as possible."

"I think it will take a lot of trying—still, I dare say I'll be equal to her," was Julia's cheerful comment. Then in a graver voice, "But you see, I do need a woman to talk to about things. Now, if I only had someone like Miss Dorr to go about with."

She paused, and Garvie, unheeding the little flush on her face, and forgetting his worldly maxims as to never praising one woman too warmly to another, answered with ready enthusiasm, "Yes, you couldn't have a better friend than Miss Dorr. She could tell you all the little things that women want to know—"

The broad-brimmed hat was shading Julia's face as she put in quickly, "Such as how not to dress vulgarly and loudly, and shew how new it all is to one? What is it Mrs. Mallock said they called it here—not to smell of money?"

Her voice was low and hurried, and seemed to break on the last words with a hint of tears.

Garvie tried in vain to read the storm signals hidden under the drooping hat-brim. Honestly shocked at the construction she had put upon his words, he hastened to protest: "My dear girl, I never dreamed of implying that you needed anything of the kind. I merely agreed with you when you said that you wanted a girl friend to talk to. Surely, when you remember that your father and mine were old friends—"

Up went the hat-brim, and a pair of angry grey eyes flashed on him through tears. "Master and workman, you mean. Oh, I don't forget it, and neither do you. Do you suppose I haven't understood what a nuisance poor father and I have been to you?"

The fresh young voice thrilled with pain and pride, and Garvie's pity for her impulsive nature kept down his rising impatience. All the same, his voice was sterner as he said, "If you will be so unreasonable I shall have to leave you, and I wanted to tell you about Mr. Thorpe, who is delighted at the chance of painting your portrait."

Like a naughty child who refuses to be mollified, Julia murmured, "I'm glad to hear that there is somebody not too grand to do it, anyhow."

Garvie, seeing that it was no use to mince matters, spoke out frankly: "Miss Praed, just try to put yourself in my place for a moment. Fortune has been good to me, and I have all the work and all the money I need. Now I happen to know a young fellow who, while he paints as well as I do, has not much of either. Don't you think it is a natural thing for me to try to give him a start that might be the making of him? If his picture does not satisfy you and your father, I promise to paint another myself, afterwards. Don't disappoint me," he pleaded. "Perhaps if I tell you that Thorpe used to be a great friend of Miss Dorr's before things went so hard with him—"

He had no chance to say more, for Julia turned to him, her eyes softly deprecating. "Oh, of course you're right and I'm ever so wrong. I don't know what got into me to be so horrid to-day. I think it was just because I was worrying at being so stupid and ignorant compared to people like Miss Dorr. But I'm so glad now that you shewed me the chance to help him. Oh, I do hope being rich isn't going to make me selfish and careless. I believe it must be having Mrs. Mallock about that makes me feel as though everyone must be mean and scheming. But I know that you just want to help father and me for old times' sake, and really, I'll do whatever you say."

A neat grey glove was held out to him, and Garvie took it, laughing, but with a new sense of nearness to the bright, changeable creature.

"You mustn't make an ogre of me," he protested. "Do what your own warm heart suggests, and you can't go far wrong. Only, to make sure, if you are perplexed about people, ask me and let me help you. You'll remember, won't you, that it's an alliance?"

As he leant forward, holding her hand in his, their appearance was sufficiently lover-like to bring a wistful smile of remembrance into the face of a white-haired lady who passed, leaning on a stick.

"Oh yes, I shan't be afraid to ask you anything, now," was Julia's ready answer. "Why is it that it is always such an unpleasant surprise to hear that another person has been afraid of us?"

"You were never afraid of me?" Garvie protested.

Julia's eyes were mischievous as she answered, "Yes, I think I always was. You see, father kept talking about you, and how you would know everything, and be so particular—"

"I don't wonder you hated me."

"Oh, I never *hated* you, exactly."

"Not personally, only just on principle. Well, you must not do so any more, in either theory or practice. But to return to our facts. Thorpe will come to see you to-morrow morning to arrange about your dress and the sittings."

"But you'll come with him?"

"No, I think you'll make friends sooner without me. And look here, this is my first word of friendly counsel; if your father doesn't go, you must take your maid with you to the studio."

"Why? He's nice, isn't he?" Julia asked, somewhat dismayed.

"Oh yes, he's all right; but it isn't thought the thing to go alone, especially over there in the Quarter."

As Garvie said this he watched her carefully, half expecting another outburst of wrath, but there was only disappointment in her voice as she considered the prospect.

"My, how awful! Jeanne just drives me wild with her *'comme madame voudrez.'* She always sniffs and says that when I want my own way."

"She probably only needs sitting on to be as mild as milk. And then if you take her about, you can rub up your French and get to know your Paris."

"So I can," Julia agreed, mentally sketching out educational excursions that would reduce the lazy Jeanne to despair.

"And I promise not to say *'Comme madame voudrez'* once if you will allow me to walk home with you," Garvie said.

Side by side they strolled up the broad avenue towards the brightness of the western sky, and as they passed one portly nurse said to another, *"Dame,* but there goes a fine couple, if you like."

VII

HER PORTRAIT

THAT evening Mr. Praed scanned his daughter approvingly across the dinner table, saying, "Seems to me as sight-seeing agrees with you. Never saw you look better since I took you away from Boulderwood."

"And please, do you remember the time when I ever did look anything but well?" Julia protested, a bit consciously.

"Well, not to say as you were pale or ill, but once or twice lately I've had a fancy you were mopy or homesick."

"The idea!"

"Perhaps it was foolish. Well, and how did you get on after I left you?"

Julia gave a casual sketch of her meeting with Andrew Garvie, which was none too casual to bring a pleased look into her father's face.

"That's right," he said heartily. "I had a silly kind of an idea as you didn't like the young man, and I was sorry."

"What ever put that in your head?" Then, without waiting for an answer; "Look here, father; you know all sorts of people at home—do you happen to know a publisher among them?"

Only one keen glance from under his heavy grey eyebrows betrayed any surprise at this sudden demand, as the old man answered, "Why yes, there is a publisher on the board of the Chiplauguin pulp-mills—don't you remember the Mr. Stratton as gave you the theatre-party when I took you to Chicago, and who came out last autumn to Boulderwood and went after mountain sheep with George?"

Now Miss Julia had good reason to remember the middle-aged widower who had shewn such an admiration for her. Of this, however, she gave no hint as she said innocently, "Why yes, he sent me that lovely box of roses from New York last Christmas. So *he* is a publisher, is he?"

"He is a partner in Marshall Brothers, one of the biggest houses in all the States. But, whatever can you be wanting with a publisher, Julie? You don't happen to have been writing poetry, do you?" And another keen glance sought for symptoms of any such weakness. A frank laugh greeted this.

"Gracious, do I look like writing poetry?" And then Julia proceeded to give her father a sketch of Sylvia Dorr's labours and ambitions. She told her story eloquently and the old man seemed strongly interested.

"Now that's the kind of girl I like to hear about," he commented heartily. "And I like her all the better for being proud and not leaning up against her friends. But what did you do?" he asked, with an evident certainty that his daughter had done something worth hearing of.

"Me? Oh well, I was going to ask Mr. Garvie how I could get about it, and then I thought, why shouldn't I work it out for myself."

"That's always the best way," her father approved. "Well, work it out, then."

"But you'll have to tell me how to set about it."

At this feminine inconsistency Mr. Praed laughed with gusto, protesting, "Not a bit of it. You just think it over and you'll hit on the common-sense way all right."

Julia leant her chin comfortably on her clasped hands, and with eyes fixed on her father, began, "Well, suppose I were to write to Mr. Stratton and tell him all about the book, asking him what the outside price of publishing it would come to, and saying that you would guarantee him against any loss—"

"Hey?"

The protest was evidently a matter of form, and Julia's only notice of it was to go on, "Yes, that is what I'd have to say—if he would make her an offer to publish the book without speaking of you or me. There, is that common sense?" she demanded in sudden triumph.

"Remarkably so," her father agreed. "Tell you what, Julie, before long you'll be a woman your old father will be proud of, and your husband too, for the matter of that."

"Oh, bother husbands. I don't need a husband," put in Julia with a fine blush.

Mr. Praed shook his head solemnly. "Yes you do, now. It's the natural way, and I hope and trust as none of my children may miss being happy as their mother and I were. Well, you write your letter to-morrow, and I'll see you through. And now let's go and find the proper place for me to smoke my pipe in this gilt-edged establishment."

Julia's mind was set on that unthankful task of playing Providence, and the next morning she sent an urgent appeal to Sylvia Dorr to come to half past twelve *déjeuner* and counsel her on an important matter. "If people have fallen out or anything, it's so much better for them to come on each other unexpected—gives them no time to get high-toned—and if deciding what dress I'm to wear isn't important, I don't know what is," she mentally justified herself.

"That tiresome dress," she went on, wandering restlessly up to a sofa where the brocade folds of the historical dress glittered. "I'm sure Mr. Garvie would think it silly and ostentatious, but I'll get it out of her, anyway."

When Sylvia arrived she was met by Julia, clad in a statuesquely plain dress of white cloth, the perfect outlines alone bearing witness to Madame Marcelle's costly skill.

"Why, you don't look as though there were anything the matter," was Sylvia's greeting.

"No, why on earth should I?"

"Only that your *petit bleu* made me fancy that something dreadful had happened, so that I left my work half finished."

"Oh, I'm so sorry; but really I did want you badly. You see, here is Mr. Thorpe coming at two o'clock about this portrait, and I haven't an idea what to wear, or what to do—and I'm shy."

Sylvia laughed out. She could not help it, though mixed with her gladness there was a shrinking from the sudden knock of fate at the door.

"And that's why you brought me away from my daily toil, you spoilt child?" she said gaily. "But what has become of the Anne of Austria dress? Oh there it is," catching sight of the sofa. "And it is even lovelier than I expected. Surely, you're not going to turn up your nose at my design?" And she lifted the brocade gown daintily with outstretched hands so that her own mayflower face looked out above it at Julia, who said:

"Oh the dress is perfect, but somehow I'm rather out of fancy for grand dress just now. I have a feeling that people might think it a silly sort of showing off, if I were painted in that. And so I put on this plain white dress to see if you thought it looked better."

A troubled appeal in her face gave Sylvia a

hint of something more at question in her mind than a mere change of dress, and guessing that she would make Julia happier if she persuaded her to carry out her first intention, she said, "You must stick to your type. Nature made you for gorgeous plumage. If you had been born a peasant you would have worn a red handkerchief and bright cottons. I'm sure that there is a natural affinity between temperaments and the colours that suit their bodies. I am afraid that I am only a pink and blue person, while all the rich autumn russets and purples belong to you. Come, do let me see you in the dress."

"After lunch," Julia said, looking well pleased. "See, here's my father coming. Father, this is Miss Dorr."

Mr. Praed had a very kindly aspect as he took the thin, white hand into his vigorous grasp. "Delighted to see you, young lady. My girl here tells me as you are living in Paris alone and working for yourself. Now there's nothing takes my fancy like pluck, and if you'll let her and me be friendly like it will please us both, eh Julie?"

For a moment Julia was afraid he may have offended the girl of whom she stood a bit in awe, but there was such a simple sincerity in his manner that it went straight to Sylvia's heart, and she answered, "Indeed I shall, Mr. Praed, and be only too glad of it too."

And so they went to lunch in great content. At table, Sylvia's quick senses could not but be conscious of frequent incongruities between her simpled-minded hosts and their showy setting.

The rooms were those of an ordinary furnished apartment of the more expensive type, and it had never occurred to Julia to make them homelike, as other women did, with books and photos and flowers. The only sign of a personal taste was shown in two or three cages of birds at the different windows, canaries, little green parroquets, and a great, gorgeous macaw, who called hoarsely to his mistress from her bedroom.

"It's always the way," Mr. Praed grumbled cheerfully to Sylvia, "never do we get to a town for a week but Julia brings home some outlandish animal. I bless my stars it's only parrots this time, and no monkeys."

Julia laughed at some memory. "Father's thinking of the dear little monkey I bought in Chicago, that ate up his pocket-book. We had to pay the man to take it back again," she explained.

"And that was'nt the most expensive part of the job," said her father.

"But what will you do with all these birds when you leave Paris?" Sylvia asked.

"Oh, I always find someone who likes to have them. Our concierge's wife will be made happy for ever with the parroquets, but as for Gorgo in there, he goes with me; do you hear, father?"

"Just what I expected my dear, but perhaps some of those slippers he eats may disagree with his constitution before that," he answered hopefully.

"It was only two."

"And not pairs at that, I'd make you a bet," her father protested.

Sylvia talked more than usual to keep down her growing nervousness at the prospect of meeting Thorpe. It was nearly two months since she had seen him, and she could not but wonder what his manner to her would be.

When they had left the table and were taking coffee in the crude red and gilt salon, she felt that anything would be better than sitting there to quiescently await Thorpe's appearance. So she made the suggestion:

"Are not we going to get the question of the dress settled? Because I really must go home soon for an hour or so of daylight work."

"That's right, young lady. Always attend to business. I expect I'll take a stroll and see what news Mr. Britski has," Mr. Praed said, and the two girls were left to their own devices.

Jeanne, the maid, was allowed no share in the entertainment, for Sylvia helped Julia to don the elaborate dress.

"There," she said, after the last touch was given, standing off for an admiring inspection. "You are a perfect presentment of a great lady of Charles the First's day. You would have defended your castle as well as did the Countess of Derby."

She was right. Julia showed a stately bearing, standing there before the long glass, the pearls twisted through the loose dark masses of her hair, the lines of neck and shoulders rising above the falling lace collar, and the full, shining folds of brocade.

At her words Julia's smile faded into wistfulness. "Me a great lady! That would be hard to fancy," she said. Then turning to Sylvia, "Tell me really, do you think I'll ever learn to be a lady? Not the imitation kind that's all right to look at—I know I'm that, now—but the sort that knows and understands about all the beautiful things in the world, like you do."

Sylvia gave a kind little laugh, as she took the girl's hand and patted it. "My dear child, you must not fancy that I am anything out of the way. It is just that I have lived about among clever people and picked up things from them. Why, of course you are a lady now, in every instinct of your nature. All you want is to know a little more of the world, and that soon comes. Why, how old are you? Twenty?"

"Twenty-one."

"And you expect at that age to know everything, you goose. No, be very well pleased with yourself as you are, and go on, all the same, taking in everything you can," Sylvia advised.

"How good you are to me," Julia said gratefully, her self-distrustful fancies scattered by the judicious words of praise.

A knock at the door, and a servant with Thorpe's card broke in on their talk.

Julia was quick to mark her friend's nervousness, and took command of the situation. "I'll feel like a fool going to receive a man I don't know, dressed up like this," she said with well-feigned shyness. "You go in and tell him I'm coming."

"I can not do that," Sylvia said in a final tone. "We will go together."

So it was; and Thorpe, standing staring absently at the cage of green parroquets, turned at sound of their coming, to see his young hostess in her bravery of apparel, led in by Sylvia Dorr, the light of eager greeting in her eyes.

"Allow me to introduce Charlotte de la Tremouille, Countess of Derby," she said gaily, and Thorpe's heart was lightened from the fear that she would greet him with sad or proud looks.

"Please don't mind her, Mr. Thorpe," said Julia, as she came forward. "It was she made me put on this dress to see if you liked it for my picture, but if you think it looks silly—"

Thorpe was holding Sylvia's hand as long as possible. "Silly?" he said. "Miss Dorr knows my tastes better than that. She knows that this is like a Titian or Tintoretto portrait, if only I were up to it. It is very good in you to trust yourself to my unknown hands, Miss Praed."

"Oh, but Mr. Garvie says that you are as clever as he is," Julia answered as though that settled

79

thought, "Oh, I've left the little jewel-safe open —just what father told me never to do. Please excuse me."

She could not stay away for long, but there was time for Thorpe to say to Sylvia, "It is so good to see you again. You understood that it was because I was down on my luck that I did not come?"

"Yes," came the soft answer, "but was not that just the reason you should have? Ought not friends to help each other?"

"I will be wiser next time."

"Yes, please."

Then the door opened to reveal Julia, one hand raised to support the gorgeous macaw, who was crooning to her in high content.

"Jove! That is perfect. Just as it is. I must have you like that, Miss Praed," Thorpe cried in frank enthusiasm.

As Sylvia agreed with him, it was soon settled, and the details arranged, Thorpe walked home with Sylvia, and she got no hours of daylight work.

VIII

FONTAINBLEAU

NOTHING helps a nice girl to make friends more quickly with a man than the knowledge that he is in love with a woman she likes. Julia and Thorpe were soon on the frankest of terms, and, in spite of the presence of Jeanne, she enjoyed the hours spent at Thorpe's studio.

He had the portrait-painter's knack of keeping his model in a good humour, and Julia talked away, sometimes telling him tales of her mountain rambles at home, and of the strange waifs and strays of civilization to be met there. At other times she questioned him of the things around her with which she was anxious to become familiar; and Thorpe would have been amused to know that often, when she went home, she carefully wrote down the names of artists and pictures which he had casually mentioned, together with his comments on them.

True, there were days when Thorpe looked haggard and spoke abstractedly, and after these Julia spared no pains to entice Sylvia into taking Jeanne's place as chaperone.

It was not always that she succeeded, but when she did, the spell of Sylvia's gentleness worked, and drove away the dark humour. Occasionally, Mr. Praed went with his daughter to the studio, and Thorpe showed great delight in the old man's reminiscences of his days of early hardship and adventure in the Michigan forests.

The portrait made rapid progress, for Thorpe worked with feverish energy, sometimes borrowing the costume to place on a lay figure. It was about half finished when Julia had the brilliant idea of giving a birthday party.

"What's it to be?" asked her father, taking up the idea vigorously. "A theatre party with supper at a restaurant? A dance? Though I fancy we wouldn't have enough people for that, unless we asked Mrs. Mallock to look them up for us."

"Bother Mrs. Mallock! It's not going to be her party. It's all my own, this time. Now just listen, and see how well I've arranged it," and she leant forward in her favourite pose of her chin on hands.

"You know you love going charging round in an automobile, and fancy your driving, no end. Well, they've got them to hold six, and that would just suit us. We can start in the morning, go down to Fontainebleau, see the old palace, where the kings and queens used to live, have lunch, take a drive in the forest that they say is just like the wild woods, and get home in time for a scramble supper here. Now isn't that well planned?"

"Splendid," said her admiring parent. "How ever did you find it all out?"

"Oh, Mr. Garvie has been down there like that, and told me about it. He knows the best roads, and if you get tired driving the thing, he can."

"Strikes me, this is Mr. Garvie's party," the old man said, with twinkle in his eye, but Julia ignored the remark.

He made a loyal protest when he found that Mrs. Mallock was not included among the four guests, but Julia was able to prove that the lady was in bed with a cold, and so the party remained as she had settled it.

There were Garvie and Thorpe in tweeds and holiday humour, Sylvia Dorr smiling under a flower-wreathed hat, trimmed by herself the night before, and Miss Oakes grimly amiable behind a brown gauze veil.

Can any band of boys and girls start out with the same determined sense of enjoyment as do a group of those old enough to have known the cares of the strenuous life, when they leave these behind them for a day, to let the joy of the world sink into their souls, with refreshment and healing? Julia was the only one of the six who had not as yet known the harder side of life, and perhaps even she had her secret problems to solve.

Mr. Praed was a proud man as he took his seat, his motor-cap pulled well down over his eyes, and started southward, crossing the river and running along the wide, leafy avenues that skirt the Invalides.

Soon the dreary southern suburbs gave place to eccentric little villas, pride of the retired Parisian tradesman's heart.

"Seems to me as they must grow an extra crop of them coloured glass balls in their gardens," Mr. Praed said to Miss Oakes, who sat beside him.

At last they were in the open country, among the first green of meadows and woods, and over the meadows sounded, piercing sweet, the song of the lark, and from the depths of the woods came the mysterious gurgle of the cuckoo. At this latter, Julia was especially delighted.

"I believe you thought they only existed in poetry books," Garvie accused her.

"Well, that's all I ever knew of them, anyway," she retorted, unabashed.

When they reached Fontainebleau some of them might have liked to make for the forest, but their young hostess held them resolutely to their sight-seeing.

Garvie was at her side as they passed through galleries and rooms once stirring with history, now abandoned to drowsy guardians and inquisitive tourists. He was curious to see what impression it all made upon her, and rather to his surprise found that she took in the spirit of the place with quick intuition.

Christina of Spain and Monaldeschi, Jose-

phine's divorce, and Napoleon's parting with
his old guard—she had some mental picture of
them all, and when she shewed a lively interest in
the salamander of Francis and the crescent of
Diane de Poitiers, he ventured a joke on her new
learning. "Have you become a disciple of Miss
Dorr's, and fallen under the spell of the Renaissance?"

Julia flushed and laughed, but answered bravely, "It's all so splendid that I can't help loving it.
Still, one needs to fancy it a perpetual summer
time, with roses and sunshine, and everyone always young and strong. Diane de Poitiers with a
toothache, or these courtiers with their velvet
and lace muddy or shabby, would break the spell
at once. Then I suppose my fancy is taken by the
contrast of that old-time gorgeousness with all
that I used to know best, the lumberman's camps
and the mining settlements up among the great,
dark mountains; the winter nights, shining and
white like Revelations; the summer thunder-
storms booming and rolling among the crags, and
the strong men fighting for civilization among it
all."

It was the first time that Garvie had heard
Julia speak out her thoughts in this fashion, and
he kept for long the remembrance of the girl in
her white serge dress, her face bright with interest, the stiff old-world setting forming a background to her young vitality.

They had loitered near a window at one end of

the stately Gallerie d'Henri II, to look down on
the stretch of formal garden below, while the
others dutifully followed Mr. Praed as he kept
close to the guide he had engaged, who was ex-
patiating in a loud voice on the frescoes of Prim-
aticcio. Mr. Praed believed in getting his
money's worth out of sight-seeing, as he did out
of everything else.

The spring sunshine came through the window, bringing out wonderful lights and shades
in Julia's black hair, against which rested the
red poppies in her hat, and Garvie thought to
himself that she was better worth looking at than
all the frescoes of the Renaissance. His mind
was rapidly dropping its critical attitude towards
the girl, and it was with full interest that he
answered, "Yes, that must be the life that makes
real men and women. I have sometimes thought
that I have fallen into a feather-bed existence
here; that if I were to have the courage to leave
these crowded art circles and go out by myself
into a fresher atmosphere, I might paint something of my own country and people—something
that would live through its reality."

There was no doubt of Julia's interest, as she
listened with shining eyes. "Oh, do, Mr. Garvie,"
she said impulsively. "Come out to us among
our mountains, and I will show you the stretches
of wild-flowers at the foot of the rocks. I have
seen the white-haired, Swedish children filling
their arms with them. And then there are the

days of blue autumn haze when one sometimes meets a half-breed woman in a dull red dress coming down a path between the yellow trees, with a big bundle on her back. Oh, there are pictures everywhere."

"And you have the true eye for them. Why, with a few words you show me the whole scheme of colour. And I begin to suspect you of being an idealist too—the children picking flowers in the spring sunshine, the tired woman in the autumn evening—you feel the meaning of both. Yes, I shall come some day, and shall remind you that, as it was you who asked me, you are bound to play showman to your mountains."

His ready response brought a startled look into Julia's eyes. "Oh, I didn't mean to ask you to come," she faltered. "Of course it's all rough out there, and I see how much more your life here can give you."

"There, it might give me the best of all," protested Garvie, who was losing his head a bit, and saying more than he had meant to say. After all, how many men when they begin to make love, do it of foreordained purpose?

Just then an impatient hail from Mr. Praed broke in on their talk and sent Julia skimming down the length of the gallery with a gay protest against the slipperiness of royal floors.

When the palace had been viewed the guide was paid, and Mr. Praed relaxed the vigour of his sight-seeing and was content to imbibe his history from Miss Oakes, nearly as true an encyclopedia of facts as Baedecker.

Thorpe and Sylvia loitered by the pond where the aged carp form an attraction to loungers. There was the breath of sun-warmed April flowers in the air, and there was the return of hope in their hearts.

"Did you ever hear the old French name for spring, *le renouveau?*" Thorpe asked, looking down at Sylvia where she sat on the stone coping of the pond. "The word has been in my mind often to-day. It seems to mean a fresh chance, a new start in life; all that I feel now I am with you. I can't help knowing that this portrait of Miss Praed's is going well, and if only it is a success and my picture gets into the Salon, I may have a show yet." He hesitated, and then went on earnestly: "I have made up my mind if things go better, to go home and have a try for portrait-work. This Paris is stultifying to a man's soul, unless he is a hero, and I'm not that, God knows. You don't like Paris, do you Sylvia?"

She looked up and spoke with unusual vehemence. "No, I hate it. I only stay here because my fashion drawings need the Paris stamp at home."

"But why shouldn't you do better work than those things," Thorpe pleaded. "That article in the *Era* on the women of Catherine de Medici's court was charming—everyone said so. Why not stick to work like that and drop those wretched fashion things?"

Sylvia laughed. "The spring has gone to your head and makes you forget the lean years when one needs a prosaic standby. To tell you the truth, I'm too great a coward to leave the safe shelter of the fashions. Good work takes time, and those drawings are turned out so quickly, and the pay is a certainty."

Thorpe's voice dulled as he said, "It's hard that you and I cannot afford the luxury of honest work."

There was a nervous questioning in Sylvia's upward glance as she said cheerfully, "Oh, yes, we can. Work may be just as honest, if it is not grand. But I often think how wonderful it is that I have got on as well as I have."

"Yes, it makes me all the more ashamed to see a frail little woman, like you, facing the world so bravely, and holding her own as I can not do," Thorpe said gloomily.

"Why should you be ashamed of bad luck?" Sylvia protested: "Bad luck, that is I trust, over and done with. Then you have not heard from the Salon yet?"

"No, but I must very soon now," and he drew a sharp breath. "I had not the heart to ask you to look at my picture when it was finished, but I know that it is good work, that they ought not to refuse. I am willing to be judged by it. What is it Browning says—my old trick you see—'I stand on my attainment?' Ah, if I might only say as he does,

> Other heights in other lives, God willing;
> All the gifts from all the heights, you own, love "

His voice shook, and his hand was near hers on the stone coping.

'Why not?" and with the words her eyes met his in sweet directness.

There was no response of lover's gladness. "Perhaps some day I may regain the right. Not now," he murmured; and bewildered, pained, Sylvia was silent.

On the pause came the summons of Mr. Praed, calling them to lunch at the Hotel de l'Aigle Noir, and thus in a short time the worthy man interrupted two interesting interviews.

After lunch came the hours in the forest, where a shimmer of vividest young green rested on the birch trees, without as yet veiling their white branches, where the downy bracken stems were uncurling their heads; and white garlic blossoms spread over the ground like snow.

But it was the rocks and pine trees that aroused Julia's enthusiasm.

"It's almost like home," she cried, and insisted on a stoppage, and a scramble up one of the jagged slopes. No one felt any desire to hurry, and it was a marvel that they got back to the Avenue Friedland before the yellow twilight had altogether faded in the west.

Then came a meal that was half dinner, half supper, altogether informal in its gaiety.

"Now ladies and gentlemen," said Mr. Praed rising, "we've had our little outing, and we've all been happy together, and I want you to drink to the health of that young woman opposite, Miss Julia Praed, who is twenty-one to-day. She ain't likely to be any better looking, or any better-natured than she is now." There came a chorus of protest against any such necessity, at which the old gentleman beamed. "Well, I daresay I agree with you on that point myself, but what we'd all like, I'm sure, is for her to go on increasing in health and happiness right up to the end." His voice sank on the last word. Then, "Julie, my dear, here's luck," and he reached across the table to clink his glass against hers, an example followed by the others.

IX

BRITSKI

IT was the next morning that Mr. Praed dropped into Britski's galleries, those wonderful treasure-houses of art, old and new.

From the outside on the Avenue de l'Opera they looked like two small adjoining shops, one window displaying two or three paintings against red velvet drapery, the other a confusion of ivory carvings, bits of old china, silverware, all in the approved state of dustiness for bric-a-brac shops. Within, there were long showrooms, the darker ones below filled with old furniture and other antiques, while in the top of the house were two sky-lighted galleries in which hung collections of old and of new pictures.

"Never mix the past and the present if you want to do either justice," the owner was wont to say.

The cream of the collection was to be found in a small room at the end of the picture-galleries, a room which Britski made his own private retreat. Here stood the most perfect *cinque cento* cabinet in the place, here hung a tiny Millet that Britski always intended to sell if he should get a large enough price, and always deferred parting with on some excuse. The man was a genuine lover of art, and looked forward to a day when he should be rich enough to keep the best of his treasures for his own enjoyment. He had angled for Mr. Praed with the skill and patience he knew how to use when the game seemed worth it. First, he was led on to acquire the habit of dropping in at Britski's in idle hours, to wander freely about the galleries, smoking and chatting with the owner, who had always leisure to answer his questions. Thus, by a series of delicate experiments, the latter ascertained that pictures had small attraction for the Canadian. He might choose to buy a moderate-priced, bright-coloured modern painting, that told its own tale of incident or humour, but he would never pay down his thousands for some dingy canvas on the assurance that it was a valuable old master, or for some weird impressionist work, because it happened to be the latest fashion.

And so it followed that Mr. Praed's steps were seldom guided towards the picture galleries, but various costly antiques were brought in his way, and their prices casually mentioned until he grew used to their value.

Then, one day, the carefully watched for clew came, when the old lumberman's eyes brightened at sight of a silver centre-piece of the time of Henri II. There were three high vases joined by a low colonnade along which were studded exquisitely worked little statuettes.

He at once threw out hints of buying the master-piece, but Britski insisted that it did not belong to him, but had been sent by a famous collector for repairs.

He promised, however, to keep a sharp lookout for any chance of buying a similar article. He apparently saw that the time had come for the fish to bite, for, on Mr. Praed's next visit, he told him the story of the impoverished daughter of a noble family, forced to sell the ancestral furnishing of her home, the story which Mr. Praed had repeated to Garvie at his dinner-table. So far Britski had said nothing more definite, and Mr. Praed was growing impatient. "If he doesn't come down to business, I'll let him know as there are more dealers in Paris than him," he fumed with an effort at self-assertion.

The conventual calm of the place soothed him, and when he found the owner carefully studying an illuminated breviary through a magnifying glass, his greeting was pacific, though to the purpose, "Morning, Mr. Britski. Got any news for me today of that there castle? It's not in Spain, I hope."

"Ah no, not in Spain, Mr. Praed," and the small, slight man laughed and rubbed his hands together appreciatively.

Voice and laugh were low and pleasantly modulated, and Britski's appearance was not unattractive. His sallow face with its aquiline features was of the Slavonic type, and through all its impassivity there was a gently sad expression that hinted at past failures.

Laying down the breviary with a lingering touch as though he loved the old morocco, Britski politely waved his visitor to an armchair, while he took a seat opposite. Mr. Praed had been shown into his private sanctum, and the heavy curtains were closed behind him.

"It is strange," Britski began in his careful English, "but I was about to write and give you the news you ask for. Yes sir, Mademoiselle de Rostrênan has decided to give you the first choice of the family treasures—treasures which I assure you are no everyday affair. I consider myself lucky that I am able to secure such a chance for you."

"That's all right then," said Mr. Praed comfortably, "and now the next question is my going to see them. I suppose you'll come and show me the way. I ain't much good at French, and you said this castle was in an out-of-the-way place, didn't you?"

"It is down on the southern coast of Brittany, a long day's railway journey from Paris, with an hour's drive afterward. You would not care to have the things packed and sent here?" Britski questioned.

"No, no," was the testy rejoinder. "Didn't I tell you that I wanted to see for myself what an old castle and its fittings-out was like? No, I'll be off as soon as can be. Would the end of the week suit you?"

Britski looked thoughtful as though weighing possibilities, before he said smoothly, "I fear that I cannot leave my business just now, but I could easily find you a good travelling servant or courier who spoke French and English."

Mr. Praed, with all a self-made man's distrust of being managed by such people, answered hastily:

"No, no, I ain't such a fool as not to be able to find my way all right, if you write out on a paper the names I want, and all that. I've done it in that fashion in Mexico. And now let's see the catalogue." And Mr. Praed prepared to enjoy himself.

Britski watched closely the effect of his words, as he answered, "I have never received a complete catalogue from Mlle. de Rostrênan. That she prefers to go over with you herself. You see, I am nothing but an agent in this matter, receiving a commission on the sale. But," and here he lowered his voice cautiously, "I have been asked to explain to you in confidence that, while the Rostrênan treasures of tapestry and armour, of medieval furniture and china, are well known to connoisseurs, the public is ignorant of the most valuable part of the collection. It seems that as far back as their records go, the Rostrênan family has always been in possession of a marvellous

hoard of silver cups and vessels of Greek or
Roman workmanship, many of them magnificent-
ly embossed with classical subjects. These things
have never been photographed or accurately
drawn, but an agent whom I can trust has seen
them and reports them of the highest value.

"If the lords of Rostrênan knew whether this
treasure were the spoil of medieval crusades, or of
some Norman pirate shipwrecked on their rocky
coast, or, like the treasure found near Rennes,
were simply turned up by the plough, they have
never said, and the local impression seems to have
been that the things were long since sold and
scattered. But I have confidential information
from the young lady that these valuable articles
are still at Rostrênan and that they must be sold
without delay. And so, you see, my dear sir, that
this matter is a larger one than is at first visible."

His keen glance sought Mr. Praed's face only
to find it bright with interest.

"That's something like." the latter said, thump-
ing his stout stick vigourously on the floor. "I
didn't want any twopenny ha' penny sort of
affair. But when you talk of cups and vessels—"
He hesitated. "I suppose you mean they are
something ornamental. Just plain silver tea cups
wouldn't be much use, you know."

Britski smiled the merest bit, as he answered,
"Perhaps they might be better described as vases
and salvers; handsome table ornaments, in fact.
I will read you the young lady's description of

97

one or two pieces: 'There is a silver dish, two and a half feet in diameter, on which is embossed the abduction of Briseis and her restoration to Achilles'—"

"What's that?" interrupted Mr. Praed.

"'Those are scenes from Greek history," was the explanation. "'Another piece is a cup called a *patère*, with reliefs representing a contest between Bacchus and Hercules, and bordered by medallions of Roman emperors from Hadrian to Geta'—this one must be of great value," Britski looked up from the letter to say with appreciation.

"It certainly sounds well," the other agreed. "But look here, you haven't said why you spoke of all this in a confidential way. I should have thought such things would be best sent to Paris to be sold with as much fuss as possible—that is if the young lady needs all the money she can get."

The objection was shrewd, and the lines around Britski's eyes contracted with keenness to meet it. "No doubt, as you say that would be the best method, if the owner could prove that the silver was not treasure-trove, dug up from the earth or washed ashore, and so liable to be claimed by the government.

"The family have always been strong royalists and clericals, and so obnoxious to the present government, especially since the peasants in their neighborhood opposed the expulsion of the Sisters. I have heard that the Préfet down there is on the lookout to catch them tripping, so this poor girl has to be on her guard."

"Well, whatever the man you mention may be, I don't think much of him to be sniffing round an orphan in that fashion," Mr. Praed broke out hotly, and with the words the strain in Britski's face relaxed.

"I fear that the French have fallen away from their old-time chivalry, at least we Hungarians think so," he said loftily. Then becoming practical again, he asked, "Shall I write to Mlle. de Rostrênan and say that you will go down on the tenth, to the nearest village—it is about three or four miles from the chateau—and see the collection? You ought to be fairly comfortable at the inn there."

"Oh that don't matter. An old lumberman like me knows how to rough it, and if you'll send along that man of yours to see me as far as the village, it will be all right. Let's see—Tuesday is the ninth—yes, that suits well enough. My daughter is busy with this portrait of hers, and won't be lonely. By-the-by, you are up in those things. Do you know a young American artist named Rupert Thorpe?"

Again the deep lines around Britski's eyes contracted as though a light had been flashed before him.

"Rupert Thorpe," he repeated vaguely, as if not remembering the name. "Oh yes, I know him. I have once or twice bought small things of his, when he was very anxious to sell. Do I understand that he is painting Miss Praed's portrait?"

"Yes, he's been at it for a week or so, and seems to put his whole backbone into the job. A clever young fellow, Mr. Garvie calls him," and he glanced sharply at Britski, whose noncommital tone perplexed him.

"Oh yes, he is clever," the other acknowledged. Then with a seeming outburst of frankness, "But if you had done me the honour to consult me, he is not the man I should have chosen to paint a beautiful young lady's portrait."

"What! what! Nothing wrong with him, eh?"

"Oh, nothing definite, only if you knew these young men of the Latin Quarter, wild and reckless, living from hand to mouth among models and such, you would see that they are hardly the kind for *comme-il-faut* young ladies to know. I trust Miss Praed does not go to his studio?"

"Well, yes, she does," was the crestfallen answer. "But then Mr. Garvie spoke well of him, and he seemed such a good-natured young chap."

"Young men will stick to each other," Britski conceded, "and I allow that he is all that is pleasant as long as things go to his liking, but let his vanity once be offended—and he is touchy as the devil—and he is off, with his work finished or unfinished, that is all the same to him. And that is the last you see of him. I speak from experience, I who tried to help him," and the Hungarian shook his head in mournful resignation to youthful ingratitude.

"Dear, dear, that's too bad! Well, if he tries any of those tricks on me he'll hear of it!"

"Ah, sir, you might as well let a will-o'the-wisp hear of it. When he vanishes, he vanishes, that's all."

"Well, he hasn't vanished yet, for I left my daughter at his studio an hour ago. And that reminds me, I must be getting home for lunch," and Mr. Praed hoisted himself out of the armchair and proceeded through the show rooms towards the door.

Without noticing two ladies who stood with their backs to the light, he spoke over his shoulder to Britski, "Well then, you'll settle it for me to leave Paris on Wednesday, the 10th, eh?"

"Leave Paris, dear Mr. Praed. Not for long I hope," said one of the ladies, in the shrill voice of Mrs. Mallock.

From behind the old man came a fierce glare from Britski, but either the light was dull or the lady was obstinate, for she held her ground, leaving her companion absorbed in the inspection of old laces.

"Good morning, Mrs. Mallock," said Mr. Praed. "Well no, I don't suppose my little trip will take more than a week or so."

"Ah, that is a comfort. I feared we were going to lose you," Mrs. Mallock said with genuine fervour. "And dear Julia, she goes with you?"

"Don't think so ma'am. You see there's this portrait."

"But you can't leave her alone in Paris. You'll have to let me go and take care of her."

This view had never occurred to Mr. Praed, who was used to consider his daughter equally capable of looking after herself in a lumber camp or a Chicago hotel. However, he had acquired the habit of deferring to Mrs. Mallock as an authority in all matters Parisian, and so answered meekly, but without enthusiasm, "I'm sure, it's very kind in you Mrs. Mallock, and Julie will be delighted to have you."

Upon this latter point, however, he had his doubts—doubts which gave him a deprecatory manner that evening until he had confessed his weakness, and received absolution in Julia's good-humoured, though resigned acquiescence.

"She *is* sly. She knew that I never would have asked her if she hadn't got hold of you first. But I needn't let her bother me much. She can take the carriage and go 'round doing the grand by herself sometimes. She loves that. It would have been so nice though to have had Miss Dorr."

Mr. Praed said nothing at this. The distrust of Thorpe implanted by Britski had momentarily cast its shadow over Sylvia too.

X

GARVIE'S MODEL

I T'S no use Virginie. I'm sorry, for you've been posing like an angel, but those eyes won't do. You're in for a hard day's work to-morrow, for we must go at them afresh."

An equable man in practical affairs, Garvie was a slow, and sometimes a fussy, painter. Hard to satisfy with his own work, he would go on trying to bring it up to his standard until his friends sometimes told him that he had taken the life out of it.

Intent on the defects of his picture, he did not look up until he noticed that no answer came from the girl, who had already changed her dress and now hovered in an uncertain fashion between the easel and the door.

"In a hurry?" he asked carelessly.

"Sapristi! No. At least—I thought you might do without me now," and her raised hands fumbled nervously with the folds of her veil.

Garvie looked puzzled.

"Yes, of course, I do not need you any more to-day. But come early to-morrow."

Virginie's sombre eyes were fixed intently on him, as she said, with a sort of dull impatience,

"I mean, do without me to-morrow—do without me altogether. I cannot sit any more."

Garvie was tired and discouraged, and spoke sharply, "But you must. Did not you hear me say that I shall have to do the eyes all over again?"

"Yes, I heard," was the sullen answer.

"And you know that this London show is an important thing. Come, be reasonable. Why, Virginie, you are crying. Whatever is up now?"

With a quick movement, he had caught her by the shoulders and turned her to the light in an attempt to see her face, but she just hung her head and sobbed, "It is only that it hurts to disappoint you, the only man who for years had treated me decently. Oh yes, I know," with a sudden flash, "they fall in love with me, and then for a time I rule them, the imbeciles, but—well, no matter. Indeed I would not go if I could help it."

And now she was looking up at him, her face softened as few had seen it, and Garvie, realizing her weird fascination, knew that it behooved him to walk warily.

"And why cannot you help it? You are free, are you not?" he asked gravely.

She gave a little laugh that had no mirth in it. "Who can say that he is free? All are bound in some fashion. But tell me, then, if I went for always you would miss me in your painting, eh?"

She had struck the right chord to stir his caution. "Miss you? I do not see how I should work without you. You have been the best part of all my last year's pictures. Those cairngorm eyes of yours must magnetize me, for I never feel tired when I am painting you," he broke out. Then with an attempt to lighten the situation, "But you are only talking nonsense. Why should you go away?"

In a vibrant whisper she answered, "I must go. I must go." Then, still holding him with her eyes, she went on, slowly, intently: "There is one way—if you needed me so much—if we could go away from Paris—anywhere—what does it matter?—where you could work. There is Venice— that is good in the spring. Then you could always have me to paint—but *ciel!* I know it is impossible."

If he had ever really fallen under her spell, Garvie might now have forgotten the grim lessons he had learnt from seeing men sink under such a life as she suggested.

"Dropping down the ladder, rung by rung."

As it was, he was able to stand firm, though he felt a genuine pity as he took her hand, saying, "Yes, Virginie, it *is* impossible. I could not leave Paris now and give up all I have gained. I have made my place here and must stick to it. But why will you not tell me what is the matter, and let me see if I can help you?"

Twisting herself away from his grasp she cried wildly, "You can give me no help. I must go! Let me go!"

"If there is any one bothering you for money—"

"No, I need no money now. Keep what you owe me, in case I ever come back. Listen, Monsieur Garvie, I have told Suzette Boulay to come and see you. She has red hair—"

"Damn Suzette Boulay! Virginie—"

"Adieu, monsieur, adieu," and with a swift rush, the girl was gone.

Garvie stood looking towards the door, and presently drew a deep breath, partly relief, partly regret.

"Poor soul. The tragic forces have turned up, sure enough. Well, thank goodness, I did not make an ass of myself. I believe it was a close shave, once. And now I think I need my *déjeuner* after all this."

The peace of his usual haunt greeted him, as he entered the dingy room at the Hotel de France et Bretagne, where the little old lady at the desk smiled a friendly greeting, and where every man in the room was an acquaintance, and many were friends. Such quiet places there still are in Paris, where the provincial or tourist seldom penetrates.

Garvie passed on to his usual seat at a corner table, where already Frye was in earnest discussion with a burly Norman, winner of last year's first medal, and with the gaunt correspondent and art-critic of an important American paper.

Frye's mind was evidently full of his topic, for

on his short greeting, he added the news, "Thorpe's picture is refused."

"Not possible? Such clever work. Strong as nails," Garvie protested.

"Clever if you like," said the medallist, "but all the same it was immature. He is young enough for the rebuff to do him no harm. A refusal or two might have been good for you and me, five years ago."

"Injustice is good for no one. It may be his last strong effort," Garvie said brusquely. He was seriously disturbed at the news.

The critic lighted a cigar, as he delivered his dictum, in the fashion of one whose words carried weight.

"Thorpe had better go out to New York and try his luck there. He will have no success in Paris."

"Why?" Frye asked.

"Can not say. But I have an idea that he has trodden on the corns of some of the Veiled Beings who have power to make or mar such as he; and if so, the gods themselves could not save him. Are you a friend of his, Garvie?"

"Yes, I have always had a liking for the boy."

"Then the best thing you can do is to persuade him to go home, and start afresh. Coming, De Fougères. Ta, ta."

The two men walked away, leaving Frye and Garvie alone.

"What did he mean?" asked Garvie, troubled.

Frye shrugged his shoulders. "He knows more than he intends to say, I fancy. There is probably some one whom he cannot offend by speaking out."

Both men sat in silence, considering the matter. It was Garvie who spoke first, "It cannot be accident when the same thing happened last year. Have you any theory as to who is at the bottom of the affair?" he asked.

The answer came in one word, prompt and uncompromising, "Britski. I know that he took nearly all of Thorpe's last summer work in Normandy, small work, I mean."

"What has that to do with it?" Garvie asked with a cynical eye on his just arrived *omelette au rhum,* as though even that might disappoint him.

"I have noticed that once he regularly takes a young fellow's smaller work, that man never gets in a position to ask big prices."

Garvie pondered this problem a moment before saying, "But surely it would pay him to push the man whose work he has bought."

"So I should have supposed, but it does not seem to be the case. He does push for all he is worth, and more, the man whose big Salon picture he buys. I know that. He is pretty deep, that little Hungarian, Pole, Jew—whatever he is."

As Frye spoke he rose and Garvie said, "Wait a bit, and I will come along with you. I must look up the poor devil, though I doubt if he welcomes me. But, see here, how did you hear of his bad luck?"

"I met that Californian boy, Howe, as I came along, just now. Their studios are next to each other, you know. He said that yesterday they went in together, and Thorpe found the notice in the concierge's den. He just read it and seemed dazed for a moment, then laughed and said, 'Well, I am going to sell my traps, buy a van, and start as a travelling photographer. Like to come?' and he went off to his room."

"Poor devil!"

Together the friends threaded one or two of the old, winding streets of the Quarter, before they stopped at a door in the Rue Monsieur-le-Prince.

"Coming up?" Garvie asked.

"No. I always thought Job might have preferred his friends one at a time. You can let me know to-morrow in what humour you find him."

But this Garvie was not destined to do, for the concierge, less ferocious than most of his kind, recognizing him as a frequent visitor, poked his head out of his dark little room and asked, "You seek Monsieur Thorpe, Monsieur?"

"Yes, he is at home?"

"Ah, that he will never be again, for, look you, to-day he brings in a man who buys his furniture. Then he stows away his canvasses in Monsieur Howe's studio, takes his poor little trunk and drives off. Oh yes, he paid me, he was not bad, *le petit* Thorpe, not like some of those *rapins*."

As the wizened old man talked, Garvie stood thinking. So then it was despair absolute that had conquered, cutting this fellow-countryman off from the future of chosen career, friendship, perhaps love itself. Surely there must have been some dark, unknown force at work to thus isolate a man from all that he valued.

As he stood outside the dingy apartment house, realizing his helplessness to do anything more, and yet hesitating to go back to his own affairs, a sudden remembrance of Julia Praed's portrait stirred him to fresh dismay. He had recommended Thorpe to them, had made himself personally responsible for him, and with a result at which Mr. Praed had a right to be seriously annoyed.

Confound the fellow and his unreliable humours. He was as trying to have to do with as Virginie herself. Virginie! And now an idea came that caused him to stand and stare so fixedly at a *blanchisserie* that a visible flutter spread among the young women behind the window panes.

Virginie! It was this morning that she had been in such hurry to go. It was this morning that Thorpe had driven off from his studio. Was is possible that a mere sordid artist and model intrigue had been made such a source of discomfort to him? And Sylvia? Garvie muttered some unpleasant word, recalling a glimpse of the girl's face as she smiled up at Thorpe on that Fontaine-bleau day, and thinking of what she might soon hear as idle gossip.

But she should never hear it through him, he vowed to himself.

Now his evident duty was to go to the Praeds and express his regret that his second-hand philanthrophy had led to such annoyance for them—a not unusual trick of that cheap article, when we indulge at a friend's expense.

It did not take long to have himself conveyed in a cab across the river to the Avenue Friedland. In those more cosmopolitanly fashionable neighbourhoods the elastic mid-day meal is apt to be nearly an hour later than in the purely French regions, such as the Quarter, and Garvie found the father and daughter at table loitering over their coffee.

His first glance showed him that Mr. Praed's good humor was over-clouded, and Julia's smile anxious; but the greeting he received was as cordial as ever.

"That's right, Mr. Garvie. Just in time for a smoke. Julie here, doesn't mind it." Then when his visitor was settled, the old man went straight to the point, "And so our young painter has skipped and left us in the lurch, eh?"

Garvie did not fancy the words, still he had resolved to eat humble pie if necessary, and tried to do so with a good grace. He was assisted in this by an appealing glance from the grey eyes at the other end of the table. Like most really pretty girls, Julia was twice as charming in her home dress, and her outline against the light was altogether satisfying to Garvie's eye.

"Yes, that is what I came about," he answered frankly. "I am sorry enough for the poor fellow; but I am deeply annoyed that he should have treated you like this, and that I should have been the cause of your giving him the commission."

"You weren't the cause of his going off in that underhand, sneaky way," grunted Mr. Praed, who even in his ill-humour could not consider "old man Garvie's son" to be in the wrong. "It was exactly as Britski warned me—soon as there's anything does not just suit him, he's off without a word, and, 'you might as well try to catch a will-o'-the-wisp,' says he. He knew him, it seems."

"Britski said that, did he?" Garvie spoke with ominous sternness, about to protest, when he checked himself. He would know more about the business before he attacked Britski; would know if he had any right to defend Thorpe. And so he only asked, "How did you hear he had gone?"

"I had a note from him this morning, saying he was sorry not to finish my portrait, but that he was too ill to work and had gone to the country. He thanked us very nicely for what he called our great kindness to him," Julia said, simply.

"Well, I shall be back in town before the Salon opens—say the end of April. Then you must let me paint your portrait myself. I only doubt if I

can make as good a thing of it as Thorpe was doing. It would have been a magnificent picture."

As he spoke, Garvie was already studying
Julia with artistic appreciation, through his half-
closed lids. He was beginning to think that he
had been a fool to depute so pleasant a task to
another. Under his gaze, Julia blushed finely,
but it was her father, who, instantly mollified by
the offer, answered heartily, "Not half so good as
yours will be. I'll bet my boots on that. It
stands to reason that the men at the head of these
things must know best. They give your pictures
a good place, and they kick this young Thorpe
out, and I, for one, am quite willing to believe
that it's all as it should be. Excuse me for a
moment, Mr. Garvie, I just want to get another
cigar."

As her father walked heavily out of the room,
Julia, with her chin on her folded hands,, leant
toward Garvie and asked cautiously, "Don't you
really know why he went away, Mr. Garvie?"

The latter felt himself in a tight place. He
wished neither to arouse strong sympathy for the
absent one nor to imply any hidden blame, for
either opinion might reach Sylvia and cause her
fresh distress.

So he answered in as noncommittal a fashion as
possible, "I assure you I am completely in the
dark. Of course I know that he was nervous and
over anxious about the fate of his Salon picture—"

He paused, and Julia's question came low and quick, "Does Miss Dorr know?"

Their meeting eyes acknowledged what their words left unsaid.

"Even that I cannot tell you. Perhaps," slowly, as though weighing the question, "you could find out and let me know."

"Do you think I know her well enough?" Julia hesitated.

"She ought to be told. You could speak to Miss Oakes," Garvie persisted.

"Very well, I'll try. I will go there this afternoon," Julia acquiesced. She had fallen into the habit of acquiescing in Garvie's suggestions. This settled, her mind went back to her own affairs, as minds have a habit of doing.

"Did you know that father is going away on Friday?" she asked.

"In search of his castle in the air? And what becomes of you?"

"I am left in Mrs. Mallock's charge. Isn't it horrid?" she said, wrinkling up her face in a delightful fashion.

"Well I suppose you could not stay by yourself, and if you rule her with a firm hand she may not be troublesome. I shall come and see how you are getting on before I leave town."

"Oh, do!" And a blush and smile emphasized her words.

XI

AT NEUILLY

JULIA was as good as her word, and went to her friend's that afternoon. But one glance into the white, stricken face raised to greet her, with a brave smile, told her that her errand was needless, and she only stayed for a few minutes of futile talk.

As she sat bent so steadily over a sketch that required to be posted for that evening's mail, Sylvia had in her pocket the letter that that morning—how long ago it seemed!—had smitten down her every hope.

How happy she had been since that sunny day at Fontainebleau, with Rupert Thorpe his old ardent, impetuous self again. How often as she worked she had found herself murmuring softly,

Other heights in other lives, God willing;
All the gifts from all the heights your own, love.

Now the words that kept echoing in her mind were the bitter phrases of that letter in her pocket. It had no beginning, but broke out abruptly:

"I am writing to say good-bye, for I am leaving Paris to-day, and I am not fit to see you again, am not worthy of your dear friendship. I have given up the fight. My picture is refused at the Salon. I am leaving art, everything, and going away into outer darkness. Think as hardly of me as you can, and never waste a tear or a regret on them. I am not worth them, but I carry with me the vision of your face, as it smiled on me last. Ah, the divine bounty of that smile. Goodbye, Sylvia! God bless you for all you have been to me!"

All through the day, since the receipt of the letter, she had been alone, sticking to her work in a dazed, mechanical fashion, receiving Julia with a dulled imitation of her usual manner. But when, late that evening, Harriett Oakes came home from a long expedition, she found her pacing her little room with the fierce sweep of a caged animal.

"Rupert Thorpe has gone away. Read that!" she said, thrusting the open letter on her bewildered friend. She was past self-control or reserve now.

"What does it mean? Oh Harriett, is it *suicide?*" and with the word, she broke down and sobbed herself into a state of exhaustion.

In grim-faced dismay, Miss Oakes soothed and tended her, until Sylvia lay huddled white and still on her bed.

Later on they talked it all over, but with small comfort, and the next day, Miss Oakes, whose wooden countenance and thirty odd years gave her much freedom, went and interviewed Frye, and then Garvie.

The result with both was equally meagre. They supposed that Thorpe had got worked up into a nervous state of suspense and could not stand the disappointment. He had probably taken himself off, for a time, to some cheap artist haunt —Grez, or such—and would be sure to turn up again after a few weeks of country air had made him his old self again. Make enquiries of the police? Certainly not. That was a thing which none of them had a right to do, at present, and which Thorpe was just the fellow to bitterly resent. Thus, with a marked unanimity, spoke the two friends, who, having held council the night before, had agreed to keep their mutual theory as to Virginie Lapierre's departure to themselves.

All the same, Harriett Oakes, who was a shrewd woman, with vision undimmed by sentiment, went away with a strong impression that Rupert Thorpe's absence was due to some unpleasant scrape. And so Sylvia Dorr was the only one of his friends left who felt quite sure that he was deserving of sympathy. But what was there that she could do or say in his behalf? Through sleepless hours she went over every incident in her poor little idyl, but without any solution of the problem. And so with tired, white face she settled down again to her work, work from which Miss Oakes would often try to entice her with every excuse for outdoor loitering that a Paris April gives.

Now it was tickets for a good Sunday concert, or for a new play; now it was a flower-show. Sometimes Sylvia yielded and went, but more often she insisted upon sticking to work, either to her researches at the Bibliothèque National, or her drawings done at home.

"It is amazing, the errands that rich friends will ask one to run. I suppose it never dawns upon them that time can mean money to us poor grubbers," growled Harriett one day, when they sat economically lunching together at the nearest Duval. "Mrs. Shatford, who had months of leisure and a carriage in Paris, discovers, just as she is starting for Sicily, that she cannot be happy unless a renaissance silver casket she had picked up, is immediately repaired by a cheap and artistic workman. Having been fool enough to tell her that I had heard of such a one, it is, 'Oh, my dear Harriett, you are such a concentration of energy and kindness, that I know you wont mind seeing to it for me,' and there I am, saddled with the business and the casket."

"What did you do it for?" Sylvia asked listlessly.

"Because I am an idiot, I suppose. But Mrs. Shatford has been good to me, and then the man may turn out 'copy.' The person who mentioned him seemed to think that he was rather a mystery. I have his address, somewhere out at Neuilly. It is a lovely day, and I have nothing special on hand. Let us go home and get the precious casket, take a Porte Maillot bus, and after we have done the errand, we can go and sit in the Bois. I shall be all the better for a look at the smart world before my next *Transcript* letter."

"I will go if you like. I did a long morning's work," Sylvia agreed in the half-hearted fashion that had grown habitual with her.

They carried out Miss Oakes's programme, and it was still early in the spring afternoon when they found themselves exploring one of the quiet, featureless Neuilly streets, with its vista of tall apartment houses, broken here and there by the wall of a villa, with stunted shrubbery of lilacs and laburnums, all glorious now with bloom. Spring's annual touch upon city streets is like the flowering of a love tale in a life otherwise utterly sordid and futile.

"This is the number, but there must be some mistake. It is not the place where a workman would live," Miss Oakes said, stopping before a high, dilapidated gate, above which a coat of arms was still visible. The walls were nearly as high as the gate, and what with them and a group of plane trees, there was a little to be seen of the house. "It is certainly No. 28," she went on, "and perhaps the man is concierge."

"Perhaps so, but if you ask my opinion, I think it is a private lunatic asylum," Sylvia said with a laugh.

"If so, one of the patients has just made his escape, for the gate is ajar. Come, let us go in."

"In spite of the fact that this is evidently the first chapter of a dime novel? What do you think we will find? A corpse, a ghost or a lunatic?"

"A silversmith to mend this tiresome casket, I

hope," Harriett said, leading the way up a tiled path much encroached on by a thick undergrowth of shrubbery. The flight of steps, the façade of the white house, and the big doorway, all shewed that the place had been a comfortable home in its day, but all revealed a state of extreme dilapidation.

"This door is ajar, too. Shall we go in?" Harriett said, her lowered tone revealing a slight nervousness.

"Here's a bell. Pull it."

The rusty wire creaked at the touch, but no bell sounded.

"I am going in," Miss Oakes said with fresh determination.

The door being pushed open revealed a large hall with black and white paved floor, and walls from which the frescoed plaster was peeling.

Of the several doors leading from it, only one was open, but a cough and the stir of someone moving within, told that one room at least was occupied.

As Harriett turned briskly towards this door, Sylvia's vivid imagination sketched a picture of themselves gagged and robbed, perhaps murdered, in this place into which they had rashly ventured. She would have dearly liked to make for the outer door again, but she could not leave her friend alone, and so mustered courage to follow her.

Harriett's footsteps brought a sudden cessation in the low sound of regular movement, as though someone had paused from his work to listen, and her sharp knock on the door was followed by a hoarse "Entrez," or rather "Angtray," in a foreign voice. "German," commented Miss Oakes to herself as she pushed the door open.

The peaceful interior revealed to them scattered at once any secret fears as to the nest of outlaws. The room had evidently been the salon of the villa, and ran the length of the house, one side being taken up with windows that opened into a patch of overgrown lawn. At the end nearest the door a high embroidery frame stood, like an easel. It was filled with a stretch of dingy canvas, on which a young woman was engaged in carefully arranging odds and ends of old tapestry, which she was picking out from a heap on a table beside her.

In the centre of the room, on a rough, unpainted table stood a beautiful object, which as far as Sylvia could see, was a wonderfully wrought gold pyx of the best renaissance period.

Before it, elbows on the table, sat a man in a white blouse. He seemed to be making measurements or notes, for he had drawing materials before him and pencil in hand. Both man and woman were young, and of a heavy blonde type that bespoke Alsatian, if not German, origin.

As the opening door revealed the visitors, the two workers stared at them in a surprise, strangely disproportionate to the cause.

"What do you wish, Madame?"

It was the woman, who, standing with a bit of tapestry in her hand, spoke, with sullen abruptness, in French, strongly tinged with a German accent. Her dress was a dull blue cotton, such as she might have worn in her own village, and heavy masses of pale blonde hair hung loosely about her face.

The man had risen and stood by his table, staring at them with big, light blue eyes. Miss Oakes, feeling that she would like to get through with her errand as quickly as possible, unwrapped the casket, and advancing towards the man, began to explain that having heard of his skill, she had brought it to be repaired. He only shook his head without looking at the casket, and the woman spoke impatiently.

"*C'est pas la peine.* He understands but a word or two of French. We come from beyond Strasburg, and we are going back there again when we have finished this work. He cannot do anything for you."

"But if you would explain it to him," persisted Harriett, annoyed that she spoke no German.

"*C'est pas la peine.*" Again that ever useful phrase. "He has promised to work for only one house while we are here in Paris. They would keep him forever if he would stay. They want him to do so much, but we must go," and a strangely hunted look stirred the stolidity of her peasant face.

During the discussion the friends had advanced

somewhat into the room, though with no encouragement from its occupants, who remained motionless in their places.

Sylvia taking no part in the discussion, had her interest enough aroused by the unusual interior to study every detail.

The large, brightly-lit room was bare of any furniture save that of a workshop. At the farthest end stood a craftsman's bench and tools, but for what trade she could not make out. In a corner lay a heap of odds and ends of old metal work.

She noted the contrast between the long delicate hands of the man, as he stood with them resting on the table—real artist hands—and the bovine peasant outline of his face, darkened now by an angry mistrust. Before him lay an elaborate drawing, both in sections and complete, which she thought was a copy of the beautiful golden pyx, a delight to her eyes. There were papers with memoranda of figures scattered around, and among these lay an envelope that flashed a familiar name on her.

It was addressed in a French hand to Rupert Thorpe at his studio, Rue Monsieur-le-Prince. It had evidently been since used to jot down a memorandum in pencil. She could not help it; she leant forward and taking up the envelope read the pencil scrawl—

"Finish by Saturday. Britski."

Turning quickly to the woman, she asked with

what composure she could, "Do you know the Monsieur Thorpe to whom this is addressed? I want very much to see him to-day, and will be glad to know where he is. I would give ten francs to anyone who told me."

With a deliberate movement, the man put out his hand and silently took the envelope from her, holding it carefully in his grasp.

Startled by this, she drew back towards Harriett, but with her eyes still fixed in questioning on the woman.

The latter shook her head in vigorous denial. "We know no one in Paris save the people in the shop we work for. That was just a message left about work. We know no *messieurs*. We only want to be let alone."

The little scene had passed so quickly that Harriett could not understand it, but seeing that Sylvia meant to hold her ground and ask more questions, and that both man's and woman's faces grew more forbidding, she took her by the arm saying, "Come. Don't you see they want us to go? *Bonjour, madame.*"

This final politeness was only answered by a surly grunt.

Once outside the big iron gate, the friends stood still and drew a breath of relief.

"Why, you look like a ghost." Harriett protested in sudden dismay. "What was on the envelope?"

"It was an old envelope addressed to Rupert

Thorpe, with an order scribbled on it by Britski. Oh Harriett, what does it mean?"

Now Miss Oakes had made up her mind that it would be poor friendship to encourage Sylvia in any fanciful theories as to Thorpe's disappearance. The sooner she left off worrying about him, the better it would be. So now she answered with cheerful certainty, "Mean? Why, that these queer people work for Britski, patch up antiques, and all that sort of thing I suppose. You know that Mr. Thorpe has had a good deal to do with him. He has probably thrown down an empty envelope in the shop, which Britski has picked up to write a message on. That is plain enough."

"Yes, but," Sylvia persisted, "why should these people have been so sulky? It almost seemed as though they were frightened of us, or angry at our coming."

"Britski has probably cautioned them against strangers, so as to keep them under his thumb and pay them less. They seem like simple country people. But we need not trouble ourselves about them any more. I have this nuisance of a casket still on my hands, worse luck. Come, I am going to take you over to that restaurant at the Porte Maillot and give you a glass of benedictine. You need something," said Harriett, inwardly anathemizing Britski and Thorpe, and the friend who had sent her on the errand.

XII

ON THE BALCONY

WITHIN the first few days after Mr. Praed's departure, Garvie kept his promise by calling twice on his daughter. Each time she was out, but after the second visit came a note from Julia, the first he had ever had.

"Characteristic," he thought as he read it. "The writing firm and clear, the words frankly to the point."

A month ago he would hardly have troubled to thus criticize the ordinary little note that asked him to come that evening.

The day had been mild as summer, and instead of sitting in the garish red and gold salon, he found Julia out in the blue-grey twilight of the balcony. She was bare-headed, but a cream-coloured cloak hung over her shoulders.

"Don't you think it's nicer out here?" she asked as he took her hand. "I love watching the long lines of steady lights and all the little twinkling moving ones, and thinking what they mean—life all jammed up together, like toys in a Noah's ark."

"I am afraid you are looking at the philosophic

instead of the artistic view of it," he said taking a chair opposite hers; "but if you could only see the effect of your black hair against the blue street vista, you would become an impressionist on the spot."

Julia's heart rejoiced that her recent studies enabled her to comprehend the latter term.

"It's a doubtful compliment," she said lightly, "for impressionist portraits generally seem painted as a veil to ugliness."

"What wilful misinterpretation," he protested. "But where is the lady who keeps you in order? Has she left you to your own devices?"

"Yes," and Julia snuggled back comfortably into the folds of her cloak, as though appreciating the fact. "She was asked to some rather swell reception. She nobly urged me to go too, but I think she was just as well pleased that I stayed at home, and I'm sure I'm glad to be rid of her. Now if you will only light a cigarette, it will have such a cosy home feeling."

Did Julia guess what witching words were those last, to come in a clear young voice to a man who was beginning to think himself tired of a solitary life in a big city?

Garvie obeyed with a pleasant warmth at heart.

"And how are you getting on with the lady?" he asked.

"Oh, she's just tiresome, that's all. Her latest excitement is a wretched little French count, who she says had an American mother, but I don't be-

lieve it. He must have had a bit more sense if
he had. He is like a little white rabbit, and
comes about up to my elbow, but he has had hun-
dreds of grandfathers."

"So have we all."

"Yes, but she says that his were crusaders,
dukes, and all that kind of things. He lives
with three aunts and two grandmothers over in
a misty old house in the Faubourg St. Germain.
She took me there."

"Now, are you sure that you counted the old
ladies right?"

"Oh well, an aunt more or less doesn't matter.
The worst is, she put the little atom up to the
hour I ride in the Bois, so that I have to go a different road every day. I'd like to trot him out
for a round-up on Tom's ranch. Oh dear, I wish
I were there." And with a sigh, Julia stretched
up her arms to clasp her hands behind her head.

Garvie did not mean to shew his disgust at her
being pestered in this fashion, so he said lightly,
"Come now, it will never do to let Mrs. Mallock
and her satellites make you homesick. Have you
any idea when your father will be back?"

"No," and the girl's voice sounded no more
cheerful. "I had a letter this evening, and there's
never a word as to when he is coming."

"Is he so interested in this collection?"

"Well, in a way." She hesitated, and then
with a forlorn little laugh, broke out, "I believe
he's more interested in its owner, this Mademoi-

selle de Rostrênan, he talks so much about. His latest idea is that, as she has no home when she leaves the chateau, it would be nice to ask her to come and stay with us. He thinks she would be a companion for me and help me to speak French. Oh, Mr. Garvie," leaning forward, "you don't think—do you—"

The rising trouble in her voice, stirred Garvie's heart to pity, and he hastened to answer her unfinished question with more conviction than he felt, "No, certainly not. You must not get such bogies into your head. You never did before, did you?"

"At home? Oh no. You see, he used to be busy all day in the office or at the mills, or would be talking to men."

"Out of mischief, in fact. Well, in spite of idle hands, we must try to keep him out of mischief here. This collection is a nuisance. I suppose he says something about it, doesn't he?"

"Oh yes, lots," she answered listlessly. "He writes two whole pages about the old castle on a river, and the big rooms full of tapestries and carved furniture, and all sorts of frumpy old rubbish," she went on, forgetting her recent æsthetic studies in her disgust. "He says that, as he is buying the whole lot, it will take him some time to have it catalogued, and that he means to stay and see it done, though Britski didn't think it necessary."

Garvie laughed. "It strikes me that the friendless orphan is likely to have a nice little nest-egg, though Britski is sure to get his pickings in the way of commission. I suppose Britski is there?"

"No, there seems to be only the orphan."

"By-the-bye, what did you say her name was?"

"Mademoiselle de Rostrênan."

"I seem to have heard the name before. And where is the abode of the sleeping beauty?"

"It's all down in father's letter. If you will come in, I'll get it for you," and Julia made a movement to rise.

Garvie put out a protesting hand, saying, "Oh no, please. Don't break the spell of the night for any such mere matter of detail. You can tell me by-and-by." Then as Julia settled herself again, "I must confess that my curiosity is stirred by the romance of the remote chateau and its orphan chatelaine. Your father does not look much like a knight errant."

"Poor father!" Julia laughed sweetly. Then, "Oh, I remember the name of the place, now. The Chateau of Rosbraz, near Trêmalo, Finistère, and father was staying at an inn, the Lion d'Or."

Garvie gave a slow whistle of astonishment. "And that same Lion d'Or at Trêmalo happens to be my very destination, when I start, day after to-morrow. I have often been there for weeks at a time. Trêmalo is a village, on the south coast of Brittany. It is still ten miles from a railway, though I hear that there is to be one there next year, which will spoil it. Now it is a bit of the middle ages set down on a river, just where it meets the tide. It is a haunt dear to artists, though none are likely to be there at this time of year. How surprised your father will be to see me. I shall be able to keep an eye on him, and to let you know how things go. You will like that, won't you?"

He was leaning forward now towards the outline, dark against the blue twilight.

"Oh, it *would* be a comfort. Somehow I feel so lonely. But are you going to be away very long?" she asked naively.

Garvie's intention improvised itself as he spoke. "I promise to return at once, if I can beguile Mr. Praed away, minus the orphan." Then, with a sudden inspiration, "But look here, I have a better idea. Why not come and keep an eye on him yourself?"

The kindly dusk hid Julia's tremour at the ardour of his tone, though there was a little catch of her breath before she answered, "But however should I get there? I couldn't be ready to go with you, I suppose—"

"No, and that might bring Mrs. Mallock down upon us as a chaperon," Garvie said, checking the simple-minded suggestion, with hasty conscientiousness. "But the journey is really quite simple. I will write out the places and hours for you, and your maid can manage the rest, all right."

"Oh, thank you," Julia breathed, relieved to have her mistake covered.

"You would be delighted with Trêmalo," Garvie went on, much taken with his scheme. "You could not have a better introduction to old-world ways. Why, there are paths over the hillsides where the wooden sabots of generations have worn foot prints in the solid granite, and out on the lonely heaths one comes on a great Druidic shaft or dolmen—"

"Dolmen." Julia said puzzled. "I thought that was an old lady's cape, trimmed with beads."

"It is a Druid's grave as well, or perhaps an old lady Druidess; That is the country of the Druids, you know."

"Is it?" Julia said, with a mental note that here was a new subject for her to master. She would go to Galignani's tomorrow morning and see what books she could get about Brittany.

"By-the-by, how would you like to be painted as a Druid priestess? You would have your hair hanging loose, and wear a long white robe with one arm and shoulder bare, while you hold up a golden sickle."

Mrs. Mallock's sneers about artists and models bore fruit now in a little fit of prudish pride.

"Oh, I don't think I'd like it at all," Julia said hastily.

"No, perhaps you are not the priestess type. Those Druidesses should be pale, with stern eyes used to look on death." Then with a more personal note, "But perhaps you will let me try an outdoor study of you some time while we are there. It would get me in touch with you before I begin the famous portrait."

"If you like," Julia murmured shyly. "What will the hotel be like?" she asked.

With somewhat of a shock, Garvie realized that this girl he had patronized a short time ago, had adroitly turned the subject back into its more practical and less personal side.

She was right, he acknowledged to himself, and answered, "You can hardly call it an hotel. It is little more than a village inn, but Marie Jeanne is an old dear, and as she is used to lady artists, she will know how to make you comfortable. I doubt if your chef could turn out a better fish *soufflé* than she can. But it is getting late, and Mrs. Mallock's sense of propriety will receive a shock if she finds me here when she returns."

As they arose to go in, he said, "I had better write out the directions for the journey now, in case I do not see you alone again before I go."

"Yes, sit there," she said pointing to an elaborate and little-used writing-table. Julia was not a girl with a bosom-friend correspondence. Garvie scribbled a few lines and then looked up, laughing, at Julia, where she stood watching him, her arms resting on the back of a high arm-chair, the full cloak of creamy cloth still hanging over her shoulders.

"Be sure you don't give your dear chaperon a

hint of our scheme, or she might feel it her duty to sacrifice herself and come too," he said.

"No, she doesn't," was the girl's resolute answer, "for I will not pay for her ticket and I'm sure she won't herself. She never happens to have change when there is any paying going on."

"Wise woman," Garvie commented. "But shall I tell your father that you are coming?"

Julia pondered for a moment, then with a laugh, "No, I think you'd better not. He might wire and tell me not to, you know."

"Then you will appear, at your own sweet will?" Garvie asked, checking an impulse of prudence that suggested the possible awkwardness of such a descent upon an amorous father.

The doubt had cleared from Julia's face.

"What fun!" she said. "By-the-by, father must think he is settled down there forever, for he says he sent to some town and got an auto for going to and from the castle. How far is it from the inn?"

"A matter of two or three miles. I have tramped it often, though I know it best from the water. I used to sail there a good deal one summer. If I can get a boat, will you let me sail you down?"

"To call on the orphan?" she jested.

"Well, I suppose you had better commence by being civil. It would not be wise to oppose your father unnecessarily," Garvie warned her.

He was beginning to foresee complications in their improvised scheme.

But Julia was without doubts. "Oh, he'll be all right as soon as I get there," she said airily.

"Well, I must be off," he said and this time he did really take himself away, having no desire to cause the enemy, in the person of Mrs. Mallock, to blaspheme.

It was the last talk they had before his departure, for, when he came again, he found Mrs. Mallock very much in possession. However, Julia's smiling *au revoir* was comfort enough, and was answered by a brief pressure of her hand.

Garvie had not yet settled with his own mind that he wanted to marry Gabriel Praed's daughter, but he was sure that it would be very pleasant to walk with her among the Breton chestnut woods and orchards, to see her proud smile at the naive display of some newly acquired knowledge, to feel the pride of a teacher in a quick pupil.

It was a dangerous role that he was choosing for himself.

XIII

VILLA MARIPOSA

I T was a fine Sunday morning, one of those spring days when all Paris turns out into the streets. The rich go to the races, the poor go to the parks, to Versailles and St. Cloud.

Sylvia Dorr was not holiday making, for Madame Marcelle had given her a commission that required haste. The designs for a bride's and bridemaids' dresses, were to be sent to America for approval, and must be ready for the next day's mail. Unfortunately, Sylvia had mislaid some directions, and without them was at a complete loss.

"What ever shall I do?" she said, brushing back the loose hair from her forehead, as she looked up at Miss Oakes, who had just come in from early church. By a queer contrast, that unemotional person delighted in the ornate ritual of a high Episcopal church.

"Let me take a note to her," the latter suggested.

"But it is Sunday, and she will be out of town. She always is," was the dejected answer.

"Oh yes, I remember hearing what a pretty

villa she has at Bas Meudon. Villa Mariposa was the name, I think. Let us go there. You have got to come out to lunch somewhere, for I am not going to pay Hotel Cleveland prices on a fine Sunday, and it won't take so very long."

"Only half the day, and the trams and trains will be so crowded;" but even as she protested, Sylvia put aside her work to get ready. Perhaps she, like other tired toilers, craved the fresher air of the suburbs, better substitutes for the real country in Paris than elsewhere.

She was right. The trams were crowded, and the friends underwent many delays before, still in the crowd, they descended at the noisy little station.

"You might as well question a mad dog, as to where somebody lived, as ask those men," Harriett said, with a contemptuous scowl at the perspiring and irate officials. "We must have our *déjeuner*, so let us find the quietest restaurant there is, and then we can ask the waiter about the house."

The quietest restaurant might have been quieter, but this was not their first Sunday excursion, and, knowing what to expect, they settled themselves at a white-clothed table in a little garden full of other such. A month later it would all be dusty and sordid enough, but to-day the lilac-bushes were towers of fragrance, and the tiny leaves on the clipped lime trees glistened like green gold. Around them was a motley crowd of students and their female following, of noisy family parties, of blue-coated soldiers, but undisturbed they finished their omelette, and *bifteck-au-pommes.*

Miss Oakes's keen eyes studied her surroundings as possible copy, but Sylvia turned from them with a tired longing for solitude.

"How I hate it all," she said wearily, her eyes fixed in languid distaste on a stout female bicyclist in bloomers and white jersey. "It seems such a pity that I was made without any Bohemian instincts. They would have come in so useful."

"You do very well as you are. Look at that tiny old peasant woman in cap and shawl. How bewildered she seems and how kind her soldier son is to her," Harriett commented.

As the pale little waiter scudded up with their cheese, Sylvia laughed. "If the men at the station were mad dogs, your waiter is a hunted hare," she said.

All the same, when he brought their coffee, he was able to tell them that the Villa Mariposa was "a little walk of a quarter of an hour up the hill at the meeting of two roads. They could not miss it."

"Madame Marcelle lives there?"

"No, it is Madame Britski. Monsieur and Madame Britski; people most amiable and distinguished." It was a pity they were so much in Paris, but to-day they were certainly at home, and had company, he knew, for his wife was helping in the kitchen.

There was a pause of perplexity between the friends as he rushed off to answer five different calls, a pause which Harriett was the first to break with the oracular remark, "I am not surprised. It is strange we did not guess it long ago."

"But what does it mean?" Sylvia wondered, nervously.

"Mean? Why only another of their trade secrets, of course. I suppose they could not so well recommend strangers to each other if they were known to be husband and wife. It must be nice, too, to step into a fresh name with your best clothes, and leave the workday one with your workday worries. Lots of the London lady dressmakers do it, I have heard." Harriett was pursuing her policy of discouraging Sylvia's mistrust until a favourable time should come for her to make a fresh start without Madame Marcelle's help. Her own struggle with life had taught her to walk warily.

The anxious shadow did not lift from Sylvia's face as she murmured, "I wonder, though, that she never told me."

"She knows that there are no half-and-half measures possible with any secret," said Harriett, leading the way out.

There was no mistaking the road, for there was only one that wound up a sloping hill, bordered by every eccentricity of outdoor restaurants.

These gradually gave place to villas, which, as they advanced, became more imposing in style and more secluded in fresh greenery.

"Here is the place. 'Villa Mariposa' is on the gate," said Harriett as they came to a branching of the roads. The three cornered bit of land was shut in by a laurel hedge, but through the gate they could see beyond the shrubbery an open lawn set with flower-beds, and a pretty white villa of Renaissance design.

As Harriett laid her hand on the gate, Sylvia caught her arm saying, "Do you think she will mind our coming? You know the waiter said that she had people there."

"But I thought you really wanted to speak to her? We can ask for her at the door, and if she doesn't choose to see us, she need not. It is on her own business, after all. Look here, you write a line on your card, saying what you came for. That will make it simpler."

This was done, and the two walked up the path that ran between borders of bright anemones and ranunculus, backed by radiant banks of azalea bloom.

"One can trace Britski's hand in the taste of everything," commented Harriett, "No glass balls or cheap statuary here. Look at that dear terrace along the front of the house, what an Italian air it has. Those Lombardy poplars are as effective as cypress. I wonder if those two have any children. They should be dowered with the *culte* of beauty, at any rate."

Sylvia made no answer. She had not plucked up spirits since the first mention of Britski's name.

"Who shall we ask for?" Harriett murmured as they climbed the terrace steps. A burst of noisy voices came to them from the open windows of a room where they saw people seated at table.

"Madame Marcelle. It is the only name I know her by," Sylvia decided.

At their demand, the flurried man-servant grinned. "Madame Marcelle in Paris is Madame Britski at Meudon. I doubt if she sees any one on business, but I can ask," and he led them into a small room that seemed half library, half boudoir.

Here the traces of a cultured taste were as visible as outdoors. The scheme of colouring was subtle, the ornaments and pictures few, but each perfect of its kind.

Miss Oakes took it all in with her usual quick interest. "Heavens, what a buhl secretaire. It might have belonged to Marie Antoinette herself. Look, Sylvia."

No response coming, she turned to find Sylvia staring up at a small picture.

"What is it?" her friend asked, going across to her.

She saw a golden sunset sky, dusky green

meadows by a river where nymphs were bathing. It did not need the signature to tell anyone learned in French galleries that this was a Corot.

"Fancy a picture-dealer keeping a Corot in his wife's sitting-room. There is something grand in it," Harriett exclaimed "But whatever is the matter?" she asked as she saw the pale dismay in Sylvia's face.

"It is not a Corot," came the protest in a hurried whisper. "Rupert Thorpe painted it, as a joke, that day we went out to Ville d'Avray. He said he meant to imitate every one of the Barbizon painters, one after the other, to see if he could not be successful with something."

"Are you sure this is it?"

"Yes, look at that dab of vermilion in the corner. I put that in myself. But he signed it— oh, I know he signed it," she said wildly.

"Hush, someone is coming."

There was a rustling of silk, a waft of scent, and Madame Marcelle glided in, smiling and comely.

No longer clad in her business panoply of shining black satin, she looked five years younger in a wonderful costume of a pearly tissue that veiled a green matching the young leaves on the lime trees outside.

Here and there a Cashmere embroidery of white and green iris outlined her draperies, and a string of pearls at her neck brought out the rosy warmth of her skin, the glow of auburn hair, evidently free from tinting.

The triumph of a woman of over thirty, as she faced such a figure in her glass, was still in her eyes and smile.

All the same, at first sound of the deep voice, Sylvia said to herself with a little shiver, "Oh, dear! She is vexed at our coming."

There was however no sign of such a feeling in her effusive greeting. "Ah, dear mesdemoiselles; but it is wonderful that you should have found me out in my little nest among the trees. Do tell me how you were clever enough to do it," and her insistent eyes demanded an answer to the gay words.

Sylvia explained with characteristic directness, that Miss Oakes, having an idea that Madame Marcelle lived at Bas Meudon, they had come on the chance of finding her, and of having the trousseau difficulties settled. "Of course we did not guess until we enquired for you that you were known as Madame Britski," she explained.

"I *am* Madame Britski," came the brusque words, with a quick and angry flush.

"Of course," murmured Sylvia, dismayed at the effect of her speech. Even as she spoke, the smile was again donned, and the gay voice sounded.

"Thousands of times have I been about to tell you of my home life, dear child, but you know how it is—" with a shrug of her shoulders. "You

and I talk for ten minutes—always of business—
and then it is, 'Madame Marcelle is wanted,' for
this or for that. And now we must settle this
trousseau matter, I suppose. Let us seat ourselves."

In a few clear sentences she and Sylvia had discussed the doubtful point, and arranged the whole
affair.

"Ah, but you have a good head, my child. You
should be making money in a business like mine,"
Madame Marcelle said presently. "And now that
our trousseau is safe, you must let me order you
some *déjeuner*. Ours is over, but they can bring
you a cosy little meal here."

"Thanks, madame, but we had our *déjeuner* at
the station, and must return to Paris before the
afternoon crowds," Sylvia answered.

Madame's light protest had little meaning in it,
and they both rose. "I am delighted that you
should have found me so cleverly, only remember," came the smiling caution, "that at Boulevard
Malsherbes I am always Madame Marcelle. It
is simpler to keep the two things separate, and
though these friends of mine—" with an outward
wave of her hand— "all know, they respect my
little secret. Then too, none of them are my
clients. I prefer to have it thus. And so *au
revoir,* dear mesdemoiselles."

She parted from them at the door with the same
graceful affability, and turned away to join her

guests. These were now scattered in bright-coloured groups about the garden.

Sylvia hurried on nervously without looking to right or left, but her friend took in the Watteau scene with critical eyes.

"The tribes of Israel, with a flavouring of the opera," she murmured. "It was not necessary for our hostess to say she did not dress them—the fact speaks for itself. Look at that tinted Venus walking with Britski. His wife would never have made that pink costume. Well, the double lives in big cities are queer."

"Queer enough," Sylvia assented drearily. Then, in alarm, "Oh, dear, Britski is leaving the woman and coming towards us. Let us hurry."

She would have done so, if Harriett had not checked her with a grasp on her arm. "No, we cannot do that. Don't be foolish. He won't bite you."

Down a side path, at right angles to the avenue, came the master of the house, raising his hat with a gentle deference. In his light grey summer clothes and Panama hat he had undoubtedly an air of distinction. He might have been a Polish noble strolling on his ancestral estates rather than a Paris *bric-a-brac* merchant, enjoying the Sunday repose of his suburban villa.

"Dear lady," he began to Harriett, "you are surely not leaving us without a bite or a sup. If you will present me to mademoiselle—" with another bow to Sylvia—"I shall try to persuade you."

There could be no doubt of the pleasantness of his manner, Sylvia acknowledged to herself, as after they had declined his offers of driving them down to the station, he stood chatting.

"I knew your drawings before I had the pleasure of meeting you," he said. "I tell my wife that such work as yours is wasted on her chiffons, and that some day I shall try to take you away from her to paint me *aquarelles*. Why do you never come with Miss Oakes to visit my galleries? There is stuff worth seeing there sometimes, though I have to tear my heart and let the best go. Ah, when I am rich that will be a different matter. But you will come, will you not?"

Sylvia could not but promise. She felt as though those velvety black eyes were hypnotising her, and it was a relief to find herself on the public road, Monsieur Britski standing at the gate watching them.

"Well, that was all as good as a play." Miss Oakes commented. "How I wish I could write a novel. I see so many strange things."

"They seem to entertain you."

"I think I shall try some day. But come, let us catch the three o'clock train."

XIV

STORM SIGNALS

MISS OAKES took good care to say nothing further to her friend as to the Corot picture and her recognition of it. She felt sure that Sylvia must understand that the mystery of Thorpe's eccentricities was revealed. To her it seemed quite clear that he had been, either willingly or unwillingly, painting forgeries for Britski, and sore and ashamed, had yielded to despair at the news of his Salon rejection.

She was sorry for him, yes; but sorry as a man might be, with a pity mixed with contempt for the weakling who had gone under.

Sylvia, she knew, would regard the culprit far otherwise, and she respected her reticence, as she generally did. It is strange that more people do not discover the moral force imbedded in reticence, and strive to attain to it. It is nearly always the most reticent of a family group whose opinion and wishes are deferred to.

And so, on the homeward way, the two talked in a mere surface fashion, of their day's adventures, and when they reached the hotel Sylvia took refuge in her own room, to face her discovery in solitude.

Bitter watches, those, when the heart pleads for the dear criminal whom the judgment condemns, when the platitudes of right and wrong are re-created in travail of spirit as living facts.

The next morning, Miss Oakes indulged in the unusual excitement of a skirmish with her landlady. Ordinarily the most pacific of mortals, she had learned in a hard school to stand calmly up for her rights, so that when her weekly bill presented some unaccountable mistakes she marched with a determined air toward Madame Comerie's office.

White-haired, enormously stout, and yet with the remains of a blonde beauty, Madame Comerie's appearance suggested the probabilities in store for her daughter, Madame Marcelle, twenty years later.

If Madame Comerie had never treated Miss Oakes to her first or second-floor manner, the two had always been on friendly enough terms, and now after mutual greeting, Harriett said pleasantly, "I came to see about some mistakes in my bill, madame. I did not dine at table-d'hote on Tuesday."

"It is marked so in Alphonse's day-book, and I have never known him mistaken," came the firmly neutral statement.

The flicker of warfare shone in Miss Oakes' eyes. "He is, this time, anyway. I happen to have kept the restaurant account. See, here it is, dated."

Madame Comerie took the flimsy paper, bestowing upon it a stony stare. "You are apparently very fond of restaurants, mademoiselle. I see that you only dined at home three times last week. Usually, my guests appreciate my table better."

The tone was significant of fault finding, but Harriett only answered dryly, "That is no unusual thing. When I am busy I save time by dining out. If you will look further down the bill you will see a mark at a bottle of wine I did not have."

The landlady noted the fact, and then fixed an accusing gaze on Harriett. "I suppose you have had *some* wine. There is only one other bottle charged. My general style of boarders use three or even four a week."

As Harriett said nothing she took a pen and changed the items in question, with accustomed swiftness. "There, mademoiselle, the alterations you ask for are made, and I congratulate you on your economy."

"Thank you, madame," and Harriett walked off, with a knowledge that her days in the Hotel Cleveland were numbered. She was evidently not intended to stay, and if she persisted in doing so, it would be at the risk of further unpleasantness.

"Of course I can't be a profitable boarder. I only wonder they did not find that out sooner," she said to herself, trying to check the doubt that there was more underneath.

She was honestly troubled at adding to Sylvia's worries, but before the friends met at noon, she had received a telegram that drove other things out of her head. A younger half-brother, all that was left to her of family ties, was ill with pneumonia in a hospital in London.

"There is plenty of time, for I can not get off before the night train. Come and help me pack," she ended, with stiff lips, as she told her news to Sylvia.

"But you need not give up your room?" Sylvia urged, as Harriett dragged out a trunk.

"I must. Comerie would not keep it for me. I was going to tell you that when I went to her this morning about those mistakes in the bill, she all but told me to go; said that her boarders were not usually so economical. Of course, I know I cannot be a paying investment. I do not wonder she is tired of me," she ended with resolute optimism. For all that, the blow struck home.

Sylvia sitting on the floor beside an open box looked up in alarm. "It is not that. It is some trick of Britski's, because you took me to Meudon; and now I shall be here all alone," she said with certainty.

Harriett, working quickly as she talked, said, "Look here. You've got nervous about it all, and I think you had better move. It is no such serious matter. Go to see Miss Cole and find out if you can get a room where she lives. You need not quarrel over it. Just say you want to join a friend."

"But I cannot; that is, until I get some money. Madame Marcelle has not paid me for a month, which isn't a bit like her. Then she persuaded me to take that grey dress at half-price, when it was returned. You remember."

Yes. Harriett remembered that it was for the day at Fontainebleau that Sylvia had got the dainty spring dress.

"So that makes less owing to me than there would be. But when my home money comes I will be all right."

She leant over the trunk, in silence for a moment before she went on, in a lower voice:

"And if I leave here, how could Mr. Thorpe find me if he ever came back?"

A sob was smothered in the depths of the trunk.

Harriett actually paused a moment in her work to protest earnestly, "Sylvia you must not expect that. Don't you see—"

"Oh yes, I see, well enough, that you all think him worthless. No one but me feels that he must be the victim of some trickery that has driven him to despair, perhaps to suicide. Who is to say that he has not been murdered?"

The last words came in an awed whisper, as Sylvia knelt upright, her head thrown back to gaze at her friend with wide, desolate eyes.

"Murdered! Whatever put such an idea into your head? What should he be murdered for?"

"He may have threatened to reveal some knavery? Who knows? I keep thinking of that out-of-the-way house at Neuilly—those queer people who were frightened at our coming. At night I see the man's long fingers." She shuddered, and hid her face in her hands.

"You poor child! You will be ill if you encourage such fancies," Harriett urged in genuine distress. "Why, if there were the slightest possibility of anything wrong, would not Mr. Garvie, who knows Paris so well, have taken alarm?"

"I don't know about anyone else," Sylvia sobbed; "I only know that I am frightened, frightened."

"I hate leaving you," Harriett murmured.

"Oh, I am selfish to be bothering you with my affairs now," Sylvia said, with a fight for her lost self-control.

"That is all right. I have plenty of time. Then you won't move while I am away?"

"No," came the determined answer.

"Well then, the next best thing you can do is to get more change in your work. You might as well be connected altogether with American houses. I think they would suit you better than French people."

This was Harriett's guarded way of advising a gradual break with Madame Marcelle.

"I am sure they would," Sylvia agreed. "And

I daresay the *Chiffons* editor in New York would take my sketches regularly if I asked him. He has always praised them."

"Yes, do. Nothing makes you so independent as having other strings to your bow. Attend to that, and lie low until I come back." Her voice shook at the words, and the uncertainty behind them of life and death. "And then we will be off to the country."

The friends parted at the Gare du Nord, with as cheerful farewell as they might.

"Be sure to go and see Miss Praed soon," was one of Harriett's last mandates. This Sylvia had no chance to do, for the next morning, as she sat over her drawing-board, Julia appeared.

"I've come to say good-bye," she announced cheerily.

"And where are you going?" Sylvia asked, as one left on a desert island.

"To Arcadia—at least so Mr. Garvie says," and with the words, Julia blushed finely, as their possible meaning dawned upon her.

She hurried on to give an enthusiastic sketch of her plan, leaving out, as in duty bound, the object of her unheralded descent upon a parent suspected of frivolity.

"Too bad," she said pleasantly, when Sylvia told of Miss Oakes's departure, "and you are all alone? Look here. Why not come with me? It would do you good, for you are looking worn to death, and it would be such a favour to me. My maid has struck, and says she always gets ill when she leaves Paris. I'll have to go alone, and goodness knows if I ever get there. I know so little about French travelling. Of course, when you come to oblige me, I shall pay the expenses. You wouldn't mind that—" she pleaded bashfully.

For the moment the vision of

> Green days in forest
> And blue days at sea

came to Sylvia with a great temptation, and then she remembered her empty purse, the work that must fill it, and, more than all, the watch she was keeping.

"I should not mind anything you wanted to do," she said, with a wistful smile, "but it is no use this time, for I cannot go. I should love to," she added.

Julia shook her head in disgust. "I feel as though some anarchist would be perfectly justified in shooting such an odiously prosperous person as myself. I'm sure *I* shouldn't blame him. Here you are, as pale and as tired as a ghost."

"Whatever have ghosts to tire them?" Sylvia put in.

"Oh well, I only meant that they are said to be pale. I never saw one, you know. But, as I say, here you are, looking worn out, and yet you must keep working away, while I go skipping off to enjoy myself; at least, perhaps I shall," and again she blushed at fear of Sylvia thinking that meeting Garvie was the anticipated enjoyment.

Sylvia laughed softly. "Fortunately there are no anarchists in Brittany; at least, none that I ever heard of, so you can go in peace, if you promise to come back again."

The words were sweetly said, and Julia kissed her, her heart swelling with a sympathy she could not express. Who but the nearest could condole with a girl whose lover had, apparently of his own free will, vanished into space?

Something of the day's brightness seemed to follow Julia, leaving the little room dull and dreary. Sylvia might have been cheered, as she bent over her drawing, could she have known of the amiable letter from Mr. Stratton, the publisher, that was burning a hole in Julia's pocket. He wrote that, having noticed the quality of Miss Dorr's recent article in the *Era*, he thought her book would probably be well worth considering, but that, as he expected to be in Paris within the month, he would wait to look into the matter personally. He should lose no time in calling on Miss Praed and renewing an acquaintance of which he had kept so pleasant a memory.

"Oh dear," said Miss Julia at this, with a little guilty giggle.

XV

AT THE LION D'OR

THE triangular Place that formed the centre of life in Trêmalo village lay drowsing in the afternoon sunshine. To-day there was no stir of market, no horse fair or conscription. The school-children had scattered an hour ago, with a great clattering of sabots. It was not yet the supper hour when they would gather to sit on the door-steps, with their bowls of cabbage soup on their knees.

The highway ran along one side of the Place, down to its narrow end, where the old, grey bridge crossed the river. Facing this, up the slope of uneven stone pavement, stood the square, white Lion D'Or, flanked by its untidy stable yard, and edged with its green benches and little painted iron tables.

Not condescending to the mistletoe-bush sign of the humbler inn, the name *Hotel du Lion D'Or* ran across its front, in large black letters.

A sordid looking building, its exterior gave the stranger no hint of the solid comfort to be found indoors, but commercial travellers, who are good judges of comfort, pressed their journeys to get a Sunday dinner at Trêmalo, and more than one artist, now fashionable, remembered the days when he had lived there on the fat of the land, and on trust until the money came.

Its presiding genius stood at the door, a stalwart woman of unusual bulk and fairness for a Breton. She wore the plain black cashmere dress and little white net cap, a costume marking a social grade higher than the peasant woman, and yet not that of the lady who wears a hat; but such marks of caste are fast passing from the land.

Her smile was beaming, but her bright blue eyes had a snap that gave warning of hidden forces, and her great shoulders and arms revealed a masculine power. Standing there, a picture of reposeful strength, she saw what she had been waiting for, as the courier's cart a three-seated open wagon, rattled up to the door.

"Here is one passenger—an *Anglais*. Hardly an artist at this season, and so a fisherman," she thought to herself, as she called in deep tones to the driver—"And what have you brought me to-day, Alain? That carpet from Lorient, I trust."

"He has brought you me, Marie Jeanne," came a cheerful voice, as the stranger jumped down from the front seat.

"*Dame!* Monsieur Garvie! And what do you here now, when the Salon is about to open, and everyone is in Paris?"

"There is plenty of time for that. I have come to be fed up with *coquilles de St. Jacques* and fresh sardines, and to get a breath of country air."

Marie Jeanne grasped his hand with a benevolent grip of iron. "Ah, Monsieur Garvie, but it is good to see an old friend like you again. I am proud when the strangers make a fuss over your panel on the dining-room wall—Lonic and her pups beside Monsieur Smith's picture of St Corentin stopping the flood at Donarnenez—what was it he called it? 'The city of d'Is.' Yes, you shall have sardines and lobsters at will. And are you come to make a picture or to divert yourself?"

"To divert myself, Marie Jeanne, if it is diversion to wade between the second and third mill, after a salmon that remains so near and yet so far. No artists here now, I suppose?"

"Ah no, monsieur. Even M'sieur Robson only tarried to finish his picture of snow on the landes up by the big stone; for we had snow this year, lying white for a week. It is ten years since it came last."

"Ah, I heard of his picture. Took it to London, didn't he? 'A lost battle;' corpses, eh, and that kind of thing."

"Yes, he had young Joseph lying up there on a sheet for weeks, with blood smeared on his face and clothes, so that it gave one a nightmare. A *Chouan*, he called him. Those were the men who fought here a hundred years ago. Why people in London and Paris should want to look at such horrors puzzles me. He was the last to leave, but, although the artists are gone, there is an American gentleman here for you to talk to; that is to say, he may be a gentleman, or he may, as Alain says, be only one of those men who buy old things, a Jew perhaps."

Garvie knew that in these days to be called a Jew in the depths of Catholic Brittany, meant an unpleasant time, and decided that his advent might be a fortunate one for Mr. Praed.

"And what makes Alain say that?" he asked.

"Well, he is strange, you see. He does not fish, or paint, but he seems to mean to stay, for he has got an automobile over from Lorient, and is always off down the river in it. They say that he goes to the Chateau at Rosbraz, and the folks there are Jews, more's the pity. Jews in place of the Rostrênans."

Garvie checked himself in the act of protesting that no strangers were yet at the chateau. It was not his business to talk about matters that Mr. Praed had kept secret, but he meant to get at all Marie Jeanne's information.

"When did these strangers come? The Rostrênans still lived there when I was last in the *pays*."

Marie Jeanne crossed her arms, and, leaning against the door post settled down for a gossip. "Yes, there was the old count then. But two years ago he died. His son, you see, had married in Algeria where his wife owned vineyards, that brought in money, and he chose to stay there and let the *manoir*—ah, the pity—to people from Paris, who, the Rosbraz folk say, come and go, now one, now another, never the same long. Their servants are foreign, and they talk but little in the country."

Garvie rapidly digested this information, which fitted in well enough with his suspicions, though he had almost doubted that Britski could venture so far as a sham family at Rosbraz.

"And this American of yours—what is his name?"

"It's not so queer as some—Praed; that is simple enough. He seems harmless, though it is not easy to tell, when he speaks neither French nor Breton."

Garvie saw that it was time to cast the mantle of his friendship over the stranger in the land. Marie Jeanne would have calmly accepted the weirdest artist freak, but a middle-aged foreigner without a hobby suggested a flight from justice.

"Yes, he *is* harmless, Marie Jeanne. He is a friend of mine from America, where he knew my father. He told me in Paris that he was coming to this neighborhood to see about buying some old furniture in a chateau, Rosbraz I suppose. He is a good soul, and you must do your best for him," he added, smiling.

Marie Jeanne acquiesced as she generally did in the demands of her favourites. "Of course, as you wish it M'sieur Garvie. But it is strange enough to me. Have you, then, no good, new beds and chests and pottery in America that you must come here to buy old ones, often when they are shabby? It seems a pity. However, it is not my affair. There are good fresh soles for your dinner, and to-morrow I shall give you a *bouilleabaise* for lunch. Those are the things that really matter," and her shoulders shook in a comfortable laugh.

"You are a true philosopher, Marie Jeanne. And here comes Mr. Praed," Garvie added, as a familiar figure turned into the Place from the river road. "Jove! His country dress makes him a younger looking man than I thought. In spite of the grey locks he might win the heart of the aristocratic orphan," he commented, watching the spare, sturdy figure in well-fitting tweeds, coming up to the inn door. "Doubt if he's any too pleased to see me," was his thought as Mr. Praed look up and recognized him, his first stare of amazement darkening into a shadow of suspicion.

"How do you do?" Garvie hastened to call out. "Don't look so amazed. Marie Jeanne is an old friend, and Trêmalo is a haunt of my student days."

At the words, Mr, Praed's face cleared, and he took Garvie's hand with all his old heartiness. "This back-of-beyond region, where the people dress like in an opera bouffe, and speak a worse lingo than French? Well, I never should have thought it, though I'm pleased enough to have you here. There are a dozen things I'm dying to make this good lady understand. Not that she isn't most liberal in her feeding, but I'd prefer some of those eatables she gives me at eleven, for a good sensible eight o'clock breakfast; a beefsteak, and some of those eggs in a pan. Eleven is neither one thing nor the other, you see. Seems to break up the business part of the day."

Marie Jeanne had turned away with a cheerful nod, and the two seated themselves on a bench.

"I'll convey the fact to her presently," Garvie said as he lit a cigarette. "I suppose, as I find you here, the collection is somewhere in the neighbourhood. How has it turned out?"

He did not mean Mr. Praed to know of his talk with Marie Jeanne. The latter settled himself with an air of satisfaction as he began, "It's turned out about as fine a thing as I've ever come across, sir. I wouldn't have missed seeing it here, in its own home so to say, for half the pay ore in the Rockies. It's been a kind of a revelation to me to see tapestries hanging on the very same walls since Henry of Navarre, you know, him as

Bound a snow-white plume upon his gallant crest,

sent them as a present to the Rostrênan folks of those days. And oak carvings—" he leant forward to shake an emphatic finger at Garvie— "there's a sort of two-storied chest that's a regular history of France. It's got a row of queens heads along the top, with kings full length down

below, while the doors—panels, they call them—
are carved pictures of things that happened, mur-
ders, and crownings, and such amusements of the
day. You shall see it, sir," and he clapped Garvie
vigourously on the shoulder.

"Thank you."

"Then there is a mantlepiece that reaches right
up to the ceiling, and every inch of it is carved and
painted with coats-of-arms, and signs, used by the
noble families round about as were connected with
the Rostrênans. And that, sir, is to be packed up
and sent out to my new house in Montreal, though
it seemed like tearing her heart out when Mam'-
selle agreed to it. It was wonderful to hear her
going over the names that belonged to each one.
But there isn't a thing about the place that she
doesn't know the story of—and mind you, it's a
regular museum. She just walks along and tells
you the history of this or that as she goes—and
everyone of them blessed objects had something
to do with her own family. It's as though she
fairly loved them all."

"But she is going to sell everything to you?"
came Garvie's practical reminder, which however,
in nowise damped the romantic ardour of the nar-
rator, who answered:

"Every bit and scrap. You see, she says as she
would rather have them go like that, all in a lot,
to some one who will value them properly."

"And you give her a pretty good price for
them, I suppose?" Garvie suggested.

The question seemed to act as a spur to Mr. Praed's fervour. "Well young man," he said, "you may just be sure that, though he's got the name of a smart business man, Gabriel Praed isn't going to bargain with an aristocratic orphan like that. No sir, if you were to see her quietly wiping away a tear when she thinks I ain't looking—well it's touching, that's what it is. Tell you what, just come and jump into my machine, and I'll run you down to the castle in no time. Mamselle's working at the catalogue that she's making out for me, with all the dates and histories concerned. We're sure to find her there in the great hall, and so you'll have a peep at her and the collection together. It's a sight worth seeing, for it seems as though they belonged to each other."

Every word the simple-minded old man spoke deepened Garvie's respectful pity for his chivalrous loyalty to a woman who must, at least, be the tool of sordid imposters. Instinctively shrinking from some discovery that might place him in an unpleasant position towards Julia's father, he urged the first excuse that came into his head.

"But I understood you that the young lady is in deep mourning. I fear my visit might be an intrusion. Had you not better first ask her if I might come?"

With a guilty feeling, he saw the old man flush as at a detected breach of good manners. "Of course, of course," he said, hastily. "Glad you mentioned it. I'm not much of a judge of those kind of things myself, you know. Now that I think of it, I did have an idea this afternoon as she might be tired of me hanging round; in fact, she rather hinted she'd like to be alone for a bit, and so I didn't go back. I was thinking of taking a spin down the river to Bellon to have a look at them oyster-beds as they call parks. A paying sort of thing, they are, from all accounts. Tell you what, sir, the French are a good deal smarter people than I thought them. Would you like to come with me?"

Not feeling inclined for the expedition, Garvie answered; "No thank you, I am a bit lazy after coming straight through from Paris. After I've had a bath, I must go and look up the *garde-champetre* to arrange about my fishing. That is what I came for, you know."

"I see," and Mr. Praed stood before him, slowly nodding his head. "Well, it will be a comfort to have some one to speak to at dinner to-night. I began to wonder if I weren't getting deaf and dumb, with everybody jabbering around me, and me not saying a word. Queer place, this square, ain't it," he went on. "Makes me feel as though I were at the theatre, and the girl in short petticoats would come out there at the side by the market-house singing—not but what they haven't all got short petticoats here."

Garvie looked at the familiar bit of old-world

life with the appreciative eyes of the newly returned. "Yes, it has a stage aspect," he agreed,
"and I suppose it has been the scene of tragedies
and comedies enough within the past three or four
hundred years. Fairs and conscriptions, wed-
ding-feasts and pardons, may contain as concen-
trated an essence of human nature as balls and
race meetings. Are you off? Well, I'll sit here
and meditate a bit."

Mr. Praed has risen, and with a friendly "So
long," stalked off to the stables, whence Garvie
presently saw him emerge in his car, and turn off
into the road to the sea.

As the hoot of his horn died away in the distance, peace resumed her reign over Trêmalo
Place, and Garvie tried to fix his mind on an up-
to-date view of the situation.

"And you have left me plenty of food for meditation, my friend," he reflected, "with Marie
Jeanne, who knows all the news of the commune,
saying that there are no Rostrênans left at Rosbraz, and with you maundering over your aristocratic orphan and her Henry IV tapestries. It
strikes me that I have made a confounded fool of
myself in suggesting Julia's appearance on the
scene, before I had investigated the orphan question. Had I better send her a wire not to come?
No, the worse things are the more she may be
needed to help in getting her father out of a
pickle, and she is plucky enough to choose to face

any unpleasantness, if need be; and I shall be here to stand by her," and as he rose, his face settled into resolute lines that boded ill for whoso disturbed the peace of Miss Julia Praed.

XVI

THE ARISTOCRATIC ORPHAN

A S Garvie turned towards the inn door, his
attention was caught by a slim woman
crossing the Place towards the post-
office. In these out-of-the-way Breton
villages, the town dress of a lady was yet, in the
winter season, a rare enough sight for him to give
a second look to the black-clad form.

"It is not the notary's wife, nor Madame the
Inspector, and yet there is something familiar
about the outline," he cogitated. "Can it be the
orphan, out on the loose, when her patron's back
is turned? I might as well wait until she comes
back and have a look at her. Better still, I will
stroll down and ask for letters."

Putting this idea into action, Garvie reached
the post-office steps just as the girl in black appeared in the doorway. Her veil pushed back,
she had paused to finish the hasty reading of a letter she held, thereby giving Garvie ample time to
look up into the pale, red-lipped face and to recog-
nize Virginie Lapierre, his lost model. "The
aristocratic orphan! Now I must walk warily,"
flashed through his mind, as his sharp "Vir-

ginie" caused her to draw back, a startled flash in her cairngorm eyes.

A quick glance to right and left told that she meditated flight, but Garvie faced her impassively at the foot of the steps and she stood staring helplessly down at him. Stifling a sense of pity, he spoke with sarcastic deference, "So this is the mysterious reason why Mademoiselle Lapierre could not finish her engagements. Some other more favoured artist has doubtless offered her more than I did."

The girl put up her bare hand to push back the loose masses of her red-gold hair, and ignoring the second meaning of his words, answered defiantly, "It was no question of money. I told you that I must get away, and I gave you the first chance. After that I was free to do what I choose."

"*Parfaitement,* but why be so tragic over it? I assure you, that I passed some unhappy hours on your account—needlessly, as I see.

The tears welled up in her wonderful eyes, and she put out one hand in an appealing fashion. "Please do not be angry with me, M'sieur Garvie. Indeed I could not help it—at least—oh, I must go. I have a long walk before dark," she pleaded.

"Then you are not staying at Gloannic's?" he asked, still holding his ground.

"No, out in the country; down the river."

Garvie gave no sign of what he guessed. "Ah, you are at the old sardine-packer's house, I suppose. A little amateur honeymoon perhaps? Well, we may meet in our rambles. A fisherman gets to know the country. So I shall only say *au revoir,* not *adieu,*" he said, stepping aside with a bow.

"*Au revoir,* monsieur," and with the old quick flutter of drapery she was gone, not down the place to the bridge, her natural way to Rosbraz if she were walking, but around a corner into an alley, leading, he knew, to a landing.

"She has come up by boat. She could never walk it in her Parisian high heels," he commented, as he went back to the inn.

Yes, he had done right, he thought, in not making her desperate. There was no telling what she might do if she knew that she was detected. Disgusted as he was at the trouble which lay ahead for Julia, he was still distressed that it should be Virginie whom he would have to run down. He was now certain that she was under the thumb of some one; in all probability, Britski. "I wish that I could get her out of this without too big a row," he said to himself. "Perhaps I can frighten her away before the thing is exposed. If only the old man were not so green. I believe he is capable of wanting to marry her," and with a vexed laugh he went off in search of his room.

Two days passed without further developments, peaceful spring days, when Garvie, making a pretense of fishing up the wooded banks of the brawling little river, more than once explored the tidal shores between the village and the chateau of Rosbraz.

The turreted grey pile, on its point amongst the chestnut woods gave no sign of what was happening within its walls, and the coast-guard men in the little white houses on the opposite bank, when beguiled into gossip, only repeated Marie Jeanne's story.

"They must be Jews," said a white-capped little woman, "for they never go to mass, not one of them."

These expeditions were cautiously made, to avoid the automobile and its owner, and the latter had so little suspicion of any curiosity on Garvie's part that he even brought him a polite invitation from the chatelaine to visit Rostrênan and its treasures.

"The plot thickens," Garvie thought, and prepared for combat. But he might have saved himself the trouble, for when they reached the chateau, a stolid youth whom he fancied to be an Alsatian, told them that Mademoiselle de Rostrênan, having a *migraine*, regretted that she could not receive them.

"Too bad, too bad," fussed Mr. Praed, "but you shall see the collection, all the same."

Garvie did see it, and here came one of his greatest surprises. A certain portion of the tapestries and wood-carvings were undoubtedly valuable works of art, while about a third were the most palpable modern imitations.

Even allowing for the value of the real antiques, there did not seem to be a sufficient quantity of bric-a-brac to justify the trouble that had been taken over the affair. Why, Garvie wondered, had Britski, not stocked the place full of sham antiques when he was playing so bold a game? With this thought, he turned to Mr. Praed, asking abruptly: "Are these all the things? From what you said, I fancied it was a much larger collection."

Looking into the heavily lined face, he saw an unwonted embarrassment, and in a flash he understood that there was something in the affair which Mr. Praed had been induced to keep secret.

"Well, yes, these are most all; that is, there are some odds and ends in the long gallery up above, but we might disturb Mam'selle if we went there," was the hasty answer that confirmed his suspicions.

It was early in the next afternoon and Mr. Praed was sitting on the bench outside the Lion d'Or, smoking a big cigar with an air of gloom. A cheery "good day" from the inn door caused him to look around to see Garvie standing there with an after-luncheon air of well being. "Morning, sir, morning," was the gruff retort.

Garvie sat down and proceeded to light a cigarette. "Sorry not to turn up for *déjeuner*," he began, "but I made an early start and went upstream to the third mill. Fortunately, Marie

Jeanne's philosophy stands any strain of unpunctuality. I had even a better lunch than usual."

Again Mr. Praed answered drearily: "One needs philosophy for mixed-up meals like these French ones. Not but what the woman does her best, I'll say that for her," and he gave a sigh, which was obviously not a tribute to Marie Jeanne's virtues.

Garvie thought it time to make inquiries. "You look dull. I hope there's nothing the matter?"

"Nothing particular, but I don't feel exactly cheerful somehow."

With a sudden idea that he was in a humour for confidences, Garvie asked, "Have you been out to Rosbraz to-day, and is the chatelaine better?"

The old man turned on him a troubled glance from under his shaggy grey eyebrows. "Meaning Mam'selle? Yes, I've been up there this morning, and I didn't see her, neither. I saw a queer little old woman, who is always hanging round. Sort of nurse or housekeeper, I fancy. She speaks a few words of English, and told me that Mam'selle was very *souffrante*—suffering, I suppose that means, and was in a desolating fever. Seems bad, don't it? Wonder if the poor girl has any one to take care of her?"

"I daresay the old woman nurses her," Garvie suggested in the role of comforter.

"That old gypsy witch," was the contemptuous retort. "Tell you what, Mr. Garvie," with a relapse into pathos, "it would touch you just as much as it has me if you once saw her, so quiet and proud like, and yet so sad and lonely."

Taking care to give no sign of his difference of opinion, Garvie agreed, "I dare say it might. We men are easily moved by beauty in distress."

"I believe it's nothing more than worrying over these things that has worn her out. I feel like a brute about it," came in dull tones; then with the interest of a new idea, Mr. Praed asked:

"Look here, Mr. Garvie, did Julia speak to you before you left Paris, of my writing her about having Mam'selle as a kind of companion to her—talking French, and all that?"

The eagerness in his face, warned Garvie how much importance he attached to the question, and redoubled his caution. Knowing that Virginie could never venture thus far, he wished to prepare Mr. Praed for disappointment.

"Yes, Miss Praed did mention it," he allowed.

"Seem to cotton to the idea, eh?"

"Well," he began, "I have found that women are apt to fight shy of ready-made friends to order. They seem to have an inherent taste for picking them out for themselves. You see, if the young ladies did not happen to take a fancy to each other it might be awkward for everyone."

The testiness of a worried man flashed into the other's face.

"Awkward," he snapped. "Not a bit of it. Why the deuce shouldn't they take to each other?

Julia's a sensible girl, and she can't help admiring Mam'selle when she has once met her. You'll see, they'll be the best of friends," he added in momentary optimism.

Garvie, still feeling bound to administer discouragement, answered: "In my experience, a woman can always help admiring the person she does not choose to admire. But, of course, I should be a better judge if I had seen the young lady."

He had been successful in turning Mr. Praed's thoughts away from Julia. "Of course, you will see her in a day or two," was the pacific rejoinder. "But, at any rate, you saw the collection yesterday. What did you think of *that?*"

Here was a fresh difficulty to be faced. Doubts must be aroused without too great friction. "You are sure that you want my opinion?"

Even this quiet question seemed to cause irritation. "Of course I do," was the sharp answer. "Though I know as you can't do anything but admire it."

"That is as may be. At any rate, you shall have it. You must remember that an artist, living for five or six years in Paris, has come across a good deal of *bric-a-brac*, both sham and real. We go without our dinners to buy it, in the first flush of youth; later we pawn it when we are hard up; we hire it for our own pictures, and criticise it in other men's; and so, one way or another, we get a certain knowledge on the subject. Now," and his voice deepened impressively, "I took a good look around, yesterday. The light in that old hall was dim, but still I feel certain that, while some of the furniture is of undoubted value, there is about a third of the stuff that is only modern rubbish. One, at least, of the tapestries, is composed of odds and ends put together on fresh canvass."

He had hardly got so far when Mr. Praed sprang up in great excitement and faced him, one hand stretched out in emphatic remonstrance. "Look here," he shouted, "what's the use of saying a thing like that, when I told you that Mam'-selle knows the history of every bit and scrap from the day it came into their own castle. Didn't I tell you how she said—"

Garvie, beginning to feel impatient, interrupted, "Oh, yes, I know she *said*, but it seems to be your business to judge between what she says and a disinterested opinion, given at your own request—"

Forgetting his usual deference for the son of his old employer, Mr. Praed broke in, "That's all very well. I daresay you mean all right, Mr. Garvie, but after all, it's only your opinion, and if you expect me to swallow one word as casts a doubt on Mam'selle's high-mindedness, you'll just find yourself mistaken, that's all." He hesitated then with a deprecating glance into the other's stern face, went on more mildly: "There, there, I didn't mean any rudeness, I'm sure. It's only that

I'm that worried, what with the young lady's illness and my feeling that no respect could be too great for her, and what with your hints and Julia's cantankerous letter, that I hardly know what I'm saying. But I tell you what, sir," with a fresh outburst of wrath, "if you and that daughter of mine have been putting your heads together to vex me just because of her silly girl's spite—"

Garvie's patience was gone, and he broke in, gravely: "I can quite believe that you do not know what you are saying, Mr. Praed, when you speak of your daughter in such terms. I will just take a stroll down to the quay while you think it over a bit."

"Jove!" he gasped helplessly, as a luggage-laden carriage dashed around the corner and drew up at the door.

Within it sat, beaming with smiles, the present bone of contention—Julia Praed.

XVII.

IN ARCADY

THERE was evidently no misgiving as to her welcome in Julia's mind. Before Garvie could hurry to her aid, she had jumped lightly from the carriage and with a gay nod to him had hurried up to her father.

"Yes, it's me, father, not my ghost," she announced with a little laugh of triumph. Mr. Praed was a picture of undisguised dismay, as he stonily accepted her embrace.

"Julia Praed! Whatever has brought you here?" he demanded in an attempt at sternness, as he freed himself from her arms. With an undaunted smile, the girl answered, "Such fun. I've descended on you like an avalanche, and managed to surprise you both at the same time."

Garvie looking on, decided that Mr. Praed was guiltily trying to work himself up into a temper, as he retorted gruffly, "I haven't much fancy myself for them sort of surprises. They seem to me a good sight more like spying upon people, and that's a thing as I ain't going to stand."

Once before Garvie had seen her flash into sudden wrath, as she did now, though there was a mingling of wounded surprise in her voice that stirred his sympathy, when she protested, "Spying on you, father? Why, what ever put such an idea into your head? What could there be for me to spy about?"

Meeting Garvie's warning glance, she checked herself, and holding out her hand to him said with an attempt at her usual manner, "So you're staying here, Mr. Garvie, right in the same house with father. Isn't that pleasant for us all, and isn't this the dearest little place that one ever saw out of *Cavalleria Rusticana* or the *Pardon de Ploërmel?* Look at those women over there in the big white caps and collars. Aren't they quaint?" and she pointed to a chattering group of Trêmalo matrons who, in all the ardour of bargaining, had surrounded a fisherman laden with a basket of eels.

"Where is your maid? Surely you did not come alone?" Garvie demanded, somewhat reprovingly. A mischievous glance reminded him of their last talk.

"Why," Julia began with a deprecating smile, "when I told her where I was coming, she said that her mother was ill and wouldn't consent to her leaving Paris. So I just came off by myself and I got here all right, you see."

"Crazy notion," muttered Mr. Praed.

"I had better call Marie Jeanne and get your trunk taken in," Garvie suggested—"ah, here she is"—as the ponderous form of the landlady appeared in the doorway.

The latter stared in amazement at the brilliant apparition of a pretty girl in smart blue serge travelling dress, apparently on friendly terms with Mr. Garvie.

"Oh, doesn't she look nice in that dear little cap," was Julia's frank comment, and with a quick movement she had grasped Marie Jeanne's hand, saying, *"Bonjour, madame, bonjour."*

The latter returned her smile and greeting, and then turned to Garvie in appeal.

"But, monsieur, can you tell me does this lady mean to stay here? For, by St. Anne d'Auray, I cannot give her a good room without disturbing one of you gentlemen."

"That's all right, Marie Jeanne. This is Mr. Praed's daughter, and she can have my room. I will take one in the attic, if you like."

Marie Jeanne's brow relaxed. "As you choose, Monsieur. The front attic is empty. *Dame,* as this is Monsieur's daughter, we must make her comfortable. Here, cocher, bring in that trunk," she shouted, and the man made haste to obey. Marie Jeanne's word was law to all travelling folk throughout the department.

The sight of the trunk being carried in aroused Mr. Praed to a fresh outburst of vexation. "Look here, Julia," he remonstrated, "whatever are you going to do with yourself here? You won't have a soul to speak to, you know. Mr. Garvie will be away all day, fishing."

Here an interchanged glance spoke questioning

and reassurance. "As for me, I'm busy cataloguing the things down at the castle. I suppose you don't want to go dancing at the country folks' weddings over there in the market."

All undismayed at this prospect of isolation, Julia laughed. "Oh, what fun that would be. I saw a wedding party at Quimperlé, and I mean to get one of those dresses with embroidered bodices. But, father," with an appealing touch on his arm, "couldn't I help you with your catalogue? That would give me a chance to get acquainted with Mademoiselle de Rostrênan."

How winsome she seemed to Garvie, as she made this effort to propitiate her father, her face raised to his with a kindly smile. It was to no use, however, for Mr. Praed's embarrassment only made him more surly.

"Well, it happens that you can't make friends with Mam'selle, just now at any rate," he blurted out. "She's ill; worn out with trouble, and I'm sure she don't want any strangers coming bothering round," here a scowl at Garvie emphasized the words. "Anyway, I ain't going to have her disturbed a bit more than I can help. I've got business up at the castle now, (Mr. Praed always gave this liberal translation to chateau) and since you've chosen to come here without being asked, you can just look after yourself. You seem to be able to chatter to the landlady, so you had better settle about your room, and rest for a bit.

I suppose you'll be going off fishing again, Mr. Garvie?"

"I doubt it. The day has come out too bright," was the casual answer, given without a glance at Julia.

"Well, suit yourself, and I'll suit myself. I'm off," and with a great show of resolution that veiled an inward sheepishness, Mr. Praed walked over toward the shed that sheltered his auto-car. Left standing there together, Garvie and Julia looked at each other and both laughed, though there was an undercurrent of distress in the girl's voice.

"What does it all mean, Mr. Garvie?" she asked helplessly. It had been a great shock to find herself for the first time powerless to influence.

Garvie would not let her see his misgivings, and answered briskly, "First and foremost, it means that you are not to run off and weep, as you have half a mind to. We'll manage to turn it into a joke yet. Everything will seem different when you are rested. Come and sit down on these benches, whence we study village life, and I will ask Marie Jeanne for some of her good coffee. Her tea is apt to be eccentric, but her coffee is above reproach. I suppose you had *déjeuner* in Quimperlé before starting?"

"Oh yes, at that dear old inn. I'm really not a bit tired, only I feel so bewildered. What ever has got into father's head to make him behave like that?'

Garvie decided to tell the truth. "The same thing that has got into the heads of silly old gentlemen before now. He can think of nothing but this girl."

"Poor old dear!"

"And you must be careful not to oppose him when you can help it, or he may be capable of marrying her," he warned her.

"Goodness gracious!" came her first cry of dismay; then with a shy little smile, "but after all, poor old soul, if he wants his share of the fun, why shouldn't he have it? There is plenty of money for us all to have a good time."

"You are very unselfish," Garvie commented, then sinking his voice in new gravity, "But I am sorry to say that this is a more serious matter than an old man making a foolish marriage with a young girl. I have found out that this Mam'selle of his, does not belong to the Rostrênan family, as she says. She is a girl, sent here from Paris to persuade your father into buying a lot of stuff that has been recently put into this old chateau."

Julia sat staring at him in wide-eyed amazement. "But how do you know?" she asked.

Garvie hesitated. Then, to his subsequent sorrow, he decided to tell Julia nothing of Virginie Lapierre. The two stood for him at such opposite poles of womanhood that he hoped to keep them apart, even in thought.

"I had not listened to Marie Jeanne's gossip

for ten minutes before I made a guess at it, and
a few questions among the country-folk soon settled the question. You see, they must have
counted on your father not speaking French, and
on there being no English or American artists
here at this time of the year; otherwise, the whole
scheme would have been detected. I heard from
the people down the river, of the tug that had
come from Lorient a month or so ago, laden
with big packing-cases, which were landed at the
chateau. Furniture for the new owners, the
workmen said. Before that the place had been
quite empty. As far as I can make out, the girl
herself has only been here for ten days or so. It
was a master stroke of Britski's to send her here
alone, and stay on in Paris. Your father would
have been far more wideawake in dealing with a
man than with a woman."

Julia had followed his words attentively, and
now asked, "But why, if you knew all this, didn't
you warn him at once?"

"I had to make sure of my facts first. As you
drove up, I was just opening the campaign, with
some doubts as to the value of the collection, but
at the first hint he flared up, and you saw what a
humour it left him in."

He paused to let his words sink in, his eyes
intent on the pensive droop of Julia's head.

"I must confess there are some things about
the business that puzzle me. More than half the
furniture and tapestries are things of real value,

on which he would make small profit and there is not nearly the quantity of stuff that I expected to see. It seems as if it could not be worth while for a man of Britski's standing to run such risks and go to such expense for an affair of no greater importance than merely selling that amount of *bric-a-brac.* For your own sake," he went on impressively, "we must move very cautiously. Even if he did buy all the stuff that he calls 'the collection,' it would matter little to you compared to his making his life wretched by a marriage with an adventuress. Is not that how you feel?" and his voice was very kindly as he leant toward her.

"Of course," came the fervent response, as wet grey eyes looked up at him. "It's not the money that matters. Oh," with a sudden flash of inspiration, "there is that money that father settled on me, more than I ever need. Couldn't we offer to pay her more than the people in Paris do, if she would go away and not let him know where she was?"

Again Garvie hesitated as to whether he should tell her of his acquaintance with Virginie, and again he made the mistake of silence.

Remembering the model's queer disregard for money, he guessed that she was coerced by some other power, and shook his head. "A bribe would be useless if she thought that she could get the whole, and it would be rash to let her guess at our fears. No, I feel sure that a waiting game is the best. By-the-by, do you think that Mrs. Mallock is in this? Did she ever shew that she knew anything about Trêmalo?"

"I think not," Julia said, slowly. "No, I am sure that the way things were going didn't suit her. Every time she saw a letter from father, she asked when he would be back, and seemed awfully put out at my saying I didn't know. Oh yes, and she kept trying to make me tell her the name of this place without asking me directly. I had great fun pretending I didn't know what she meant, until one day I found her reading the address on a letter I had written him. 'I was just looking to see that you had put the department correctly, my dear. So many English people spell Finistère with two r's and without the accent,' she said sweetly.

" 'Well, perhaps I spelt it right because I'm not English,' I said. She would try to find out too, what father said about this girl and the chateau. No I think she is not in this game," she ended.

"All the better. It makes one less to fight. But how did you get along with her?" he asked.

Julia smiled as at quaint recollections. "Oh, we got along well enough. At first she was inclined to snub me, but when I saw that she was fidgetting at father's not coming back, I thought she might want to borrow money from him, as she had done before. So I offered to lend her some, and she took it down at a gulp. After she found that I had a separate banking account she just crawled round on all fours. It was a nuisance the way she bothered me to buy things; but, on the other hand, she rather dropped the little French count. I fancy she thought she would keep all the cake for herself."

The careless fashion in which Julia told her tale, did not lessen Garvie's indignant sympathy. "You poor girl, to have such a creature on your hands," he said. "Why did you not turn her out?"

"Oh, well, I suppose it was best to have some one, and she was useful in a way. I had learnt her tricks, and would rather put up with them than start in with a set of new ones. There has always been some one of that kind ever since we got so rich," she added sadly.

"And yet you keep your kindly faith in human nature."

"Oh, I wouldn't want to live if I didn't," she protested earnestly. "Look at father, now. It's just because he is sorry for this girl that she has got round him."

Garvie was careful to suppress any signs of a more masculine opinion, knowing there was some truth in her view.

"Then there is Miss Dorr," she went on eagerly, "who I believe would like me better if I hadn't a cent."

"And my poor self. Might not I be counted in the category of faithful friends?" Garvie asked, with sudden intentness of voice and eyes.

A blush and dimpling smile answered him. "Haven't I proved it by descending on you with all my troubles? You are one of the knights-errant we used to read about at school."

Pleasant as was the response, Garvie might have liked it to have been a little less ready. He made his next words lighter in consequence.

"I am vowed to your faithful service. But you have not told me how you shook off your chaperon."

Julia laughed. "She was an amazed woman when I told her that I was going to join some friends from America—that was true, you know —and suggested that she would prefer to go back to her own apartment. She protested at my going alone, but when she saw that I didn't care what she said, she went off quite amiably. I think she understood that she would never get in again. So that's the end of her. Now for the other one."

"The other one must, I fear, be as I said, a waiting game."

"But is there nothing that I can do now?" Julia asked.

Garvie saw that it would be hard to keep her to an inactive policy. "The first thing to do, is to get your father into a good-humour again. That should be easy for you to manage."

"Poor old soul, yes," Julia said with a tender laugh. "He is most likely already conscience stricken at the thought of my spending the rest of the day weeping, alone in a strange room."

"I hope that is not your intention."

"I'm sure it's not. Why, I want to set off and explore this queer, lovely country as soon as ever I can. Which is the very nicest place for me to go first? I'm a great walker, you know."

Garvie looked down into the frank face with its lurking tremour of mischief, and answered unsmilingly, "I am afraid it is hard to direct you. You really need to take a guide. The country is a network of lanes and paths. If we cross the bridge, we can go along the quay and out into the shore meadows where the banks are yellow with primroses."

"Oh, I do want to see them growing wild!" was the eager interruption.

"Then if we go straight up the hill from the bridge, and turn off by a path through the chestnut woods, we come to the ruins of Rustifen chateau," Garvie went on in the monotonous voice of a guide.

"Ruins? Oh, are there really ruins?"

"Or if we go up the river bank, we can climb the hill to old Trêmalo chapel and *calvaire*—"

"Oh, don't, you bewilder me," she protested gaily. "Take me anywhere. But I forgot, you are going fishing."

Garvie answered the challenge with a calm contradiction. "No, you did not forget. You knew that I was not going to leave you here alone. Shall we go now?" and he looked down at her feet to see if she were prepared. Yes, the trim skirt was quite short, and the well-shaped boots were solid in make.

"You forget that I'm a mountain girl," she triumphed. "Oh, you don't know how glad I am to be in the wilds again."

And so, side by side, they set off into what was to Julia a new world of delight.

XVIII

MRS. MALLOCK ON THE WAR PATH

AS Mrs. Mallock drove off from the Avenue Friedland apartment, which to her represented the land of plenty, her honeyed smiles hid a tempest of baffled fury. She was in such a rage with everyone that she could not decide where first to concentrate her wrath. Julia had practically dismissed her, but she suspected Andrew Garvie, or even Sylvia Dorr, of having prompted the deed. Mr. Praed, her own discovery, had vanished into the wilderness like St. John the Baptist, but was not Britski responsible for spiriting him out of her grasp?

Worst of all, there was this mysterious girl at this mysterious chateau, whom she suspected of being the main cause of her discomfiture. Why, oh why, she mourned to herself, had she ever admitted those rapacious wretches to a share of the spoils?

Lamenting thus, she ignored the fact that she had no choice in the matter. Her fortunes had been at a low ebb, and if she had not returned from America with plump prey there would have been no more comfortable dinners at the Hotel

Cleveland, no smart dresses from Madame Marcelle, no commissions from Britski.

She was shrewd enough to know that she had got the worst of it, but she did not intend to give up her hold without a struggle and she lost no time in taking her grievances to Madame Marcelle's show-rooms.

There, the stream of ornamental life was flowing on smoothly, with a coming and going of smartly dressed women. Madame Marcelle's welcome was not effusive, but presently, when the day's rush seemed over, she came across to where Mrs. Mallock was forlornly studying a model on a stand, and suggested a retreat to her own sanctum.

"I always take a rest and have tea or a *syrop* after these exacting ladies go, and before I look over the day's orders," she said, as she settled herself in a deep arm chair. In this high-tide of Parisian spring life, the day's work done by Madame Marcelle might have exhausted a strong man, but she looked as fresh and unruffled as she had been eight hours earlier.

"And what has your young woman been getting travelling dresses for?" she asked, with unusual directness.

Mrs. Mallock had not enough quickness to hide the ignorance which revealed her loss of power.

"Has she?" she gasped, then recollecting herself. "Oh, I remember she did speak of something of the kind. Two, wasn't it?"

"Yes, two," and Madame Marcelle's smile told that she marked the lucky guess. "But where is she going?"

Mrs. Mallock's grey-green eyes met hers suspiciously. "Oh, she has just gone down to Brittany to join her father for a week or so. He wanted her to see this furniture he is buying," she said airily, adding, "Britski should get a big commission on it."

"I suppose so, if it was he who arranged the sale," was the indifferent answer.

"And this girl who owns the stuff. I hear there is talk of the Praeds bringing her back with them."

Mrs. Mallock had certainly known more of her letters than Julia suspected.

Was it fancy, or did Madame Marcelle's high colour waver, and the lines of her mouth tighten? At any rate, it delighted her adversary to think so, though she was unaware of the cause.

She remembered however, rumours that Madame Marcelle's weak point was jealousy, not, it was said, without cause.

"I haven't heard Britski speak of her. We are both so busy at this time of year that we hardly see each other," the dressmaker explained.

"Ah, my dear, you are a wonderful woman. I do not see how you manage to keep so fresh, working as you do. And now tell me," with a fawning smile, "do you think that you could make me a chic little costume, foulard or crepe,

or something of that kind, for the Auteuil races?
There are some newcomers, South Africans, at
the Cleveland who I think would take me, and I
could tell them who had made it."

"They have been here already," was the dis-
concerting reply, "and I am weeks deep in orders now. I can undertake nothing more before
the Grand Prix."

Under her paint, Mrs. Mallock flushed with
rage. This was as good as a refusal of any further contributions, and how could she fish in social waters without suitable array?

"The Grand Prix! But that is two months
off," she quavered.

"Exactly so. And I shall be working night
and day until then. Must you go?" for the other
had risen. "Well," with a final relenting, "if
I have any misfits I will let you know."

"Misfits!" The word seemed the last insult,
the final stamp of failure.

In a nervous tremour of temper, Mrs. Mallock
fled, turning down the boulevard towards
Britski's. In calmer moments she stood in some
awe of the cynically inscrutable man, but the horrible conviction that she was being flung aside as
a useless tool gave her a false courage.

This courage swept her on its tide until, reaching Britski in his sanctum, she poured forth the
vials of her wrath. It was she who had discovered the Praeds. It was she who had taken the
girl to Marcelle, "and a fortune she must have

194

made out of her." It was she who had brought Mr. Praed to Britski, "and what return do I get?" she screamed; "you take him out of my hands, and send him off under the influence of some creature of your own." A flash of rage lighted Britski's impassive face. "Why couldn't you have sold him all the rubbishy stuff you wanted to here in Paris instead of swooping him away like this?"

Britski, who had been sitting contemplating her as he might a dubious piece of *bric-a-brac,* now leant forward his delicate white hands lightly interclasped on the table.

"And why couldn't you have kept him?" he demanded. "You had the first chance. If you had been up to your work, what could I have done against you? If you had been ten years younger, and prettier than you ever were, you would have had the western patriarch under your thumb to-day, so that all the powers of darkness could not have stirred him. And if you were not strong enough to bewitch the father, why could you not have kept the daughter? I never interfered there. It is the same old story, I suppose. As soon as you felt sure of the girl, you treated her like a fool; sniffed and sneered at her, and never saw that every day she was learning to do without you.

"You could have made yourself necessary to her if you had taken the trouble to see that she enjoyed herself. Instead of which you try to play a double game with those mummies from the Faubourg, and to get a commission for introducing their grasshopper of a son. A girl would be a fool, indeed, to look at him.

"Why come whining to me because you failed? If you had secured the father, I should only have taken my pickings through you. If he had married you, we would have held our tongues about Alphonse." Here the woman's face waxed ghastly. "As it is," and he brought one hand down on the table with sudden emphasis, "he is my prey and I claim him, and you can do nothing but hold your tongue and try to do better if you get another chance."

Could any words be more maddening than these, to a woman who knew their truth?

"But I shall not hold my tongue," she screamed, all caution forgotten. "And I may yet spoil your game for you. What is to prevent my following these people to this Breton village, and finding ont what is going on there? This Mademoiselle de Rostrênan may prove interesting company for me as well as for that doting old idiot."

Though this last dart was a random one, she saw that it had struck home.

"*Nom de Dieu!*" broke in Britski in a fierce voice, little above a whisper. "You had better understand that you interfere at your own peril. Your unpaid hotel bill and Marcelle's nice little account for clothes will make pleasant reading for you over your coffee to-morrow."

With a limp relaxation of mouth and arms, Mrs. Mallock sat staring at him. She had never thought that he might thus disavow all agreements. "But," she stammered, "it was always understood that the business I brought you offset those accounts. Look at what I have done."

"You have no written understanding to that effect, and could not prove it in any court," was the remorseless statement.

A wise man knows the right moment to make peace, and Britski, seeing that the woman was crushed, assumed a more placable air.

"*Voyons,* what is the use of squabbling like this," he said. "It is wiser to help each other along. I have this western Crœsus in hand to-day, you may have someone else in hand to-morrow. All roads lead to Paris, luckily for us. Come, let us renew our alliance."

With a benevolent smile he held out a hand to the wretched woman, down whose painted cheeks a few tears had straggled, making strange traces in the paint. Thoroughly cowed by this terrible sense of the passing of her day, the worst blow of all to a woman, she stammered, "I am sure I meant no harm. I only wanted to be fairly treated."

"And so you shall be. What is it, Joseph?" as a servant appeared with a card. "Yes, I am coming. Excuse me, madame," and with a polite bow, he followed the man out.

Left alone in her humiliation, Mrs. Mallock

looked around on the few costly treasures which the little room enshrined, with a futile desire to rend and destroy. She longed to thrust that sharp steel paper knife through the tiny canvas that represented thousands of francs. How easy it would be to lift her sunshade and crash that old Venice mirror into sparkling atoms; easy though impossible, for she knew that she was afraid of Britski, and dared not do it.

Ah, perhaps there was means of a subtler revenge in that bunch of keys left hanging in the half-open drawer of the writing table.

With a noiseless swoop, she was across the room in Britski's seat, ransacking the contents of the drawer. Receipted bills, auctioneers' catalogues, these she had no time to investigate. But still the eager hands sought on, every sense on the alert for a coming footstep. What was this little bundle of photographs at the very back of the drawer? Quickly snapping off the band that held them, she shuffled them over like a pack of cards.

She had often heard of Britski's skill as a photographer, and amateur photographs have been, before now, revealers of secrets.

Her first glance showed that these were all from the same model, though with a variety of costumes. Where had she seen that face before, she wondered, that heavy-jawed, angular face, with its big eyes and full lips, and framing masses of light hair?

Ah, they were neatly labelled in Britski's min-

ute, unmistakable writing. A fussy tidiness in
these small things was a characteristic of his.

"Virginie in the Quarter," shewed the smartly
dressed girl who is oftenest seen in the most Parisian of Paris streets. She strays little into the
broad avenues of Cosmopolis.

"Virginie as chatelaine." It needed a second
glance to make sure that this demure *jeune fille*
with primly arranged hair and plain black dress,
whose whole drooping pose bespoke a sad shrinking from notice, was the same person as the reckless daughter of the streets; but the features were
too marked for any possible mistake.

Here was the third, and no one who had ever
seen Sarah Bernhardt play *Theodora* could mistake the dress. "Virginie as A— G—'s model,"
it was labelled. Open-mouthed, Mrs. Mallock
stared at this last photo, various scraps of overheard talk sorting themselves in her mind. A
freak of memory recalled words that had drifted
to her at a crowded reception: "What is Garvie's
picture this year?" asked one man, and the other
answered, "Same old thing. Virginie Lapierre
with variations. *Theodora* this time."

How plain it all seemed now. This Virginie
Lapierre, known as Garvie's model, had been sent
to Brittany to play the part of the last of a noble
family, and so work upon the old man's suscepti-
bilities as to secure a good sale for Britski. Mrs.
Mallock had as yet suspected nothing more than a
big commission coming to him from a genuine

sale, and now she paid tribute to the daring of the scheme with a passing thrill of admiration.

There was hope, too, for surely in such troubled waters there was prey to be had for the seeking.

There were many puzzling details in the matter, such as what influence had been strong enough to take Virginie away from her congenial Paris life to the wilds of Brittany, and presumably set her on opposite sides from Garvie. This however, might be explained by the tempting bait of a rich old man to be hoodwinked; but that problem could wait later solving.

With hands that trembled with excitement, she rearranged the drawer, slipped the little package inside her dress, and went fourth into the outer galleries, leaving a message for Britski to say that she would not wait now but would return soon.

"A little interval for reflection will do him no harm," she added to herself.

Without yet having decided on any profitable course of action, she felt exultantly sure of holding winning cards.

She took a cab, and as it hurried her through the cheerful bustle of the streets, she found herself murmuring:

> Negligence,
> Fit for a fool to fall by.

In her far off American girlhood, before she had met so many of the world's buffets, she had known her Shakespeare well, and the words of the great Cardinal came naturally to her mind.

But there were more practical matters to consider than the astute Britski's mistake in labelling such tell-tale records.

What was she going to do with them? She knew too well the hopelessness of trying to win back the old man's good-will with proofs against this woman who had ensnared him. But Britski's words had revealed her error in regard to Julia. Was it too late to convince the girl of her disinterested friendship?

At first inclined to look on the daughter as unimportant, she had acquired a new respect for her on finding that she had the independent control of an income settled on her by her father. If Mr. Praed persisted in his infatuation, Julia would doubtless quarrel with him, and might then be glad of a chaperon.

Ah, but there was Garvie! If she were to marry him, what need would she have of Mrs. Mallock?

And then, all at once, came a vision of the double use to be made of the photographs.

If they were sent to Julia, would she not first rush to her father, and, in attempting to convince him of Mademoiselle de Rostrênan's real identity, be sure to quarrel with him? Then, acting on the suggestion that Garvie had followed his model to Brittany, to pursuade her back to him, would she not have an indignant scene with Garvie, and shaking the Trêmalo dust off her shoes, hurry back to Paris, and to the waiting arms of her faithful friend?

"It would be best to get her away on a little tour as soon as possible," that lady reflected, in a blissful day-dream. "Let me see, it will be just the right time for Venice, and from there we could go to the Italian Lakes. I haven't had a trip like that for years," and with a smile of anticipation, Mrs. Mallock spread forth her best letter-paper.

XIX

THE SERPENT IN EDEN

JULIA was right; as soon as Mr. Praed had recovered his temper, his conscience troubled him sorely about Julia. It had been as great a shock to him as to her to find that his daughter, the companion of so many journeys, was no longer welcome to come to him when she chose.

When he knocked at her bedroom door before dinner, he had resolved to eat the necessary amount of humble-pie. It was all the greater relief to find, instead of a tearfully accusing or forgiving daughter lying down with a headache, a girl freshly dressed in white serge, radiant with exercise and the interest of her new surroundings.

She had wheeled a big armchair to the window which overlooked the Place and now sat enthroned there, gazing down in great content on the panorama of evening village life. As Mr. Praed stood in the doorway, he asked with brusque awkwardness:

"Got settled all right, eh, Julia?"

Their fashions with each other had never been expansive, and on both sides this was taken as full *amende honorable*.

"Oh, splendid," was her gay answer. "I haven't felt so happy since I lost sight of the Rockies. Mr. Garvie took me the lovliest walk through the fields, up to the ruins of a castle that was built long before Columbus discovered America. Just think of that! And then we went on until we came to pine woods, real pine woods, with big grey rocks, just like home. And look at those primroses and bluebells I picked, all growing wild in the fields. And I'm as hungry as ever I can be, and that bell means dinner, doesn't it?"

"It does, and I'd keep some breath for it, if I were you," and Mr. Praed laid his hand on the one she had slipped through his arm, with a greater sense of well-being than he had known the last two days.

Surely, such a nice, sensible girl as his Julie couldn't help making friends with Mam'selle, and what an ass he had been not to remember that nothing could better help on his pet scheme of a match between Julia and Garvie than such days in each other's company. Here, when they had most likely been thinking of nothing save enjoying themselves together as young folks did, he, like an old fool, had been suspecting them of all sorts of schemes against himself.

"I must be getting into my dotage," he decided, little guessing how many people were agreed with him on that point. And so it was a cheerful party of three that sat down to one of Marie Jeanne's best dinners in the dark inn dining-room, panelled with sketches by men, some of whom were already known in New York and Paris. After dinner, they sat before the hotel door in the golden twilight, that brought out strange blue shadows on the white house fronts, and sombred the encircling hills into velvety duskiness.

The drowsy murmur of the river was heard at intervals between the shrill piping of the *binous* in the open market-shed, where the unending *gavotte* was being danced by old and young, with mirthless faces and uncouth movements. The shoemaker's daughter had been married, and a three days' feast was being held.

Julia had strolled over with the two men to have a look at this bit of old-world festivity. The two pipers sat on chairs raised on a platform of barrels and loose boards, and one or two oil lamps in brackets against the pillars gave enough light to dance by. The women were nearly all in their Sunday clothes. Their broad white collars and the stiff wings of their caps were lace-edged, and their black bodices shone with silver braid and many-coloured embroidery.

"I must have a dress like that," Julia decided, as they returned to the comparative quiet of their bench. "It's strange," she went on in a dreamy tone, "that unlike as this all is, it somehow reminds me of home, and sitting on the verandah, and hearing the miners' children playing around their houses, and the river gurgling down in the gulch. Do you remember old Joe's concertina, father? It didn't sound unlike those bagpipes over there, did it? Oh, it will be nice to get home and see it all again!"

"Why, Julie," protested her father, not over-pleased. "I thought you couldn't have enough of everything over here."

"So did I, not so long ago," answered Julia. "But I think getting away from the towns has shewn me how homesick I am. I suppose the maples will be turning when we get home, father."

"How can I tell?" was the testy retort. "If you had ever worked as hard as I have, you wouldn't be in such a hurry to end the first holi-day of your life."

Julia had been talking in accordance with a suggestion of Garvie's, that she should try to turn her father's mind back into the familiar channels of his home life and interests.

Garvie now came to her rescue with a welcome diversion, "Have you been in England yet, Mr. Praed?"

"No," was the interested answer, "and that's a thing as I've been planning all along to do this summer. I've been saving it up, on purpose. London now, one couldn't get anything better than that, I fancy. And then there's the country my father came from—that's in the north—York-shire, that is. I want to see the old farm as he used to tell me about, and the graves of the Praeds for generations. For we come of decent farmer stock, sir, though my father did get contrary over something when he was only a boy, and went off with not much more than the clothes he stood in. Well, I haven't been a discredit to him or to them, and there's a town out there, called after me, as will make our name live in the new country."

His voice had grown reminiscent, and, as he ended, the others did not break in on his train of thought.

Presently Garvie turned to Julia, saying, "Are you good for a day's fishing to-morrow? Coffee at seven, and an early start. I've ordered the little cart at half-past seven, to drive to the second mill. There you will find rocks and woods to your heart's content. It's all wild country up the river."

"Oh how lovely!" Julia cried, "But how did you know I fished?"

"Do not you remember shewing me a photo of your struggle with a salmon? I brought an extra rod on purpose," he triumphed.

A softly breathed "Oh," was her only comment, but it appeared to satisfy Garvie.

With an afterthought of duty, Julia appealed to her father, "Couldn't I help you, at the chateau to-morrow father? Or would you like to take me a run round the neighbourhood in your auto?"

"Eh, what?" and the old man roused himself from rosy visions. "No, no. I'd better be going down alone to the castle to-morrow. That is," with a touch of compunction, "unless you're specially wanting me, Julia."

"Oh no, don't bother about me, father. Mr. Garvie says that he will take me fishing," she responded demurely.

Two days passed, with weather all that April can be on those southern shores of Brittany.

Each golden hour of daylight was, for Julia, full of the joy of existence. Too proud to give Garvie any chance of feeling her presence a drag, she one day made excuses to let him go off alone sallying forth soon after to explore the country on her own account. Climbing the steep orchard bank behind the hotel, she found herself out on the open hill country, where the bare granite cropped up every here and there through its golden veil of gorse and broom.

Below her wound the river, a blue streak between red-brown mud banks, banks that had been painted in every variety of light by every variety of artist.

At length she found herself leaving the barren heights, and descending into a little slope of orchard that embosomed a tiny gem of a grey Gothic chapel. Making for this, she came sharply round a corner on Garvie, white umbrella, easel and all, absorbed in painting a bank where the wild flowers had run riot. A mutual word of surprise was followed by a laugh.

"So this is what letters to write means. No sooner is my back turned than you set off on your own account, regardless of the dangers of savage old pigs in the woods, of wicked sailor-men on the roads. Are you aware that the valley you have just passed is the famous one where the wolf ate the postman?" Garvie demanded.

"I've walked wilder places than this alone," she asserted gaily.

"But why this taste for solitude? What had I done to be banished?" he persisted, half in jest.

"O I thought you might be getting tired of me," Julia said, with a blush and laugh.

"I do not ask for people's company if I am tired of them," he answered with a look into her eyes. "Come now, for punishment, you shall sit on that bank and pose for me as the spirit of the spring morning, as the 'joy of life unquestioned.' That white serge will carry on the scheme of colour to perfection. How is it that you always wear just the suitable thing?"

Julia smiled responsive. Why does a woman so love praise of her clothes from a man? Is it that in her mind, she makes them a subtle expression of herself?

"And if you are very good," Garvie went on, "you shall have a share of my lunch. It is over there, under the apple-tree."

"Ah, but I've got some of my own," she triumphed, producing a neat sandwich-case.

"There is no catching you at a disadvantage," he grumbled, though seeming well pleased. And this was the last of Julia's efforts at self-reliance, for the present.

Was she selfish in forgetting the coming trouble between her father and herself? Perhaps so, but then for some wise purpose of her own, Nature has provided youth with the armour of egotism. How else could the young find courage for the ventures they must essay? Later they will learn to sympathize and heal.

And so a day or two passed, and one evening at bedtime, as the three came in from the quay where they had been lounging, Mr. Praed handed Julia a letter, saying: "I clean forget it when the postman brought it this afternoon. Seems heavy."

Seeing the Paris stamp, Julia waited until she had reached her room to open it. It was from Mrs. Mallock, and contained a little package of photographs which could be nothing of much interest. So she took a stroll about her room, bestowed a caressing glance on a little study which Garvie had given her, and then, letting down her hair, proceeded to brush it and read the letter at the same time, without looking at the photographs.

But soon her brush lay on the table disregarded, and with painfully intent face, she was staring at the letter as though it were some treacherous thing, with power to wound. And so it had, for it ran thus:

My DEAREST JULIA—Feeling sure that you cannot but understand how warm is my interest in you, how heartfelt my gratitude for the many kindnesses shewn by you and your father to a poor wanderer, I am taking the risk of being suspected of mischief-making, and writing to warn you of what I fear is treachery. These enclosed photographs came into my hands yesterday, and will, I think, tell their own tale. I do not know whose the writing on them is. I have never seen Mr. Garvie's—but you must see for yourself what they mean.

You may remember Mr. Garvie's irritation at my harmless little joke about his well-known, red-haired model. Here you see her in street dress, and as he has painted her for this year's Salon—what the third picture means you may guess better than I. I have heard, as gossip, that his leaving Paris at such an unusual season was due to her sudden vanishing. It is said that he is gone in search of her, so if you come across him *là-bas*, she may not be very far away. Can the third picture mean that this clever young woman is now posing as a certain orphan chatelaine?

I should hate, dear girl, for you to think me interfering, but I feel it my womanly duty to tell you that Mr. Garvie has been boasting of his approaching marriage with an heiress—apparently the model would be no bar to that.

Dear Julia, do send me one little line to tell me that you appreciate the honesty of my motives. Longing to see you back in Paris, always your loving friend,

Maud Mallock.

Once or twice during the reading of this precious epistle, Julia had paused to study with painful eagerness the three photographs which lay before her. Never in all her young life had she known such a fierce pang of hatred as came over her while she met that sombre stare of the pictured face. So this was Mr. Garvie's model, of whom she had so often said to herself that she would not think.

Could it be also, the mysterious girl down at Rosbraz against whom he himself had warned her? Oh! (with a sudden cry of pain) she remembered how he had urged her to try to get her father away without any open exposure. That was what she had been brought here for, then. He might have spared her that indignity. But there was worse than that; and with eager eyes she turned back to where Mrs. Mallock told of Garvie's boasts. She was now quite past reasoning as to the value of Mrs. Mallock's testimony, or any motive for such action on Garvie's part. A primitive passion of jealousy swept her away.

O how happy she had been these last few days, and, as if to remind her of it, a few white violets, which Garvie had that afternoon picked for her, dropped faded from her dress and hid the cruel eyes staring up at her. At sight of them, the tempest of her tears was unloosed, and, like a child grieving for a broken toy, she mourned her lost faith and hopes.

But there was sterner stuff than that of a love-lorn maiden in this child of western solitudes. Before she lay down that night she had planned out a line of action for the next day.

First of all, she must see, face to face, this girl who was hiding herself down at Rosbraz. If her father would not take her to the chateau, she would go alone, and somehow force an entrance, even if it were to a sick-room. A woman could not be so easily shut out as a man.

One glance would tell her what she wanted to know. If this so-called Mademoiselle de Rostrênan proved to be the girl in the photograph, she would lose no time in confronting Garvie. Ignoring any personal question between him and her, she would demand that he immediately keep his promise, by denouncing this audacious fraud upon her father, and threaten to do it alone, if he failed her. Then came the question whether she could convince her father, or would only arouse his anger. Well, if she failed, she would cable for her eldest brother to come to the rescue, and then, whatever happened, she would return with him to her beloved mountains, and never leave them again. And with this vision of perpetual hermithood, she strove to console her sore heart.

The first light of dawn was stealing into the room before she dropped asleep, the tears still on her cheeks.

XX

THE CHATEAU

MEANWHILE, how were the mysterious tenants of the chateau at Rosbraz faring? There were no signs of life at the little landing amongst the big boulders. None of the people from the coast-guard station opposite now drew up their craft there. As the boats, laden with sand or fish, went up with the tide to Trêmalo, sweeping close around the wooded point from which the chateau faced the river, the sea-folk would cross themselves, and mutter, "The cursed Jews come even here, nowadays. No wonder the sardine fishing fails."

A walled-in courtyard faced south, though its great entrance was gateless now, and here, on the steps of the doorway with its arched Gothic fretwork, sat the incongruous figure of Virginie Lapierre, in a soiled cream-coloured dressing-gown, with fluttering green ribbons. Her wonderful hair fell unkempt about her shoulders, her high-heeled shoes were down at the heel, and it was only her feline grace that saved her from utter sordidness of aspect. Basking like a cat in the early sunshine, she was nibbling at a *brioche* which she dipped in the bowl of chocolate on her knees.

A little, bent old woman, of eastern aspect, her head covered with a black silk handkerchief, appeared in the doorway, from whence great ladies had watched crusaders go forth to war.

"Ah, *marraine,* it's lucky that you can make Austrian bread. I should starve if I had to eat their sour stuff here," was the girl's greeting.

"Folly!" snapped the old woman. "As if we hadn't both eaten black bread in our day. As if we may not have to eat it again. Talk no more nonsense, but listen. Louis has been to the post and brought a letter. There are orders, sharp enough. Since your being ill has not hurried that old fool, you are to be well and see him again—him and his catalogue."

"*Sapristi!*" came in a disgusted tone from Virginie.

"But with the daughter and that Monsieur Garvie about, we cannot be too careful," the old woman went on. "You are to do all you can to hurry the *bonhomme* into finishing up the business, and we are to be ready to leave at any moment, by sea perhaps, as soon as the cheque is signed. Heavenly powers! If I should be as seasick as I was in coming!"

Virginie meditated a moment in perplexity. "This is a new course he is steering," she muttered.

The old woman answered what she had left

unspoken. "Yes, I fancied you were to have fooled the old man to the top of his bent, and that we should have lived in riches. But I doubt if he thought you clever enough."

Virginie flushed angrily. "Clever or not, I could do it now, if I chose," was her sullen answer. "But I don't want to be bothered with the old fool. I can get all I want in Paris among the artists, without being bored to death as I am here," and in proof of the fact, she yawned prodigiously.

"You leave the artists alone, just now," was the sharp mandate. "You are more pig-headed than a child of ten. When you know that you should not be seen you were roaming the woods yesterday looking for that American."

"I was not," protested Virginie with a scowl, but the old woman went on:

"And now, here you are, in broad daylight, where anyone might come along and see you; the old fool himself, who knows, and you looking like nothing save a girl from the Quarter."

"Well, what else am I?"

"And hardly the greatest imbecile of a foreigner could suppose that the lady of a chateau would wear dressing-gown and slippers like yours, or never put a comb near her head in the morning. What if I write to tell *him* how you are risking his plans?"

The threat had an instant effect. Paling, the girl caught at her skirt, pleading: "Oh, *marraine,* you would never do that? He would be so angry with me."

A spark of something like affection shone in the eyes of the old hag, as she answered briskly, "Well, then, be good and attend to the task set you. You can be sharp enough when you choose. And get indoors now and dress like the girl in the picture he gave you to copy. You'd look like a fine fool if the old man were to come puffing up the avenue in his machine. And see here," as Virginie moved to obey her, "you are to tell him that your aunt in Auvergne has written offering you a home, and that you must get this business settled and go. Ah, it is too bad that you may not get a few diamonds out of him first; but such are the orders. You are to try for nothing more after the bargain is made."

"And Heaven knows, I never wanted him," Virginie reiterated in a last protest, as she retreated within.

Meanwhile Julia, having accomplished her aim, was speeding with her father along the road to Rosbraz.

Instead of going down as usual to the dining-room for coffee, she had a tray brought up to her bedroom, sending to Garvie a little note to say that she could not go on their planned expedition, and to her father a message asking him to come and see her.

There are dressing-gowns and dressing-gowns, and Julia's drapery of white crepe was a very dif-

ferent affair from poor Virginie's dingy flannel.
As different were the two faces above the garments. Though some of the first young hopefulness had gone from Julia's face since yesterday, it
was replaced by a courageous self-control, far removed from the reckless cynicism of the cairngorm eyes and red lips.

Sitting at her open window with her break-
fast-tray on a table beside her, Julia looked winsome enough to persuade a man to anything.
But at her appeal to take her to Rosbraz, Mr.
Praed bristled up suspiciously, and it required
all her powers of persuasion to get her way.

She succeeded at last, and dressed for the
drive, taking, however, one or two peeps through
the curtains to watch Garvie going down the
Place, his painting-traps over his shoulder. Never
had she liked his looks better than in that shabby
corduroy jacket and broad-brimmed Panama. A
few tears fell at thought of the flower-fringed orchard, where she was to have spent the day with
him.

Brushing them proudly aside, she hardened
her heart by scoffing to herself. "*One* model is
surely enough for any man. I could let him have
my white serge if he wants it for the red-haired
girl, to 'carry on the scheme of colour,' as he
said."

There was no white serge to-day, only a busi-
ness-like grey dust-cloak, when she took her place
beside her father. If only the day had not been

so joyous a one she could have borne it better, she thought, as they crossed the bridge beyond which the river rippled in the sunshine.

Up the hill they went, and turned seaward into the open country, where every apple tree was a mass of crimson buds, with here and there an open pink blossom; and the great grey chestnut trunks were crowned with domes of richest green. Above the young wheat hung larks in an ecstasy of song, and from the hillsides came the warm, soft scent of the gorse. Everything, save herself, glowed with young life and happiness.

From the meadows they skirted a belt of pine lands that have stood untouched since the days when they sheltered Druid rites.

"There's the castle," Mr. Praed said with an air of proprietorship, and, rising above masses of chestnut woods, Julia saw with a thrill of nervous anticipation, the pointed turret-tops of Rosbraz. A neglected avenue, sloping up under stately chestnut trees to the sturdy grey pile that spoke of days of siege and foray. Then the car stopped, and they picked their way along a rough path to the dilapidated courtyard with its flanking outbuildings. Every detail impressed itself on Julia's state of nervous expectation, and she wondered why the noble family of Rostrênan had been so little endowed with a sense of tidiness.

In the doorway stood the bent form of Mère Suzanne, who, with her parchment face and snakelike eyes, was not a figure to reassure a nervous stranger.

At their approach she began in a queer voice a jargon of broken English. "Ah, M'sieur has fetched the pretty demoiselle to Rosbraz. But my petite will be glad! She goes better—she can see and talk to-day. M'sieur will come," and with a beckoning hand, she turned to lead them within.

A glance at her father showed Julia that he was strangely agitated. As in a dream she followed through the great hall, with its yawning chimneys and raftered roof lost in the shadows. Here were the ghostly figures of armour that she had jested about, and vaguely pictured tapestries, and heavy bits of carved oaken furniture.

Without pausing to call her attention to these, her father hurried after Mère Suzanne up the dark winding stairs, built, like all the rest of the chateau, as though for a race of Cyclops.

Never would Julia forget the sight that met her as she emerged from the shadows of the stairway into the comparative brightness of a long gallery, running the whole length of the chateau front, its Gothic windows letting in the morning sunshine. Full in the light stood the embodiment of her disturbed night visions. There were the masses of red hair, curbed into demureness; there was the plain black dress emphasizing the pallor of the face, and the red line of lips; and yes, there was the hostile stare that recalled a wild-cat she had seen brought to bay in its mountain lair. The very pose was the same as in the photograph.

There could be no further doubt that Mademoiselle de Rostrênan was Virginie Lapierre, the Paris model.

An indignant shame for her father was Julia's first definite sensation, as she marked the feeling in his voice.

"Now this is something like, Mam'selle," he began, "to see you back here among the things. But we won't have you overdoing it again in a hurry. And here's Julie as I've told you about, come to see you herself. And I hope you two girls is going to be good friends—I'm sure, Julie—" and he turned to his daughter with what was meant for a threat, but was only an appeal, in his voice. Even the masculine certainty that his women folk cannot help liking the object of his affections, failed him in that crucial moment.

"I'm damn glad to see you," came the incongruous words of greeting, in broken English, as the model held out her hand.

Julia could not hide a little start, as she forced herself to put her hand into the clawlike one outstretched.

"There, there, Mam'selle," Mr. Praed protested with an awkward laugh. "There's that word again as I told you English ladies don't use, nor American either, for the matter of that. You see, Julie, Mam'selle had a bad lot for an English teacher; at least, he must have been all that to have ever allowed a girl to hear such words, and she, knowing no better, can't all at once get out of the way of using them. Not that we mind, do we?"

The wistfulness of this explanation brought a lump to Julia's throat. How could these people dare to so treat her father.

Then and there, she began her fight for him, as she said, "Oh, not at all. Then you were not brought up in a convent, Mademoiselle?"

A flash of impatience under the assumed meekness told that her shot had gone home.

"Alas, my dear father would not have me go. We were always—what you say—*ensemble,*" the strange creature answered in studied tones of woe. It was then that Julia noticed the newness of the crepe-trimmed dress. It could hardly have been worn half-a-dozen times.

"There, there," Mr. Praed put in testily, "don't be reminding the poor girl of painful things, Julia. And see here, Mam'selle," his voice softening on the word, "don't you be a tiring of yourself to-day with the catalogue, and you just out of bed."

With a gentle touch he took a paper out of the girl's hand, and laid it on a table, where Julia saw that written lists were spread out.

"Here now," Mr. Praed went on, pushing forward a dilapidated Louis Quinze arm chair, "you just sit yourself down and be comfortable, while I give Julia a peep round at all these old family things of yours."

Julia had before this noticed that the gallery was well filled with a semblance of the accumulated treasures pertaining to an ancestral home. The walls were hung with tapestry, between which were trophies of arms, and here and there a dim old portrait. Great carved chests were loaded with bright-coloured pottery, and one splendid black oak cabinet held nothing but Celtic and Merovingian ornaments, fibulas, and torques in gold and silver.

As the red-haired girl sank languidly into the offered chair, sniffing at a smelling-bottle, Julia's keenest desire was to turn on her with contemptuous words of denouncement. Keeping a tight rein on herself, she looked from one object to another as her father complacently pointed them out.

"How well it was all done," she kept saying to herself, wondering whether this girl had been capable of the arrangement, or if there had been others behind her.

"And them china dishes with the snakes and frogs on them," said Mr. Praed, pointing to some Palissy ware, "is one of the rarest kinds ever made in France. What did you say a dish like them sold for in Paris, Mam'selle?"

"*Sacristi!* The Cluny museum did buy one last year for ten thousand francs."

Julia did not know that French ladies do not say "*sacristi,*" but she noted the parrot-like repetition of the words, as with a tiresome lesson.

"I don't think that they are as pretty as the

things they make at Sèvres," she murmured in an
attempt at intelligent connoisseurship.

She and her father had made an expedition to
the Sèvres factory and had been much interested
thereby.

"Sèvres!" snorted Mr. Praed. "Them things
were all modern, and these were made by one of
the first Protestants as was ever in France. They
wanted to burn him, didn't they, Mam'selle?" he
appealed.

"So said my dear father. What should I
know?" was softly breathed from the arm chair.

"Exactly so," Mr. Praed agreed, and a momentary silence fell upon the little party.

The poor man had a disappointed consciousness
that the visit was becoming an open failure.

It was all Julia's fault, he thought. Why
couldn't she be bright and talk away as she always
did, instead of standing there like a great school-
girl.

A desperate desire to save the situation led him
on to reveal his precious secret. He would wake
these girls up, he said to himself.

"I was thinking, Mam'selle, that now Julie is
here, it might be just as well to shew her *everything*. She's a clever girl and wouldn't go talking to other people about things as we want to
keep to ourselves—"

Ourselves! So it had come to her father having secrets from her with this creature of the
Paris streets! Stung into protest, Julia spoke

quickly, "Oh, please don't let me interfere with any secrets," and stepping across to one of the narrow casements, she stood looking down on the green sea of encircling chestnut woods, and on the blue streak of river beyond. It was some solace to look on the outer world and long to be away, anywhere in the pure air uncontaminated by this woman.

She thus lost sight of the girl's start of alarm, followed by a malicious grin.

Virginie was saying to herself, "This should finish up the tiresome affair." What she did was to rise with the languid grace learnt in posing under trained eyes, saying, with purring softness, and a ludicrous imitation of some Irish artist's brogue:

"Devil a bit of a secret is there from your daughter in Rostrênan, Monsieur."

Julia had turned from the window and now broke into an irrepressible laugh. She knew it was undignified, but she could not help it. The contrast between manner and words was too ludicrous.

"Dear, dear!" her father fretted, but unconscious of her mistake, Virginie swept across the room to a recess, and drawing back a heavy stamped velvet curtain, revealed a row of shelves on which stood eight or ten silver bowls and vases.

"Behold the Rostrênan treasure," said the girl with a theatrical gesture, and poor Mr. Praed puffed his admiration.

A few weeks ago, Mr. Praed had, with Julia, hunted out the Bosco-réale silver in the Louvre. and having seen it, enabled her to guess at the rarity and value of the things before her. Their beauty she felt.

"But these must be worth a fortune," she murmured, understanding at last the magnitude of the affair.

A laugh of triumph came from Virginie, and Mr. Praed clapped his hands together emphatically, shouting, "That's it, my girl. You've hit the right nail on the head, this time," and then he went on to repeat Britski's carefully prepared story of the possibility of government confiscation, the Préfet's persecution of the Rostrênans because of their Royalist sympathies, and the consequent need of secrecy.

Julia followed the tale intently, but could detect no inaccuracies. "Mr. Garvie will know," she said to herself, before she remembered that henceforth there was to be no more appealing to Mr. Garvie.

As if he read her thoughts, her father said, "And mind now, there's to be no talking about this, not even to Mr. Garvie, until I've got all this silver shipped from Nantes or Brest. That's what I'm a-hanging on here for, and that's why I wasn't too pleased to have Garvie poking round and asking questions." He paused with a vague sense of saying the wrong thing.

A flush was on Julia's face, but she looked

steadily into the mocking eyes confronting her, conscious of their malevolence. In that moment she knew that this girl hated her as a rival, and the knowledge was exceedingly bitter to her pride.

"I am not likely to trouble Mr. Garvie with our affairs," she said gravely, "and I think, father, we have tired this young lady enough for to-day."

Fortunately, her enemy only wished to end the interview.

"I am *desolée*," she sighed, "that I am so stupid, but I cannot think well yet."

This was enough. Even Mr. Praed was glad of a chance to separate, and with many cautions to rest, bade farewell to his divinity.

"I'll take a run down this afternoon," Julia heard him say behind her, but she did not care. Neither did she care that he was surly all the way back.

Her enemy's parting words rang in her ear, "You will come again to visit me, dear mademoiselle, *n'est ce pas!*"

What an insult they seemed.

XXI

DISCORD

GARVIE'S painting in the flower meadow did not make much progress that morning. The vaguely sketched white figure mocked him with its illusiveness, and in momentary irritation he seized a *pochard* and began a fresh study.

Eventually this was scraped out, for to-day was one of those destined to see no success. Resolute against the desire to give in and go back to *déjeuner,* he finally stretched himself on the grass and took refuge in a pipe and in meditation.

He was by now enough in love with Julia to know, with the lover's sixth sense, that her curt note indicated offense, and he pondered most uncomfortably over any possible cause.

It was not so long ago that he had felt it somewhat noble in him to meditate parting with the ideal wife of his dreams, half great lady, half sympathetic art-critic, and wholly beautiful and loving, in favour of this untrained Canadian girl; and now here he was, dismally contemplating his abandoned work, and realizing that henceforth life would be a poorer, drearier thing, if it were to be spent without her. If ever success had made him a bit fastidious, he was atoning for it now, certainly to his present discomfort, probably to the eventual good of his soul. He could not yield to offended dignity when he knew that Julia stood in need of his help; and so, with self well in abeyance, he vowed to do all that man honestly could to make her his wife.

This point settled, he came to details. He longed to hurry back to the hotel and lie in wait for an interview, but his boy had just brought his lunch, and he felt bound to go through the form of eating it.

He was pretty sure that Julia would not succeed in enticing her father into an all-day expedition, and that he had the best chance of finding her about the hotel in the after *déjeuner* hour.

So the small boy Louis was disappointed of his usual half-hour's gossip over the wonders of the outside world while his patron smoked a cigarette, and was hurried off instead with his basket.

As soon as he was out of sight, Garvie packed his painting things and started for home. Luck favoured him, for as he came along the shore path where the river narrowed in amidst its grey boulders, he happened to look across to a rocky, pine-crowned knoll where he and Julia had once or twice sat and talked. There he spied above the gorse-bushes, a red spot which he knew to be a poppy-wreathed hat worn by Julia Praed.

It did not take him long to deposit his painting-traps, and then start across the bridge and along the quay in pursuit of his game. The path among the gorse bushes rose so abruptly that presently he found himself looking up into the face of Julia, where she sat on a little grassy patch. Yes, his fears were right. There was a storm-cloud in the sombre eyes that met his without any of their old glad light.

Forgetting his prepared greeting, he demanded abruptly, "You are ill?"

Her society mask was over her face as she made quiet answer, "Ill? No, I am never ill."

He was on the level now, and flung himself down beside her, with the words, "Why are you so pale then, and why did you throw me over this morning?"

This carrying the war into Africa roused her into a counter-attack, though with pride sounding its tocsin at her heart. "If I am pale, it may be because I am worried. I could not go with you this morning, because—well, that will wait."

"No, let me have it now. You must have had some reason," he persisted, choking down his sense of injury.

"If you want the reason, you shall have it. There it is."

Her voice hardened as she handed him the packet of photographs which she had been holding in her hands. As he opened it, she added, "I went to Rosbraz this morning to see if this Mademoiselle de Rostrênan were really Virginie Lapierre, the Paris model."

Her words revealed to Garvie the full measure of his mistake in not making the whole story known to her.

"And you are angry with me for not telling you?" he asked, with insistent eyes on her face.

"I have no right to be angry," she said with a tremour that told of hurried heart-beats, "but I have a right to decide not to trouble you any more with my affairs."

"No, you have no right," he broke out hotly, "to banish me from your friendship without a reason. You did trust me—"

"And while I trusted you," she interrupted, letting loose her anger, "you talked to me about this girl, all the time hiding from me that she was an old friend of yours. You won't deny that you knew who she was, I suppose?"

"I found it out within an hour of my arrival, when I met her at the postoffice door," he answered with more dignity. "But may I venture to protest that the term 'old friend' scarcely suits my model?"

"Use any word you like. What do I know of it?" she put in scornfully.

"Why should I have told you anything about the poor creature," he went on with more vehemence. "What have you to do with such as she?"

"It looks as if I had a good deal," was her dry comment.

"I would have kept you apart if I could."

"So it seems. I suppose it was on her account

you advised me to try to get my father away without any open exposure."

"That is hardly fair, Julia," he said, and the quiet words hurt her sorely. "I confess that I do pity her," he had the courage to acknowledge. "I have good reasons for believing that she is a tool in cleverer hands, and I hoped to use my influence to make her give up the game, only I have not been able to get at her."

Julia rose, and poised herself for departure, as she said, "I am sorry if our little excursions have hindered your missionary work. I am sure you can influence her all right, and hope for poor father's sake you'll soon choose to do it."

Garvie jumped up and stood staring at her aghast.

Could this haughty young woman, who taunted him with such finished insolence, be that same undisciplined girl who a few weeks ago had taken his word for law? He was not the first man to wonder at the swift maturing of a woman under the force of experience.

"Wait," he said in so peremptory a tone that she involuntarily paused. "Can't you see that by quarreling with me you may be playing into the hands of whoever sent you those photos? Who was it, by-the-bye, Mrs. Mallock?"

Julia's start told him that he had guessed correctly. The suggestion that she needed his help was so true that it stiffened her pride against yielding.

"And if it were?" she asked.

"Surely you would not take her word against mine? What can I do to convince you that your interest counts with me before everything?"

Under any other circumstances he would hardly have smothered his wrath at her behaviour, but, for all her determination, there was a forlorn youthfulness about her that reminded him of her helplessness if he should leave her.

She looked like a girl of sixteen as she stood there in her short navy-blue skirt and loose silk blouse, a long braid of hair hanging down her shoulders. Her eyes met his steadily, as she said slowly:

"There is only one way to make me that sure you were ever my real friend. No, just listen," as he made a movement to interrupt her. "Go to my father when he comes back from there to-day," and she slightly waved her hand towards the hills that hid the Rosbraz turrets, "and tell him all you know about these wretched people who are cheating him. All, I mean, that concerns us. We have no wish to pry into your secrets," she added.

Garvie was beginning to realize his helplessness in face of her attitude.

"Cannot you see," he urged, "that I have no secrets in the matter? The girl was my model. All at once, she deserts me with a half-finished picture on my hands, saying she must leave Paris.

233

I know nothing more until I meet her here. Do you not believe this?"

Julia lost courage to point out the interpretation she put upon those facts.

"I daresay it was so," she admitted, "but you have not answered what I asked you."

"You want me to go to your father and tell him that this Mam'selle of his is only a Paris model?"

"Yes." There was no hesitation in the word.

"And you think he will believe me?"

"He must," she cried impatiently. "Even he cannot help seeing what a sham she is. Why, she swore dreadfully at every second word to-day, and he kept repeating some ridiculous story about her English teacher."

Garvie smiled involuntarily. "Poor Virginie's language *has* a studio flavouring," he acknowledged.

The smile, the familiar name undid any progress he may have made towards reconciliation.

Julia flushed hotly.

"I suppose he enjoys those kind of things, as I see you do. But that is not my affair. And so you don't mean to do what I ask?"

"Can you not see that if I quarrel with your father I only put myself out of court?" Garvie remonstrated. "Listen to me for a moment, please. There is nothing in those photographs to convince Mr. Praed against his will. The best chance is to frighten Virginie into giving up the game. I will try that first, and if I fail, will go to Paris and threaten Britski with exposure. Does that suit you?" he demanded.

Julia grew very white and her mouth set in ominous lines.

"You may do whatever you like," she said. "I'll play a lone hand in the future, thank you. I expect Britski will know how much your threats amount to."

"He will, I hope," was the grim retort. "Only remember that if your father becomes the laughing stock of every Paris and New York paper it will be your doing. He may find out that a little discretion on your part would have saved him, and I leave you to picture his gratitude."

"If this is a second try at keeping me quiet, I think it is scarcely worth while," she said, with a sudden weariness of it all.

"You must not say that," he protested sternly.

"I shall say what I like," she flashed out petulantly.

"Very well. I shall leave you to do so," and, his patience at an end, he raised his hat, and turned to scramble down the knoll, and take himself off to his studio.

Julia meantime was left to realize the wreckage she had made, with much the feelings of a naughty child, who, its paroxysm over, looks around on broken, erst-beloved toys, and says "I don't care," even while it realizes its first heart-ache.

XXII

WITCHCRAFT

GARVIE did not find the latter part of the day any pleasanter than had been the beginning.

An equable man, who did not take fire easily, he was apt when once roused, to be somewhat unyielding. As he marched up the hill to his studio, hired from an artist friend in the erstwhile manor-house, he was in a fine temper at Julia's injustice; but hardly had he finished one meditative pipe before he began to relent. She might be, she certainly was, self-willed and hasty, but how helpless, how unskilled to struggle against the snares and nets which encompassed her and her father.

It were poor manliness in him to let any personal smart drive him to take her at her word and go away, leaving her to fight her own battles.

No, he would set to work now with all his skill to get to the bottom of, and break up, this wretched conspiracy which threatened harm to both father and daughter. When that task was fulfilled was the time to ask the girl to become his wife. If even then she refused him her trust, well, he would be a sadder man for it; but now he must see to his task before claiming his reward.

Knight-errantry was a new profession for Garvie, and though he gave a sigh of regret for the pleasant days just passed, yet it was with a certain sense of exhilaration that he prepared his scheme of warfare.

The first thing was to get face to face with Virginie and do his best to bully her out of the neighborhood. It was then about four o'clock, and as the old fool—poor Mr. Praed was given that name by all parties alike—would most likely be still at Rosbraz, he must wait. The tide had only begun to rise as he came up from St. Nicholas, so he could get Ivon, the boatman, to take him down after dinner, when Mr. Praed would be safe at home. Now the question was how Julia would meet him at dinner. He sincerely hoped that she would have enough sense to hide their difference from her father, but, remembering her impetuosity, he doubted it. Dinner time, at once anticipated and dreaded by two people, came at last.

Garvie and Mr. Praed were in their seats, talking across Julia's empty place when she made her appearance.

A glance shewed Garvie that she had strengthened herself to face the situation with a smart gown. "Always wear a pink dress when you are unhappy," said a female philosopher, and she had followed the maxim.

Her face was smiling, and for all his artist

study of complexions Garvie failed to detect certain skillful touches that doctored the traces of recent tears.

"Good evening," he said, pulling back her chair for her, "what a brilliant apparition you are to-night."

"Oh, well, one must do something," she answered disconnectedly, looking round the table, and bowing to the local official who belonged to the Breton *petit noblesse* and entertained secret longings to essay one of the *petit flirtation Anglais* which he so often saw going on around him. He and Mr. Praed were in the habit of holding conversations, one speaking in French, the other in English, and neither really understanding the other.

They now embarked on such a social effort, and Garvie took advantage of Mr. Praed's monologue to say in an undertone to Julia, "I expect to leave for Paris before you are up to-morrow morning. Have you any commissions for me?"

He had turned in his seat enough to watch the bent head and lowered eyelids, but could see no change in her face, as she answered, "Nothing, thank you. I don't suppose that we'll be here long ourselves now. I want to get father to come to Venice and Florence."

"And then I'll be done with you and all the rest of them," was the implied ending to her sentence.

"That would be very nice. I suppose you know

what I'm going for?" he demanded in the same lowered tones.

"Dear me, no. How could I?" she answered innocently, but still without looking up.

"I am going to try to find some way of ending this wretched affair for you. Perhaps if I succeed you may have a little higher opinion of me."

In the earnestness of his purpose, he had let the stiffness go from his voice and its depth made Julia tremble nervously.

What unlucky perversity was it that drove her, almost in her own despite to answer lightly, "Oh, please don't trouble. I'll get along all right, I expect."

"Is it at seven o'clock you want the dog-cart to-morrow morning, Monsieur Garvie?" came Marie Jeanne's resonant tones in at the doorway.

"Yes, to catch the express at Bannalec," he answered, and then there were explanations to Mr. Praed and regrets from the official. The little party had acquired a habit of loitering over the table, but to-night, as soon as dinner was well over, Garvie rose, saying:

"I must go up to the studio before dark, and so had better say good-bye now, or rather *au revoir,* I hope. Good-bye, Miss Praed. I am sorry our fishing is over for the present."

How much else was over, both thought, as their hands met without the warm clasp of friendship.

Julia felt a quick, hard pressure as hers lay limp in his. Then he was gone, and she was confusedly trying to agree in French with Monsieur Kerval's expressed opinion that Monsieur Garvie was *tres gentil* for an artist. The poor man had suffered much from varieties of the species.

Meanwhile Garvie, in an equal tumult of regret and wrath, was striding down the Place to the quay, where his old friend, Ivon the boatman, awaited him.

The tide was brimming high, and the water held the picture of sky and hills in its heart. It was a relief to leave the noisy evening groups on the quay and drift down the river, past the fields and the open hillsides of heather and gorse.

The evening peace soothed Garvie's smarting sense of loss, and he took courage to fix his mind hopefully on his next move.

All sense of compunction towards Virginie was gone, and in fear of the harm that she might work the girl who would not give him even one kind glance at parting, he was her determined enemy.

Ivon was an old companion of his on many a river day, and while content to be silent and watch the curves of the current, he was equally ready to talk if once started.

"Rosbraz? Was Monsieur going to land at Rosbraz? Did he not know that there were spies there, Jews whom the government had sent to watch the farms and see that none of the good sisters whom the soldiers had turned out, were given shelter at them? It might not be safe to go there at such an hour. What if the heretics were to use a knife? It was easy enough to fling a body down into the old well in the courtyard, where it would never be heard of again."

Garvie laughed. "Well, stay in your boat, Ivon, and you will be quite safe. I am not afraid."

"*Dame,* it was of you I was thinking, M'sieur," the man answered with a certain rough dignity; "though that is not to say that I am not afraid of witches and korrigans, and such like powers of darkness. And the old woman there is a witch for certain. The other day Alain Glue's children met her, and signed themselves as their mothers had told them to do, and she made figures with her hands at them and strange noises. They ran away, and their mother has got them all new scapulars."

"That was very wise," Garvie commented.

"But worse than that, M'sieur," Ivon went on earnestly, "they say that this old woman can turn into a girl with red lips and green eyes"—Garvie's face became graver—"and that she meets people in the woods and bewitches them. There is that rich old man at Marie Jeanne's, who runs about the country in the machine. She has put a spell on him, so that he cannot go away. She sits there and calls him, and he comes, puffing. Do not go there, M'sieur."

These last words were spoken with desperate earnestness.

Garvie saw that he must explain his visit, if he

wanted to keep the respect of his village friends.

He wished now that he had walked—it did not take more than an hour across country—but it was too late to think about that. He knew that Ivon was intelligent enough in his way, and trusted to making him understand.

"Look here, Ivon," he began. "I know all about this girl with the red lips. She is no witch, but she is one of those who make fools of men, as she has of this American. I go now to tell her something that may frighten her, and make her leave him alone, so that his daughter may not be unhappy. You see?"

"Ah, the pretty young lady! As lovely as the figure of St. Anne at Auray. You are a *'brave,'* M'sieur Garvie," was the appreciative answer, "but take care to stand well out in the open or with your back to a wall. Knives come from behind."

"There won't be any knives," Garvie assured him.

They had rounded the last point, and a soft breath of sea-wind met them as they put in towards the cove above which the outline of Rosbraz towered dark against the sunset, amidst its enfolding chestnut woods.

"Gently, Ivon. Make no noise at the landing," Garvie murmured.

They crept up the rough stone steps, built in among great round boulders, and Garvie jumped out and climbed the rough path.

The stately beauty of the old place touched him even through his absorbtion in his coming task.

"What a home might be made here," he muttered to himself as he looked up at the stern grey pile that had sheltered one race for centuries. For a moment his imagination played him a trick. He saw a joyous, active, young chatelaine, beautifying her home, loving the country, sailing, riding, lounging on the warm sea-sands on summer noons, or by great wood fires on winter nights. Two together, "man and woman created he them."

Then the vision faded before the reality. A yellow sunset glow was full on the chateau front, and, entering the gateless court yard, an incongruous picture revealed itself to him.

On one of the lower steps of the doorway sat Virginie Lapierre, demure mourning dress discarded for a scarlet dressing-gown, her hair tumbled about her shoulders in wild disarray.

She had spread a picnic meal on an upper step, in the same fashion that Garvie had so often seen her set out her lunch in any convenient corner of his studio.

There was a bottle of red wine, a loaf, and Bologna sausage, a crisp white onion cut in halves, and a slice of coarse Dutch cheese. She was attacking these provisions with the hearty gusto of any street gamin, every movement bespeaking the joyful reaction into liberty after the day's masquerading.

So absorbed was she in arranging slices of sausage and onion on a piece of bread, that she never heard Garvie's footsteps on the grass. When she did, her knife and her improvised sandwich dropped disregarded while she stared at him in dismay.

A weird creature she looked in the lurid afterglow, and Garvie felt that Ivon, had he followed him, might have felt justified in his fear of witches.

What was that strange gleam in her eyes, hate or fear? All the wistfulness that had at times shewed through her recklessness was gone, and she was simply a wild creature brought to bay.

"*Sapristi!* So your pretty young lady has sent you here already. She loses no time," she scoffed, after the first panic-struck pause.

With a sense of relief he saw that they were to come to the point without skirmishing.

"I have known that you were here, ever since the day I met you at Trêmalo," he asserted.

"But you didn't tell *her,* until she found it out for herself to-day," she jeered again, with what seemed to him fiendish insight.

"It does not matter what I told anyone," he insisted. "I have come here to warn you to drop this crazy fraud of Britski's, and see to your own safety. You should lose no time in getting away from here. The game is up, I tell you."

Decided as were his words, he saw that they had missed their effect.

244

"Since when?" she asked, lounging back on the steps in a splendid pose. He could not but mark how the loose sleeve fell away to shew the flesh tints of her arm, how her body took that long curve under her clinging red draperies.

"So you want me to go, do you, you and that great wooden-limbed doll?" she shrilled, deliberately working up her temper. "Take care then that I go alone. You would look cheap, you and she, if I waltzed off with the old *bonhomme* and his cash. Hey, but if I once got him to Vienna the shekels would fly!" And with the words, she sprang to her feet snapping her fingers over her head in a splendid Bacchante gesture.

"And what would Britski say to that?" he asked, striking desperately at a venture.

Her arm dropped to her side, and she stood facing him, trying not to betray the check.

"Britski is all right, if only he gets his pickings, and there would be plenty of pickings going," she asserted with an attempt at defiance.

"Britski and you might be anything but all right, if it came to a trial for swindling and forgery," Garvie retorted.

"A marriage would make me safe from that. Hey, then, how would that Diana of yours fancy me for a *belle-mère*?"

"That would be the quickest way to cut your throat," he answered with a more coolness under the insult than he felt. "In America there are divorces for the smallest things. As soon as Mr.

Praed understood what you really were, he could turn you off penniless."

"And who would make him?" she panted. "Not you, or I shall tell this Mademoiselle Nitouche some pretty yarns of the Quarter. What matter if they happened to you or others."

"Look here, Virginie, I've had about enough of this," he interrupted. "I came here to-night to give you a chance of getting quietly away before the smash-up."

"But you are angelic!"

"And if you won't listen, you'll be sorry for it. Do you know," and he began to lie skillfully and boldly as befitted the present crisis. "Do you know that Mr. Praed's son, a shrewd business man, is on his way from America to have you all arrested. Do you know that there have been tales spread round the country until the peasants are ready to mob you for witches? If a child, or even a horse or cow, were to die suddenly, your lives might not be safe for an hour. Have you never heard the old people tell of what such peasants as these have done when once they were mad with fright?"

He paused to let his words sink in.

"Anything more?" she asked hoarsely. She had drawn herself up to her full height, braced back, a vivid line of red against the grey stone of the doorway. She seemed at the same moment to shrink from and defy him. Garvie could read in her distended eyes the gruesome recollection of fierce tales of peasant riots heard in some far-off land.

His heart might have smitten him for this bullying of one who had been almost a comrade, but the shadow of Julia's distress was over him, making him pitiless.

But behind the girl in the doorway there appeared a figure that recalled Ivon's tales. Under the black silk shawl that covered Mère Suzanne's head, flashed a pair of wrathful eyes, first on him, then on Virginie. A clawlike hand grasped her arm, and a torrent of abuse in an unknown tongue descended upon her. Whatever the words might be, they cowed the girl, who slunk back into the house without a glance in his direction.

The old woman equally ignored him, slamming the great door behind him. He could hear the heavy bolts drawn.

"Well, that's no go," he muttered to himself, as he turned away. The sunset glow was gone, and the world was merged in a blue-grey twilight.

"Lucky for us there is a sea-breeze to take us up against the tide," said Ivon, setting his bit of sail.

The next morning Garvie left for Paris.

XXIII

THE SCHWERER PORTFOLIOS

SYLVIA, left without her friend, realized that she must rally all her forces against depression. She tried to absorb herself in an illustrated magazine article on the Bonaparte women, spending hours at the Bibliothèque Nationale. Daily she took a long walk in the early morning when the air was freshest, and the spacious avenues all but deserted. She did not mean to fall ill if she could help it. It was her regular habit to call twice a week at Madame Marcelle's, and on the customary day she went as usual.

"Madame is in her sitting-room. She said for you to come there," was the mandate that met her.

In this temple of fashion, the carpets were so deep, the portières so heavy, that every movement was noiseless. Madame Marcelle seemed not to notice her entrance, lying back wearily with closed eye-lids amongst a pile of cushions.

Was it fancy on Sylvia's part, or did she really look worn and harrassed, her whole pose bespeaking dejection?

'All her old liking revived by the thought, she

said quickly, as she came forward, "Dear madame, are you tired or ill?"

Alertly erect, the smile back on her lips, the dressmaker demanded, "Why ask that? Do I then look old and ugly?"

She reached out to take up a silver hand-glass from the table, and stared at herself critically.

"I had the *migraine* last night, but I shall take a drive at lunch time and that will make me look all right. Ah, I envy those fine ladies nothing save fresh air. When I was a child, at home in Normandy—but what does that matter now, when there are a hundred different customers to please?"—she checked herself. "Come and sit down and talk things over," she added, pointing to a chair. "How dainty you look this morning, in your little grey alpaca. To think of you, who supply ideas for some of the costliest dresses in Paris, wearing a ready-made, Bon Marché blouse."

"The Trois Quartiers, madame. The Bon Marché is too far for busy folk like me. Don't you like it?" Sylvia asked smiling, as she stroked down the discussed garment.

"It does," was the acknowledgment. "But I'd rather see you in proper clothes. You wear them well. See, then. Owing to you, that American trousseau is such a success that I should like to give you a present. Let me make you a little summer silk, something useful if you like—black-and-white, or dark blue. I should give you an air so *distingué*."

Sylvia shook her head. She had to smile very hard for fear of revealing the distaste this proposal aroused.

"Ah, dear madame, you are all that is kind, but indeed, I have so little use for such clothes. I hope to spend the summer in some quiet country place where a blouse and a ready-made skirt are all that I need."

"Indeed," and Sylvia felt that this scheme of hers had been weighed and disapproved of, before Madame said cheerfully, "Well then, it shall be for next autumn."

Knowing that many things must happen before that, Sylvia did not gainsay her. They discussed some orders for a while, and then Madame shoved aside their papers, saying, *"Ciel,* I forgot that I am due at Britski's this half-hour. I am to look at some rare laces from Antwerp. I want the first choice of them. Yes, and he told me to bring you to see some wonderful portfolios of drawings of court beauties from the time of Henry IV to the Revolution. It is the Schwerer collection, just bought by a Russian princess, and he only has it for a week or two, so if you do not come now you may miss the chance."

Certainly, something must be wrong with Madame to-day, for as she spoke, her manner was forced, her colour came and went, and she watched Sylvia narrowly. The latter hesitated, half-ashamed of the feeling that made her shrink from going to Britski's. She instinctively guessed, however, that she could not refuse, and remain on quite the same friendly terms with her employer, and Harriett's warning recurred to her. Besides, she felt grateful for Madame Marcelle's kindly offer and anxious to please her.

So she agreed, and presently they were driving the short distance to the Avenue de l'Opéra, in a neat little carriage.

On these spring mornings, there were strangers of all nations to be found in Britski's outer shop where the least valuable articles were displayed.

One or two appreciative glances followed Madame Marcelle as she swept through and on to the upper galleries. In her fair maturity she was like one of Ruben's richly-coloured, full-curved women, and the type is ever a favourite one in Paris.

On every side were things that Sylvia wanted to pause and study. In the diffused daylight of a room lighted from above, they found Britski, loitering before a small picture on an easel. Had he expected them, Sylvia wondered, as he moved forward to meet them, with his usual gentle deference.

"So you have brought your little Cinderella," he said to his wife. Then to Sylvia, "Ah, Mademoiselle, I can promise you a sight that makes it worth your coming. But, as this is your first visit, let me take you for a stroll among my treasures."

Treasures they were indeed that she saw, as she followed him down the long gallery. On the dull red walls hung modern pictures, each placed where it could be seen to the best advantage. No overcrowding here.

Beneath the pictures stood choicest articles of furniture, from the heavy black oak chest, rudely carved in Celtic design, to the slim inlaid cabinet or work-table, wrought by Buhl or Caffieri in the days of the fifteenth Louis.

On these were placed enamels or porcelains of the rarest kinds.

"This Henry II vase and that Capo-di-Monte dish, are likely to be bought by the state for Cluny," Britski said, pointing impressively to two insignificant pieces of china.

Sylvia could not but respect the knowledge which every word revealed as he passed from one object to another. He treated her, too, not as a good-looking girl, but as a fellow connoisseur, who could appreciate his comments, could sympathize with his love for these things brought together by his own efforts.

The latent hope of finding some traces of Thorpe caused her to keep a keen eye on the pictures though her guide gave them less notice in passing than he did the bric-a-brac.

Her watch was rewarded by sight of a small pastel, the weird study of a red-haired child gathering apples in a russet-tinted orchard, a study he had shewed her with a frank delight in its originality.

A quick glance discovered the monogram R. T. with which Thorpe was wont to sign his lesser work.

She caught her breath in an effort at composure, before she said, "I see you have a little thing of Mr. Thorpe's there?"

Britski's smiling eyes were full on her face as he answered suavely, "Do you think that is Thorpe's. Well, it may be. It was bought for me at a studio auction in the Quarter. I sometimes send a man to such sales. One picks up clever studies at them, now and then. Some collectors have a liking for studies. More individuality, they say."

Resolved not to be headed off in this fashion, she asked with a beating heart, "Do you know where Mr. Thorpe is now?"

Britski laughed as though the joke were excellent.

"*Sapristi,* I wish I did. He owes me for frames, as he owes for nearly everything else, I hear. His friend, Mr. Howe, thinks he has gone to America, but he is just as likely to be in Venice or Capri, or any cheap place where artists gather. Anyway, his day is done. He can never show in Paris again."

With a resolute hold on herself, Sylvia checked the indignant protest that rushed to her lips. It would be folly to let these people see what Thorpe's good name was to her.

Just then, Madame Marcelle made a diversion by announcing that she could waste her working hours no longer and would go down stairs to inspect the lace. "I will rejoin you in your little room in half-an-hour. It is there that you have the precious portfolios, *mon ami?*"

Britski assented briefly, and led the way towards the end of the gallery, where heavy curtains divided off his own sanctum.

A queer type of the man, Sylvia thought it, as she noted the luxury of two deep armchairs; the small Millet, a sombre sketch of village roofs against a sunset sky, that hung well in view of Britski's seat; the shelf of pale green jade carvings against a red background; the heavy safe door in the wall, which told of hidden treasures.

On the table of massive carved oak, lay three purple morocco portfolios, stamped with a gilt monogram.

"Ah, here are my choicest gems—would that they were really mine," Britski said as he shoved forward one of the armchairs for her.

"I knew of this collection, that was the life-long hobby of a Vienna banker, but when it came into the market, a Russian princess was too quick for me. Now, I am tantilized by having these portfolios in my hands for repairs."

He unlocked the clasps with a little gold key from his watch-chain, and then Sylvia forgot everything else in what she saw. There was, as he had said, a unique collection of coloured prints, pastels and water-colour drawings. Many a fair, frail dame who had dabbled her white fingers in the history of nations to leave a lurid stain, was here represented.

Some of the faces and costumes were familiar to Sylvia from her researches; others were entirely novel, and aroused her keenest interest. What a help they might have been to her in the writing of her book. "Ah, if I only could have had the use of them," she breathed, half to herself.

"I am *desolé*," Britski said softly, "but I am sworn to let no copy be made—however—"

"Oh indeed, I never meant that. I know that it would be impossible," Sylvia protested, red with annoyance.

"I was about, though, to ask your help," he went on. "You see," taking up a book in the same purple binding and opening it to reveal pages of minute handwriting—"this is a catalogue of the collection, but in four places, marked thus with a red cross, the drawing is missing. I have the four names here on a slip of paper. They are all Frenchwomen, and I have been asked to have these blanks filled up with modern replicas from the Paris museums.

"It is no easy task, and requires both knowledge and skill. I mentioned my perplexity to Marcelle and she, like the creature of resources

255

she is, immediately declared that you, Mademoiselle, were the person to help me. You will not disappoint me, I am sure."

As Sylvia looked up into the keen, intellectual face, she knew that the request was a genuine one, knew too, that there were not many as competent to do the work. Harriett's warnings and her own misgivings were forgotten in the spirit of her craft.

"I am sure that I could find pictures of all these four without much difficulty," she said, fingering the paper thoughtfully. "This last— Lucille Desmoulins—I know a charming print of her in the Bibliothèque, and I could copy it in water-colours."

"Then you will undertake it?" Britski asked, with an eagerness too quiet to startle her. Sylvia had already turned back to the fascinating portfolios.

"Oh yes, I will undertake it," she answered, as though it were a foregone conclusion. Then with a little laugh, "It is a bold thing to put myself in competition with work like this." She held out a delicate pastel of the wistful-eyed Louise de la Vallière in all her court bravery. "How rare this must be. I have never even seen a copy of it."

"I think there is another of her in convent dress. Poor Louise, she was the earthen pot among the brass ones," Britski said, turning over the sheets.

They were in full swing now, and each portrait

brought its own comment or discussion. With the interest, Sylvia's languor was gone. A pink flush transformed her face, and she talked freely and cleverly.

Her armchair was drawn up to the table, and on the other side of it, his back to the curtained doorway, Britski stood, leaning forward with one hand on the table.

"Ah, if only I had bought these portfolios. what a book we might have made from them, you and I, Mademoiselle. I should have spared nothing to make it a gem worthy of your name."

As he said the words, Sylvia saw a gloved hand part the heavy curtains, and a face appeared between their folds. Was it only an effect from the dark red hangings that made that face show white and rigid as a Medusa head, to Sylvia's bewildered vision? Surely it was fancy, she thought, as Madame Marcelle's cheery voice rang out, "*Mon Dieu*, are you two still over those pictures?" and Madame's handsome self sailed in. "I fear that I must tear you away, *petite*. My fine ladies will all be on strike," she urged, but Sylvia protested.

"Ah, madame, give one little look at this Watteau dress. It is an idyl."

There were a few moments more loitering over the portfolio, and then Madame Marcelle took Sylvia by the arm and gaily insisted that she must carry her off.

"Just a minute for business." Britski said,

"See then, Mademoiselle," and he produced a little package of tinted papers. "Of course you understand that we must have no crude white paper jumping at the eyes here. These are samples to choose from for your work. I have had the town searched for the nearest match to these time-softened fabrics. Send me a little word to say which you wish and you shall have it at once."

The words were carelessly spoken, but Madame Marcelle stood watching as though the little roll which he handed Sylvia contained her fate.

Perhaps her intentness irritated him, for Britski asked sharply, "Did you decide about your laces, Marcelle?"

The latter started before she answered gaily, *"Bien sûr.* Though you may think that I have taken the lion's share, *mon ami."*

"Ah, well," was the answer in renewed suavity. "Your customers and mine both want the best, and they are willing to pay for it, or they would not come to us. That is so, is it not, Mademoiselle?"

"I suppose so," Sylvia murmured. The portfolios were closed and the spell was broken. Once in the carriage again with Madame Marcelle she was aware of an impalpable breath of discord. Not that it found any open expression, for the lady volubly spoke of her pleasure that her little friend should be of use to her husband, of the lucky chance that had given Sylvia the commission. "And where are you going now?" she asked, with a swift turn, fixing the girl with her bright blue eyes. "Shall the carriage take you home?"

"I am going home, but, please, I would rather walk," Sylvia pleaded, with an undefined desire for solitude. Then feeling that she had been abrupt, she added, "My first task must be to try some colours on these samples, and find out what I need. I suppose I had better write to Monsieur Britski about it?" she asked timidly.

"No, I will send Joseph to you this evening; you can give him the list," came brusque as an order to a servant.

XXIV

PITFALLS

SYLVIA now spent most of her days in the hunting-grounds already familiar to her, the wonderful national collections of Paris.

The smoke-coloured drawing-paper had come, and in faint-hued water-colours she completed her copy of the hapless Lucille Desmoulins' portrait.

Of a less known beauty she had found a rough little print that she hoped to work up into a picture.

In her enjoyment of the congenial task she came nearer to forgetfulness of her anxieties. The hours spent in quiet old galleries were so short for all that she wanted to unearth of that past, doubly dead through its futility. What a much saner, less turbulent world it will be when more women shall have learned the soothing powers of the day's impersonal work!

It was near closing time in the Bibliothèque Nationale, and Sylvia was making earnest use of her last half-hour, when a note was brought her from Britski, saying that he had obtained the loan of a rare book of pre-Revolutionary portraits, among which was one of the missing dame.

Would she come and see it when she left the library?

Thinking nothing save that this was another step towards the successful ending of her task, Sylvia left the cool stillness of the big building to plunge into the glittering stir of the streets. At four on an April afternoon Paris life surges at high tide, and as she sped along, a demure little figure, Sylvia's thoughts fled wistfully from the noisy streets to a certain familiar spot in distant New England where the blue-green waves would be lapping among the brown sea-weeds on the granite ledges, where the west wind would be seeking out the sweetness of the hidden arbutus amongst last year's birch leaves. Ah, those days of youth and idleness in the homeland! Could she never creep back there, a tired woman, to end life where she had begun it?

She roused herself from these unprofitable dreams at Britski's door.

There was a quiet over the show-rooms, the cosmopolitan customers of the earlier part of the day being now out at race-courses and in the Bois.

She seemed to be expected, for a shopman led her up stairs, and then the whole length of the galleries towards Britski's private room. The silence, the loneliness of the place made her nervous. Dark figures in armour seemed to threaten her from shadowy corners. A gilded Bhudda smiled across at a gigantic, many-coloured mummy-case, with its calm face and crossed hands, as though pitying this western waif for her ignorance of all the secrets of life that they two knew. A level ray of sunshine pierced a square of Nuremburg glass and drew a lurid red stain down the neck of a white bust of the Princesse de Lamballe, as though recalling the September day that saw that fair head cut down.

There was no room for such fancies in the cosy little sitting-room, with its window open to the outside air, and to the stir of the street below. Sylvia stood for a moment, glad to be alone and to recover her breath.

"What a fool I get when I am tired," she murmured, giving hasty little touches to her hair before a round mirror that hung on one wall. The mirror gave her back a pale face, with the jaded look of a worker at the day's end.

From a side door Britski appeared, with his usual quietness of movement, and any vague uneasiness which Sylvia may have felt was soothed by his businesslike directness.

"I, too, have not been idle, you see, Mademoiselle," he said with a wave of the hand towards a book on the table. "This is a rare history of the diamond-necklace affair, and there is a portrait of the Countess de La Motte, which is what you want. I have to return the book to-day, and if you could make a sketch now," he suggested.

"Oh yes," Sylvia said, opening her note-book and sitting down. Her weariness was forgotten as she studied the piquant little face of the woman doomed to the ordeal of torture.

"I wonder if when she was a child she ever dreamt of the rack and awoke shrieking," she pondered.

Meanwhile Britski was standing watching her and presently asked, "You have been all day at the Bibliothèque, Mademoiselle?"

"All day, Monsieur."

"And your *déjeuner?*"

"Oh, I ran out to a *crêmerie* for a bowl of chocolate and a roll," she answered, her head bent over her book.

"If you would honour me—you see, I am half Russian in my habits, and have tea at all hours, so that they bring it whenever I want it. It is five o'clock, and I know your English ways. May I not give you a cup of tea now?"

As she came in, Sylvia had noticed a white cloth covered side-table on which stood a Russian samovar and cups of egg-shell china, and a plate or two of dainty cakes. She did not know why the idea of this little meal alone with Britski was a shock to her, but with the shock came the knowledge that she must hide it.

"It is kind in you to think of it," she made smiling answer, "but you forget that I am an American, and have no English ways. I really never take tea in the afternoon."

She was looking up at him, and marked a pe-

culiar contraction about his eyes that deepened
some strange lines.

"Pardon me," he said in a silkier voice than
ever. "I know that I have no right to try to turn
a business interview into a friendly one. I am
afraid that some of my customers spoil me and
make me apt to forget that I am only a shop
keeper."

To her dismay, Sylvia saw that the man was
genuinely annoyed, and with the old instinct of
good-breeding, she tried to atone.

"But I am not a customer, only a poor little
work-girl, about whom it is very kind in you to
trouble." She had overdone her humility, she
saw by the flash in his eye, but it was too late now
to retreat and she went on.

"I daresay you are right, that tea would do
me good, for I have a *folle* headache from those
musty rooms. I shall be glad of a cup, if it is no
trouble."

"Trouble!" he said in a deep voice, then turned
aside to ring and give an order, while she went
on with her work.

Her sketch was finished as the tea appeared,
and it was bodily ease to lean back in her armchair, nibbling at a dainty *langue de chat* and sip-
ping tea such as she had never before tasted.

"It is caravan tea," Britski said, as she commented on it. "I have a friend who sends it to
me from Moscow. I believe in taking a little
trouble to have the best."

"You always have the best, it seems to me," she said, feeling this a safe topic. "Your house at Meudon is nearly as full of beautiful things as these galleries."

"And why should I not have my own pleasure in the things I love, the things it is a grief to me to sell to ignoramuses, to *nouveaux riches?*" he said ardently. "That little villa is nothing to the home I mean to have some day, in Sicily or Corfu. It is good enough in its way, though. Tell me, you will let Marcelle bring you there some Sunday—next Sunday, eh?"

He was leaning forward, his arms on the table, his eager eyes fixed on her face.

There could be no more self-deception. She must walk warily with this man. It was not her first experience of the kind, since she had faced the ordeal of bread-winning. Many a bitter tear had been afterwards shed over the humiliation which, at the time, she had faced with cool contempt. More than one good offer of work had been rejected because they had been proffered in that same vibrant voice, with those eager eyes, that intense smile.

The cold fury that came over her cleared her mind, and shewed her the harm that this man's enmity might do to her.

If only she could get away without a scene, she would take care that he had no such chance again.

With the smiling chill of her old society armour

she answered, pushing her chair the smallest bit backwards:

"A thousand thanks, Monsieur. It is lovely out there, away from the streets. I am sorry, but I have promised to spend Sunday with an American friend."

"Can you not put her off It is 'her'?" he asked, sharp as a flash.

If only he would take those piercing eyes off her face. A horrible fancy that he was hypnotizing her, brought a clammy dampness to her forehead.

"Yes it is 'her,' but I fear I must not break my promise," she answered as lightly as she might, though she heard the quaver in her voice. Why could not her woman's body answer to the courage of her woman's soul? Just then, she heard a shuffling step in the corridor, and knew that the longed-for interruption was at hand.

"May I come in, Monsieur Britski?" sounded a piping masculine voice.

The contraction of the latter's eyelids alone told his annoyance as he answered, "Certainly, Monsieur Naftal. Do me the honour to enter,"

A shrivelled old man with a terrier-like face ambled in.

Mr. Naftal still called himself an artist, though it was many years since he had produced a picture. If he had any use in the scheme of existence, it was to act as a link between art and society in Parisian-American circles.

He took people the round of the studios, got little paragraphs about young artists into the papers, helped wealthy dames to pick up the bargains their souls loved, and made himself so generally useful that he seldom had to pay for his own dinner.

Sylvia knew him, and knew him, too, as an inveterate scandal-monger. She caught his glance of discreet amusement as he took in the tea-table with their intimate group, and she knew that the situation would lose nothing in the telling.

With a great show of cordiality, Britski rose and offered his armchair to the newcomer, but Sylvia saw that he had taken the chance to close the book that lay open on the table, and to shove her sketch-book to one side.

She took this as a hint that she was to say nothing about her commission before the visitor. At any rate, she would get away while he was still there; that she was resolved.

"La-la, it is too bad that Louis of yours did not tell me you were engaged. And here I am breaking up your little party," fussed Mr. Naftal, his eyes sparkling with mischief.

"You are not breaking it up, Mr. Naftal, because I was going," Sylvia said, pulling on her gloves. "We had finished our business, Monsieur Britski and I, and as I was tired from my work, he was kind enough to order tea for me. I shall remember that caravan tea, Monsieur," she said as she rose. It was quite safe to be amiable now.

"If only you remember to come soon and have some more, Mademoiselle," he said deferentially.

"And what charming creations are you concocting now?" Mr. Naftal asked with an inquisitive glance at her sketch-book.

"A ballet of Queen Mab and her fairy court," she retorted airily. "Good-day, Mr. Naftal. Ah Monsieur," as Britski followed her, "do not disturb yourself. I know the way down."

"It is nothing," was all the notice he took as he persisted in going.

She brushed on rapidly past some crowded furniture, but presently the greater space of the gallery gave him room to walk beside her.

"To-morrow must be given to search for number four—Agnes Sorel," she said, feeling words better than the silent companionship of intimacy.

"And where do you hope to find her?" he asked.

"I must explore the St. Genevieve library. I have leave to study the engravings there," she made answer, not thinking of any reason for keeping her movements unknown to Britski.

She thought of it, though, the next afternoon, when, walking down the sombre Rue Soufflot, that leads from the scholastic shades of the colleges to the stir of the Boul. Mich, and the cheerful outdoor life of the Luxembourg, she came on Britski strolling casually along. She made no attempt to conceal the nervous surprise with which she greeted him, and he indirectly answered it by saying:

"Behold me, Mademoiselle, in the regions where I pursue the wily artist. It is the hour when they begin to gather at the cafés of the Boulevard. You are walking that way. May I join you?"

"I am only going to take a Clichy-Odeon bus at the corner," was her repressing answer.

They both knew that this being the end of the line she would not have to stand about, but could at once on reaching the arcades of the theatre, step into a waiting bus.

Britski took a comprehensive glance at the inobtrusive grey figure before he said with gentle pertinacity, "Why should you hurry from your day's work into one of those stifling omnibuses? Come and sit for a little minute under the trees in the Gardens, and tell me of your search to-day. If you are so economical of time, it will save you a letter or an interview to-morrow."

There was a thinly veiled sneer in the latter words, and perhaps they stung her a bit, for she paused to face him, as she said, "I am sorry, Monsieur, but I really must hurry home."

"At least come for five minutes to the *pâtisserie* at the corner—just five minutes to eat a *baba* and drink a glass of *syrop*," he persisted.

The flush deepened on her face. Did this man think that she, Sylvia Dorr, was one to go about the restaurants of the Latin Quarter with him?

"It is quite impossible, Monsieur," she said, disdaining any further excuse as she walked on.

"How proud you are," he murmured, with a glance of wrathful admiration.

"I need to be, alone as I am," she asserted, her eyes fixed ahead, her chin well atilt. They had reached the stir of the Boulevard, and she was just poising herself for the perilous crossing, when amid the stream of cabs and motor-cars and busses, she caught a glimpse of a watchful, lowering face, at the window of a closed cab. Madame Marcelle was spying upon her husband's movements. Could it be on her account?

The thought steadied her, and she found herself deftly threading her way among the horses' heads and the puffing motors, while Britski was checked on the pavement.

Had he seen his wife's face? She did not know, she did not care. All she wanted was to reach the shelter of a public vehicle.

In a step or two Britski was again at her side, but there was small chance of any continued talk as they were swept on with the Boulevard stream.

Already there were noisy groups of students and overdressed women at the tables before the café doors. It was Thursday, the day that a military band plays in the Luxembourg Gardens, and the Quarter had responded to its call. A mortal loathing of all this sordid brightness came over Sylvia, and she could scarcely veil her nervous irritation, to answer her companion when he asked,

"You will not then give me a few minutes?"

"I'm afraid not, Monsieur. Ah, there is a bus ready to start."

The conductor was on the platform as she darted forward, and with a hasty *bonjour* to Britski, jumped up, and climbed the narrow steps to the roof.

Here she subsided on a bench in a tremour of wrath and fear. The big omnibus thundered over the rough pavement of the dark old streets, by the grim, historic churches of St. Sulpice and St. Germain-des-Prés. By the time it had reached the Pont du Carrousel, and the river breezes fanned her face, Sylvia's passive courage had revived, with her self-confidence.

What harm could this scheming man, this jealous woman, do her, unless her own weakness supplied the means? She would go home and work night and day to finish up this commission that had been made the excuse for intercourse, and would then carefully avoid any more such traps.

She was not afraid of anyone, she assured herself; but, all the same, she felt desperately forlorn as she reached her own room and looked around with a longing for the familiar presence of Harriett Oakes.

XXV

THE SNARE IS BROKEN

FOR two days, Sylvia worked steadily, hardly leaving her room save at meal times. Then, her task finished, she took her drawings to Britski's, at an hour when she guessed he would be absent at *déjeuner*.

There was a very real sense of relief in knowing that the affair of the portfolios was ended, and she did her best to put out of her mind the remembrance of Britski's eager eyes, of his wife's haggard face.

It was a day or so later, when, returning from a walk, she opened the door of her room to see the waiting figure of a thin old lady, with the stamp of genteel poverty on every inch of her meagre garments.

This was Miss Cloude, an old family acquaintance, who found the occupation of making meet the two ends of a very small income a little less sordid under foreign skies and among strangers.

Her inquisitive pessimism was often a strain on Sylvia's nerves, but she always did her best at a cordial welcome, and never, if possible, let the poor soul go without whatever food she could offer her.

"Now this is nice. You and I will have a cup of tea together," she said as cheerfully as possible, but was met by a mournful shake of the head.

"Ah, my dear, it was not for tea that I came. As an old friend of your family, I felt it my duty to warn you."

This unpromising opening chilled Sylvia's hospitality, and presently she found herself listening to a remarkably unpleasant tale. One of Miss Cloude's greatest joys was an occasional Sunday lunch with a certain kind-hearted member of the American colony. At the latest of these functions, Mr. Naftal had been also a guest, and he had entertained his hostess with a lamentation over the Bohemian tendencies of American girl students in Paris, as instanced in Sylvia Dorr, whom he had found having tea, alone in his office, with Britski, "who, when all's said and done isn't much better than the old clothes man who goes round calling 'marçant's d'habits'—"

"He said, my dear, that you had cigarettes; but that, I assured him, was impossible."

"No, there were no cigarettes," Sylvia said wearily.

"And Mrs. Lyle said that she was disappointed to hear that you were that sort, on account of your family."

"Look here, Miss Cloude, I know you would help me if you could."

"Yes indeed, child," and the thin hand patted hers.

"Well, then, I want you to go to Mrs. Lyle, and tell her the true story," and Sylvia gave a little sketch of the incident, "and tell her, too, that I shall take good care never to have tea alone with Monsieur Britski again.

"That's right, my dear, for—I didn't mean to tell you—but Mr. Lyle joined in and said that if half the things he had heard of Britski were true, no lady should have anything to do with him, business or no business."

Sylvia was both startled and wounded at this, and her voice was tremulous as she tried to answer lightly, "It's not so easy to be a lady and a work-girl both. The lady must go to the wall, sometimes."

"Oh, my dear, and your mother one of the Rockford Troubridges!"

Sylvia did her best to cheer the woman who had the misfortune to belong to the old dispensation of feminine incapacity. She fed her with tea and biscuits and sent her on her way, in a twitter to defend the girl.

Then, when the door closed, she turned back to her solitude in utter desolation of spirit. So she could not even fight her battle, bear the humiliations that honest toil brings to such as she, without the jeers of gossips, the cruel comments of those who should defend her.

Mechanically moving about to tidy the remains of her little tea-party, she noticed an unstamped envelope on her table, addressed in Britski's flowing Italian hand. Taking it up, she found it to be soft and fat, and sealed with a big red seal. On this seal was the impression of a bare arm clutching a dagger, with a motto in an unknown tongue running round it. Within were two bank-notes of a value that made her stare. She had not expected to be thus paid for her work.

There was a flowery letter expressing the satisfaction which her drawings had given, and saying that he would be always ready to take as many more of such drawings as she could supply him with, at the same prices.

"There is a demand for that style of water-colours to go with Louis Quinze drawing-room furnishings," he added.

A rapid calculation told Sylvia that a month or so of work paid at that rate, would mean more than she had ever earned, and for a moment she wondered if it might not be possible to undertake it. It was but for a moment, and then as she realized that Britski was paying her more than the market value, her cheeks burned with shame that she should have harboured the temptation.

There was one of the samples of smoke-coloured paper lying on the table, and taking it up she studied it with absent-minded intentness, her thoughts all on the problem as to how best to refuse this offer, without bringing about a rupture with Madame Marcelle.

What a subtle tint of age was on this paper,

and how curiously rubbed and blunted its edges were. Surely Britski must have unearthed some veritable old pile hidden away among artists' materials.

What pains he took about trifles, for after all, it was a mere trifling detail to give these modern drawings such a look of age.

Was it a trifling detail, though? And then she caught her breath, as she saw the trap into which she had so blindly stepped. The tale of the Russian princess must be all a fabrication. Those portfolios had been bought incomplete, and were now, thanks to her, to be sold as a complete collection. No wonder he could afford to pay her well. No wonder he could offer her more such work, work that would all be sold under false pretences.

Dazed with horror, she wondered if the little tea-party had been part of the plot, and if Mr. Naftal had been purposely allowed to come up and find her in intimate converse with her employer.

With Madame Marcelle's jealousy aroused against her, with slander spread amongst her fellow-countrymen, she would be a helpless tool in Britski's hands.

Would she, though? And amidst her desolation, the tonic of righteous anger stirred her into a new force. Lucky for her, in that moment, that she came of a sturdy stock, used to facing the strength of the sea. But Rupert Thorpe?

Did not the game that had been played with her shew how he may have been entrapped?

There was that signed Corot in the Meudon villa, which she had seen Thorpe paint as a joke. Had it not been innocently sold, with perhaps such a subsequent order given as had come to her to-day, until, with debts and the threats of of revealed forgeries, he had been securely caught in the toils, every effort at independent work baffled by Britski's underhand influence. Ah, how he must have bled under the slow torture before he had taken refuge in flight.

Where was he now, alive or dead? And with the recurring thought of suicide, she wrung her hands in momentary despair.

Would it not be better for her, too, to get away out of Britski's ken? There are some cases where an honest woman must own herself defeated. Did it not seem now as though that time had come for her? A cable to her sister would, she felt sure, bring her the passage-money to reach home. Then she remembered her brother-in-laws's illness, the young baby, and knew that there could be no spare funds in that household. No, there were, she knew, orders and letters with money coming to her, and she would hold her ground for a bit, and perhaps Harriett would soon be back. At thought of that tower of strength, the first sob came, and it was almost a luxury to let the grief storm sweep over her, unresisting.

Poor Sylvia, with the blonde masses of her

hair all tumbled against the shabby chintz of the armchair, just a lonely, heart-sick girl.

But even then her fate was on the turn, for that day Julia's friend Mr. Stratton had arrived in Paris. With as little delay as possible, he had hied to the Praeds' apartment, only to find his divinity absent. Then he bethought himself of the friend in whose welfare Julia was so interested.

An energetic business man, he had already informed himself as to the quality of her work, and was satisfied that an illustrated book, by her on the history of costume would be worth the taking up.

All the same, he might not have been so prompt a visitor without the ulterior motive of news of Julia.

As it was, Sylvia, pale from last night's storm, had barely settled herself to her morning's work, when his card was brought to her.

Mr. Stratton? The name conveyed little to her, the appearance of the burly, black-haired man still less.

But she liked the steady grey eyes, the stolidly honest face, and at the first words of his purpose, she was aglow with hope—hope, all the more precious for the inky darkness it scattered.

He had seen her illustrated article in the *Era*—had made inquiries about her with the object of getting her to do some such series for the magazine connected with his firm, but, hearing of the book which she had in preparation, had come to ask to see it, with a view to publication.

Presently he was looking over the precious portfolio, with judicious words of praise, and it was arranged that the manuscript should be sent to the hotel.

"I have a man whom I employ as a reader when such things turn up here. Though I am out on a holiday now," he added with a smile.

The friendliness of the smile encouraged Sylvia to ask how long he expected to be in Paris.

"That depends," he answered. "I thought of taking a run down to Venice—favourite place of mine for a lounge—but I may wait to see some friends I expected to find here," and then he went on to speak of the Praeds, and to learn all that Sylvia knew about them.

"And you will promise us something for the magazine—an illustrated series that would make up into book form later. The women of the Bonaparte family and their friends, eh? Couldn't be better, that. We'll take the first part as soon as you have it done. Pay on delivery. Good-day," and he was gone, leaving a very different Sylvia from her he had found.

Within an hour, she posted a simply polite note to Britski, acknowledging the money and saying that she would be too busy for a while with some magazine articles to undertake any fresh orders.

She had hesitated about returning the money, but finally decided against doing so. It might be a mistake to shew her hand so plainly before she had reached more neutral territory than the Hotel Cleveland could possibly be.

But that night she fell into a more peaceful sleep than she had known for weeks, with visions of fragrant meadows and cool streams.

XXVI

VARNISHING DAY

WHAT'S wrong with Garvie? He doesn't look as though he were getting the full change out of his success," said one of a group of English speaking artists on Varnishing Day. It was the crowded hour of the early afternoon, and already the year's successes and failures were decided on by the makers of opinion.

Frye looked across to where Garvie stood, his hand effusively grasped in congratulation by one of the honoured masters of his craft.

"He hardly seems up to the occasion," he acknowledged. "Perhaps he thinks it good form not to betray his ecstasy. Or perhaps he is shy." A general laugh greeted this suggestion. The laugh would have been louder if anyone had ventured to hint that the reasons for Garvie's ill-concealed grimness were sentimental ones; but it was, nevertheless, the fact.

On this day of triumphant achievement, it all seemed stale, flat, and unprofitable to Garvie, just because a certain wilful young woman was not there to share it with him. Was it always to be like this, he wondered, with a dull pain at heart, and was the taste gone out of everything henceforth? And then he set his face and determined that he would not spoil the fruits of his long effort because an ungrateful girl chose to believe the first hint of evil against him.

His Theodora was already one of the sensations of the season—the pallid-faced, red-lipped woman in her dull purple draperies and heavily jewelled Byzantine tiara leant, in a palpitating white heat of interest, on the marble balustrade of her balcony to watch the chariot-races of the rival factions, blue and green. There was a cruel joy in her eyes, as though they beheld the downfall of a long-hated foe.

The picture was hung on the line in the big room, and had already a crowd round it.

On every side Garvie was greeted by the warm congratulations of men who knew the worth of the work, the continued toil it represented.

"May I add my humble voice to the paean of praise?" came in honeyed tones from Britski, well-dressed, with a leisurely air of good-breeding.

Garvie's face hardened, as he met the glint of mockery in the grey eyes.

"Thank you," he said brusquely. "I think some share of the praise so kindly given me to-day should go to my model. You know her, I believe?"

Britski's glance gave back the cold hostility of his. "The face *does* seem familiar to me," he acknowledged. "Let me see—is there not a girl named Virginie Lapierre?"

"Exactly so. What a good memory you have," was the grim comment. "I was surprised to find the young lady in Trêmalo the other day," Garvie added.

Not a quiver told that the shot had hit the target. "Indeed! With an artist?" Britski asked in a politely conversational tone.

"No. She was going by the name of Mademoiselle de Rostrênan—that of an old family in the neighbourhood."

"Strange freak, that."

"Very strange."

"You are sure that there was no mistake?" I myself, have corresponded with a lady of that name."

"Exactly so. There was no mistake. I met and talked with her. Look here, Britski," and his voice took a tone of haughty superiority. "I think the little game is about played out, and the lady had better retire with the honours of war; otherwise she may lose the chance of retiring at all."

For a moment the two men stood looking into each other's eyes, and then with an open snarl, Britski spoke: "If Mr. Praed thinks differently, the opinion of Monsieur Garvie may not matter."

"That remains to be seen," was the cool retort. "I may have more forcible means of expressing it than you know. For instance," and his voice sank impressively, "I might express it by cable to Mr. Praed's sons, whose enquiries might start a Paris scandal involving the most unexpected people."

"That would be all very fine, provided that none of these people happened to be friends of yours, *'ce petit* Thorpe, for example," Britski sneered. "Might it not be wise to consider first if you wish to see him imprisoned for fraud? And a certain fair American, who copies old pastels so charmingly, what about her?"

"You damned scoundrel!" Garvie muttered.

"And the other young lady might not be so good a match, if her father were driven into a quarrel with his family," went on the venomous voice.

Fortunately, Garvie's stick was in safe keeping down stairs, or it might have left its mark across that taunting face. As it was, his arm was raised before he remembered the folly of being drawn into a brawl with this adventurer.

With a great effort at self-repression, he turned away, choking down his wrath with thought of the coming days of retribution.

As he shoved his way through the crowd intent on soothing his ruffled composure with a solitary cigarette, a friendly hand grasped his arm.

"Hello, Garvie, may lesser fry address your grandeur to-day?" came in the cheery tones of

Howe, the Philadelphian, whose studio had adjoined Thorpe's.

Here was one who might aid the purpose of his righteous wrath.

"You are just the man I wanted to see," Garvie said, drawing the young fellow into a quiet corner. "Look here, can you give me any news of Thorpe?"

"The very thing I was going to ask you," said the other. "Confound the fellow. He has kept us running around, playing games of questions for a month now. You see, it is this way. I fetched his rejected Salon picture back to my diggings before the framer could lay hands on it for his bill."

"Britski?"

"No. He didn't want that wily spider to know about it. Owed him money, I suppose. Well, there it stood until the other day, when a seraphic cousin of mine, given to good works, fetches along a wandering millionaire to see my infantile efforts. To the dear woman's sorrow, he falls upon Thorpe's picture and insists on owning it at any price. I said the man who painted it was off mountaineering somewhere or other in Algeria, that I had lost his address, or never had it,—anyway, I got him to hold the bargain open until Thorpe should reappear, but, naturally, with every studio in Paris gaping at him, he won't wait for ever. Pity, isn't it?"

Garvie's mind worked busily while the other

was speaking. Thorpe's continued absence, gave substance to the fears aroused by Britski's open defiance. On Sylvia Dorr's integrity, he would have staked his all, but in Thorpe was there not some fatal vein of weakness, nullifying his best gifts? Was it not possible that, disheartened by failure, he had allowed himself to sink into becoming Britski's tool?

These misgivings bid Garvie walk warily in his inquiries.

"I thought he would have turned up by now. Still brooding over his sorrows in some country village, I suppose," he said casually. "He ought to face the music like a man. If you should hear anything of him, let me know, will you?"

They parted, and Garvie went on to fresh greetings, to a smart restaurant dinner, and an evening at the opera.

The next day at Monroe's bank he brushed against a quietly dressed girl. Something familiar in the outline made him take a second look. It was Sylvia Dorr, wan and thin, but with face spiritualized by days of steady constancy, of solitary waiting. She was unmistakably glad to see him, and something in the quiet eyes, raised to his, gave him a choking feeling as he recalled Britski's calumnies.

In his student days, he had been in love for a whole winter with the dainty school-girl, and this boyish admiration stirred him now to sterner purpose of vengeance on her behalf.

"I heard you had left Trêmalo," she said, as he greeted her.

"How?" he asked startled.

"I had a letter from Julia yesterday," she said demurely, and he asked no more, though he meant later to have a try at finding out the contents of of that letter.

"You look as though you had been working too hard, and needed fresh air," he commented. "I want a talk with you, and it is a lovely day. Don't you think you might be very nice and come and drive up to the Bois with me?"

Sylvia felt a pleasant sense of security in the presence of this fellow-countryman who had known her in her own home.

The lonely terrors that had surrounded her seemed all at once to become vague as a remembered dream. She too wanted a talk with Garvie, and so it was very readily that she went with him out into the sunshine.

A little open cab took them up the Avenue Friedland, and on into the wider spaces beyond.

Garvie was keenly impatient to know if the marks of strain and stress in her face had anything to do with Britski's threats, but not wishing to startle her, he bided his time.

"And how have things been faring with you?" he asked, as they drove along, and there was no perfunctoriness in the question.

"Oh, with a mixture of good and bad, as life usually is, I suppose. But there was one bit of genuine luck—" and she told of Mr. Stratton's visit and its result.

He congratulated her warmly, adding, "That is the last of wasting your time on fashion-plates, I trust. But you spoke of mixed good and bad— won't you tell me what the bad has been? We are old friends, you know."

It had been perhaps the memory of that long-dead boy and girl flirtation which had caused Sylvia to shrink from the helping hand that he had tried more than once to give her. Now that she knew of his admiration for Julia, she felt free to revive the old friendship—besides, she had been so desperately lonely of late.

With a sudden impulse of confidence, she began and told him all; her visit with Miss Oakes to Meudon; the Corot picture; Madame Marcelle; the portfolio of portraits. She even, after a desperate gulp of hesitation, forced herself to tell, with flushed cheeks, the incident of the Schwerer portfolios, her tea with Britski, Mr. Naftal's gossip and Miss Cloude's repetition of it. "They all seem little things in themselves," she ended half-apologetically, "and perhaps I was foolish to be frightened, but I was all alone."

"They were not trifles, and you were quite right to be frightened," Garvie interrupted. "He is a beast of prey, and deserves no more mercy than one."

And then, he in his turn, proceeded to tell the story of the Rosbraz chateau.

"No wonder poor Julia's letter seemed low-spirited," she commented.

"Was it low-spirited?" he demanded, as though the news were not unwelcome. "She has foolishly allowed some of the gang to poison her mind against me, which makes it so much harder for me to help her. They have told her some cock-and-bull story about that wretched girl, Virginie Lapierre."

They had by now left the cab and were sitting in one of the quieter alleys of the Bois, amid all the bravery of young leafage. Garvie was prodding nervously at the gravel with his stick, and Sylvia, watching his downcast face, found courage to reassure him.

"She does not really believe any harm of you. She said she knew you had done your best to help her, and that she had been horrid to you. I think she is sorry. Do not be angry with her," she pleaded.

Garvie looked up with a very kindly smile on his face.

"What a charming advocate you make! I am not angry. I only came away because I thought that I had a better chance of attacking this wasps' nest here. Your story makes me all the more determined. What we want now," and he leant forward impressively, "is proof of fraud, positive enough to induce Mr. Praed to prosecute Britski. And I believe that if we could only find Thorpe we should get that proof."

Sylvia's face was transformed as, with wet, eager eyes and trembling lips, she cried:

"Oh, will you really try to find him? I have been sure from the first that it was Britski who drove him away, but I could do nothing by myself," and she caught her breath in a sob.

Garvie watched her with grave compunction. He knew enough of women to be careful to give no hint of the theory he had entertained as to Thorpe's and Virginie's simultaneous disappearance, but there was one question that he must ask, painful though it might be to her.

With carefully averted eyes, he began, "Tell me—do not be vexed, please—have you ever thought that he might be in fear of an exposure; that he had been drawn into some fraud?"

As he spoke, he saw creep over her face the ghastly shadow of an old, sickening doubt, a doubt that, scarcely acknowledged even to herself, had yet power to haunt her night and day, to draw those pathetic lines on her face.

Her hands were intertwined nervously, as she murmured, "Sometimes—I have been afraid that there might be something—that someone has a hold on him."

His pity for her distress urged him to spare her, but for her own sake, for Thorpe's, he must get at what truth he might, and so he told her as gently as possible of Britski's threats.

She could not have grown paler than he was, but with a swift, beautiful glow she flashed out:

"He may have been unlucky, but I am sure—oh I am sure—that he has never cheated anyone."

"That is right," Garvie reassured her, even though he had his own masculine doubts on the subject. "Then you are not afraid of my trying to find him?"

It was the crucial test, and she quailed before it. Then, drawing a deep breath as though gathering all her forces, she said, quick and low, "No, I am not afraid."

"Well then, we will do our best. And—you must have thought it all over. Can you give me any hint as to where he would be likely to go?"

She shook her head silently; then, after a moment's thought, told him of the queer silversmith at Neuilly.

"Strange," Garvie muttered. "I have heard nothing of any gold or silver in the Rosbraz affair."

If only Julia had been in a more trustful humour on that last afternoon by the river, the tangle might have been the sooner unravelled, but so the Fates had ordered.

"Well, anyway, I will explore the place, and then I will have a look round his haunts in the Quarter. And now I want you to do me a favour," he added.

"I will do anything you ask me," she breathed fervently.

"Do not be too sure. I want you to leave Paris at once. There, I knew you would not like the idea," as a swift "oh!" of dismay followed his first words.

"But why?" she protested.

"Do you not see that if I were to hear where Thorpe was, I might want to be off at once to see him quietly, and find out the true state of affairs."

"Yes, but—"

"And after what you have told me, how could I feel quite happy in leaving you alone here, right in the midst of the gang? The first hint of exposure may make Britski turn, venomous as a cornered rat. His wife is jealous of you, and there you are, working for her and living in her mother's house. I can only have a free hand if I know that you are out of reach of any harm from him." He hesitated for a moment, and then went on, "And there is a way that you could help me, too."

"Oh, what is it?" she asked eagerly.

There was a touch of awkwardness in Garvie's manner as he said, "You told me yourself that Miss Praed's letter shewed her low spirits, and you must realize what an anxious, a painful position she is in. Now, if you, who have more knowledge of the world than she can have, were with her, surely it would strengthen her hand and make her less unhappy—and me too," he added with a passing smile.

The protest was gone from Sylvia's voice. "You are right, and I am a selfish creature. She urged me in her letter to come, but I just chose to fancy that I could not. I will go as soon as you like, and she and I will carry on the fight down there, while you—" she paused anxiously, and Garvie filled the pause:

"You can trust me. I will do my very best to give Thorpe a new start, free from the toils. We are friends, you know," he reminded her.

"I trust you fully," she smiled at him. "When shall I go?"

"The sooner the better. Day after to-morrow? Can you manage that?"

"I think so. I must pack and store everything, you know. Oh, and now I can send Britski back the money for those portraits. I was frightened to, before. I am not afraid of him any longer."

"You never shall be again," he assured her fervently. "But do not send the money. Give it to me at the station when I see you off. Yes, I mean to see you out of Paris with my own eyes. And look here. It is an expensive journey, and—"

"Oh, I am quite rich," she interrupted. "You know it was at the bank I met you. Surely it must be nearly dinner time. I ought to get home," and full of their purposed campaign, they sought a cab and drove townwards.

XXVII

MARCELLE'S TRAGEDY

SPURRED by new hope, Sylvia lost no time in carrying out her plans. On their homeward way, she and Garvie stopped at a post-office and wired Julia that she was coming. That evening, carefully avoiding Madame Comerie, she left notice in the office of her departure. Then she slipped out to leave a note with Madame Marcelle's concierge, to say that, as she was going to the country for a holiday, she would not be able to do any more work at present. Without giving it any farewell character, she tried to make this note express something of the gratitude she had once felt; indeed, still, in a fashion, felt towards the dressmaker. Who has not known a severed friendship where, trust and confidence gone, the instinctive liking of natures sympathetically atuned lasts, and awakes at every meeting? The companionship of the friend who has failed us under stress of weather, gives nearly the same old pleasure that it did before. So now with Sylvia. The strain of personal fear once removed, the thought of evil days that Britski's exposure might bring to his wife, aroused her generosity towards the woman who had befriended her, and she resolved, if possible, to get away without an interview between them.

This resolve was defeated. She was busy the next morning in her dismantled room, packing away her belongings, when a knock came at the door.

Scarcely leaving a pause for a response, the door was flung open, and Madame Marcelle appeared. Her hat and wrap were worn with less dainty precision than usual, and the raindrops of a heavy shower shone unregarded on her shoulders, while she held her gloves in her hand, together with an open letter.

These tokens of a disturbing force were emphasized in her face by a dismayed pallor, veiled with a tremulous smile.

"*Mon enfant*," she began, and through all her troubled haste the woman's gracious charm still revealed itself. "*Mon enfant*, what does this mean? Why go off and leave me so suddenly at this, the busiest time of the year? You know I cannot spare you now."

She held out the letter as though it were an accusing fact, and Sylvia saw that it was her own.

"I am sorry. I feared it might inconvenience you," she said, as she stood by an open box, her hands full of a sheaf of drawings.

"*Dame!* It is more than inconvenience. But you will stay, now that you know?" and she laid her free hand on Sylvia's arm with a persuasive gesture.

"I cannot. I am sorry," Sylvia reiterated.

"See, then. I will pay you double for everything if you will wait until after the Grand Prix."

"Dear Madame, it is no question of money."

"What is it then?"

The keen question came in a flash that matched that of the blue eyes.

Sylvia had long ago settled it with her Puritan conscience that absolute truth was not always possible in dealing with Parisians. The honester party suffered enough disadvantage without that added one. So now, with steady gaze, she answered:

"I cannot go on working any longer. I do not eat or sleep, and the doctor says that I must have complete rest and change, otherwise I shall be ill. And that, you know," she added with a wistful smile, "is a forbidden luxury to busy folk."

Her wan face corroborated her words, and Marcelle for the moment seemed to believe her.

"But you will promise to come back soon? How soon do you think it may be?" she urged, fighting every inch of ground.

For all her feeling of pity, Sylvia had no intention of yielding one point.

"Ah, that I cannot say. If I can find material for some magazine articles, I may stay all summer in the country. One can live for so little in out-of-the-way places you see."

A look of desperation came into the French-woman's eyes as she asked, "Then you mean to give me up altogether?"

"I may give up drawing fashions, but I shall never give up the thought of your kindness," was Sylvia's answer. It was the best she could do. Marcelle's eyes filled with sudden tears, and with both hands outstretched, she pleaded:

"Ah, do not go at all. Let me take you out to Meudon. There you can be all day in the fresh air and sunshine. You need only work when you choose."

Sylvia was profoundly puzzled at this persistence. She could see that the other's distress was genuine, and yet—surely she could not have been mistaken about the watchful face at the cab window, that day by the Luxembourg. Did the other woman read that memory in her face as she answered with a gentle shake of her head:

"There would still be the atmosphere of Paris. I must get away where I never see or hear of fashions."

A little forced laugh came pitifully from Madame Marcelle.

"Well, then, you shall see and hear nothing of them at Mariposa. You shall wear reach-me-downs from the big shops, if you wish. I will put them on myself whenever I come near you. Heavens, what a bundle I shall be. There, will that content you, little one?"

It was the last time that Madame Marcelle

ever called Sylvia "little one." With the next words the chill of the girl's gentleness seemed at last to reach her.

"Dear Madame, you are kind to suggest it, but please do not press me any more. I want to get away altogether from Paris. My plans are made. I have promised to join an American friend at the seaside."

"Where?"

The brief question was almost sullen.

"She is to let me know our destination to-morrow."

The tightening lines of the other's mouth told that she took in the full significance of the evasion.

"Does Britski know that you are going?" was her next question.

"Not unless you have told him," and Sylvia's voice was harder.

"*Mon Dieu*, no!" came with a hoarse cry of despair. "He will be furious with me when he hears it. Ah, what shall I do? He will think that I have been alarming you, and driven you away."

"Why should he think that?"

Sylvia was very pale, but her voice had no faltering in it. Her pride was beginning to find the situation intolerable.

"Because he will be angry, and when he is angry he can be cruel. Ah, I know that. You say I was kind to you once. If ever you thought so, come out with me to the villa to-morrow, only just for Sunday. That can do you no harm."

The appeal was wild, and might have stirred Sylvia's pity but for her sense of outrage. No harm to pass a day under the roof of such a man as Britski!

"I cannot do that," she said without any further attempt at excuse.

"Because you have quarreled with him?"

"I have not quarreled with him."

"You refused to do any more drawings for him, and he said that it must be my fault and that I had stopped you."

"You know the reason I refused to work for your husband?" Sylvia demanded, her words like bared steel.

A confused hesitation came into the other woman's face.

"No. How could I know?" she faltered.

"Yes, you do know," Sylvia persisted, letting loose at last. "You know that those drawings were to be sold as forgeries, just as those I did for the Schwerer portfolios have been. I was to be entrapped, as Rupert Thorpe was trapped, and you were aiding him in it."

"On my honour, I could not help it," the wretched woman protested. "He forced me into it, as he has already forced me into so many things. I was always honest with you until that evil day you came to the villa, and he saw you and went mad about you. Ah, what a torture my life has been since I first knew him."

"Is it not possible that you only fancy such things?" Sylvia asked with the same chilling quiet. She was sorry enough for the poor soul, but she had to put a strong control on her wrath at Britski's wife daring to be jealous of her.

Madame Marcelle stood, monumental in sullen despair.

"It is no fancy that he is realizing all the money he can, and getting it out of the business. He has sworn to me that it was not so, but he cannot deceive me in business affairs. I know that he is laying his plans to go away and leave me. Has he given you any hint of that?"

There was a new touch of insolence in the words, and Sylvia frankly recognized it in her answer.

"You have no right to ask me such a question," she said. "I have not seen your husband since I finished those drawings. I hope never to see him again."

"Do not be too sure of that. He will not lose sight of you so easily. Sooner or later he always runs down his game." She paused, and then, defiance changing back into despair, said. "He has been devilish this past week. If you can, for pity's sake tell me what is happening about that '*bonhomme* Praed' to disturb him so?"

Sylvia hesitated for an instant, during which

her assurance of Britski's approaching defeat conquered her prudence, and she said:

"It can only be that he fears exposure. I suppose you know that he has filled that chateau in Finistère with antiques, supposed to belong to an old family, and has sent down a Paris model to play the part of an orphan reduced to selling her ancestral inheritance."

"*Mon Dieu.* No, I knew nothing of it," Madame Marcelle gasped, and to her surprise, Sylvia saw that she was speaking the truth, and that the tidings were a grievous blow to her.

"What is the model's name?" she demanded, with strange eagerness.

"Virginie Lapierre," Sylvia answered.

The other's face grew haggard as that of an old woman.

"*Sacristi!* That creature of ill-omen," she moaned.

A sudden hope of getting at some information came to Sylvia.

"Who is she?" she asked briefly.

"I do not know. I am afraid to know," was the hoarse murmur, then as though anguish drove her into words, she went on.

"She came, like him, from Poland or Hungary—who knows which? I think she is a gipsy. When I first met Britski—unlucky day for me— he was a photographer, with a small place near the Gare Montparnasse. She helped him with his work, and posed for the photographs he sold to artists. I do not suppose you know the kind, but I have seen them. Then, little by little, he began to buy and sell pictures. It was my money that started him in the Avenue de l'Opera. In return, he has nearly ruined me with his mad extravagance. The villa is only the smallest part of that. How I worked to help him on! But," with a new purpose in her tone, "for all that, I shall never turn against him. Promise me that you will not try to harm him," she implored.

Still Sylvia faced her with that steady quiet of settled purpose.

"Will you tell me, then, where Rupert Thorpe is?"

"He does not know. That is part of his ill-humour, for he misses him. He has made search for him. I think he is afraid that it means suicide."

Instead of faltering before the dread word, the spectre that had haunted her night hours, Sylvia flashed out:

"If it does, he pays for it. See then, madame, I loved Rupert Thorpe as you loved Britski. I believe that at first you meant me no harm, and I am sorry for you. But I shall do all that I can to find Rupert Thorpe, dead or alive, and to punish those who wronged him. I am your husband's enemy and may yet have to be yours. What is the good of talking any more? We only hurt each other."

"Are not you afraid that Britski may find

means to stop your leaving Paris?" Marcelle whispered, with a furtive glance over her shoulder at the passage. There was a hint of dark fears in her words, and Sylvia shivered. Then, remembering Garvie, with the powers of the American embassy behind him, took courage.

"I am not afraid of any harm he can do me," she said.

"You do not know him as well as I do," came in the same frightened whisper. "But, see," in a firmer voice, "he shall have no chance to harm you, for I shall not tell him you are going. He may be angry with me," with a hopeless gesture, "but, at any rate, you will be safe out of his way. I am a fool, but—well, I always fancied that the little girl baby I lost might have grown up to look like you—and so you won't think too hardly of me?" she ended with a sob.

Sylvia was genuinely touched.

"Dear Madame," she said, taking her hand, "I shall always remember how good you were to me. But surely, if he is cruel to you, it would be a good thing if he goes away and leaves you to make a fresh start for yourself. You are so clever that you could do it."

A strange smile lit the older woman's face, as a stormy sunset lights a desolate landscape.

"Ah, you have not yet learnt to love as I have *malgré tout.* Lucky for you, perhaps, if you never do. And now I must go. No, do not touch me," waving off Sylvia's proffered hand.

Without further word she was gone, leaving a strange chill behind her.

In spite of all reassuring thoughts, and a carefully locked door, Sylvia was nervously alert throughout the night hours. But dawn came early, and with the dawn the old fears became unreal, and were left behind like outworn garments in the garret room of the Hotel Cleveland.

Garvie met her at the station, and his friendly farewell was in her ears as the train glided out through the fortifications.

On they went into the open country, where there were no Paris schemers, no Britski or his like.

"I never, never, want to live in Paris again," she murmured, as she settled herself in her corner.

XXVIII

THE PRODIGAL

GARVIE'S researches in the Quarter left him with reduced hopefulness. Nowhere in the studios could he gather word of any one, artists or models, having heard of Thorpe. The picture-dealers had not the slightest sketch of his among their stock. Not a man in the colour-shops had received a country order for paints or brushes.

"And if *ce peteit* Monsieur Thorpe is still painting, he would send to me. He never trusts those country shops," said old Alain, familiar to generations of students.

"I believe he has gone touring with a photographer's van. He always said he would take to that if other trades failed."

This was volunteered by Howe, the Philadelphian, and was the sole suggestion Garvie received. Thorpe had simply disappeared as so many men do disappear in big cities, leaving no trace behind them.

Neither had his hunt for the silversmith at Neuilly been more successful. No 28 was converted into a spic-and-span establishment for English young ladies wishing to acquire a Parisian accent, with all the comforts of home life, under the care of a French Prostestant *pasteur,* with black beard and finger-nails to match.

This worthy, who changed from servility to brusqueness when he discovered that Garvie had no youthful female relatives available, knew nothing as to any former tenants.

The baker at the corner was more communicative. "Yes, those Germans had taken themselves off, one day, as quietly as they had come. Just as well, perhaps, for every concierge in the street was persuaded that they were spies. Money? Yes, they always had money. The woman often changed a gold piece when she bought provisions. What did blue-blouses like them do with gold pieces unless they were spies, or coiners perhaps. There was always smoke coming from one of the chimneys. All the street had seen it. No, he did not know where these people came from. The butcher asked the woman once, and she muttered something about the Moselle country, but they were Germans sure enough. The butcher's wife said so, and she had once been to Strasburg."

The man seemed willing to talk indefinitely, but to little purpose, and Garvie went on his way, more disappointed than he cared to acknowledge. It was nearly a week since he had left Trêmalo, and what anxieties might not Julia be suffering?

He had stayed late at the club that evening, and as he went up the quiet Rue d'Assas, he had an uneasy feeling that someone was following him.

When he reached his door, he looked over his shoulder to see a furtive figure coming along in the shadow of the houses.

He rang, and as the door swung open in the mysterious fashion of Paris doors at midnight, the man behind brushed past with a whistle that had been a call in Julien's studio.

"Here! Who are you," Garvie cried out sharply.

The night was one of alternate storm clouds and moonlight, and now, as the stranger turned, the moon shone forth, and Garvie found himself looking into the missing man's face, ghastly in the white light.

It was Thorpe, sure enough, but Thorpe bearing signs of fatigue and exposure, perhaps even of want, in shabby clothes and face that seemed all eyes and cheek-bones.

"Heavens above! Is it you? Why, I have been searching the country for you."

As though to make sure that even now Thorpe should not evade him, Garvie grasped him by the arm, and felt how thin it was.

"Do not be afraid, I am not a ghost. What there is of me, is real, anyhow. Yes, it is me, all right. May I come up to your place for an hour or so?"

There was nothing visible of the morbid pride in defeat that Garvie knew to be a characteristic of his. Instead, his attention was caught by a new sturdiness, that seemed to set the man above his travel-worn aspect.

"Of course you are coming up. Do not think I am going to lose sight of you again in a hurry. Wherever have you been hiding yourself?"

"I will tell you presently. Look here, can you give me some food? Anything will do. I have had nothing but a cup of coffee and a roll to-day."

"The food is there all right. Come along," was all Garvie said as he led the way up to his third floor flat. He felt, with an inward groan, that every evil prophecy was being fulfilled by this return of the prodigal.

A short laugh greeted him.

"Yes, I am just a common tramp, that they would set the dog on at home and I am half famished and footsore at that. But do not look so shocked. I tell you, I have got a lighter heart than I have known for many a day. I ran away under fire once, like a coward, but now I have come back to face the music. If you will back me up, I will make you the instrument of justice," he added, with a wistful look into the other's face.

"I will back you up, all right," Garvie answered, and their hands met in a pledge given and received. That new purpose in Thorpe's face made him give the promise without misgiving.

"Thanks. You won't mind my locking the door?"

Without awaiting an answer, he crossed the passage to do so, explaining, "I would just as soon that no one knows I am in Paris yet."

Garvie watching him, remembered his request

for food, and turned to explore. He produced from a cupboard a crock of *paté*, bread, a slice of *gruyère* and a bottle of Burgundy.

"That is the best I can do," he said. "But look here, I can go over to Clairons' and get you some stew. They are always open, you know."

"Why, this a feast for a king. It is evident you do not know how tramps fare," Thorpe pronounced with glistening eyes, as he fell to. At his first pause he spoke:

"You did not mind my locking the door? I do not know that I really mean to hide. You will be better able to tell me if I need to, when you have heard my yarn. I am not going to shirk any of the penalities of my own folly, if only I can jump on a certain reptile and choke the life out of him."

"Meaning Britski?"

"Exactly so. How did you guess?"

"Oh, well, things have been happening—"

"Have they?" and Thorpe looked up, a vengeful light in his face. "They are welcome things if they reveal his cloven hoofs. But say, wont you talk while I eat? There is such a lot I want to know. How is Miss Dorr?"

His voice shook on the name, and Garvie took care not to look at him.

Obediently he began and sketched the story that Sylvia had told him in the Bois. It was not long before his listener had dropped any pretence of eating, and more than once, explosive *sacrés*, mingled with forcible Anglo-Saxon swear-words, interrupted the tale.

As it ended, a brown, weather-worn hand seized Garvie's in a vigorous grasp.

"Good chum! May I live to pay you back for befriending her. That settles it. I will get the knife into Britski, no matter what the cost is."

"Will the cost be heavy?" Garvie asked gravely. Britski's threats were strong in his mind.

"That remains to be seen. Anyway, I will pay the cost all right. And so you sent her to the Praeds at Trêmalo? I rather fancy that old gentleman is to be my weapon of retribution. He and his collection come into the story that I have to tell. But give me your version while I finish this *gruyère*. Jove, it is marvel the difference a meal makes in a man."

Gravie told the tale of Virginie's conquest of Mr. Praed, and his listener laughed out heartily.

"It is no laughing matter to have Miss Praed in contact with that girl's deviltry," Garvie protested with a touch of irritation.

"You are right. It is not, at least it would not be, if their sublime impudence was not about to meet with a downfall. When you have heard my story, you will understand," Thorpe said, settling himself for his narration.

"Have a cigarette?"

"Thank you." And when he had started it, he began.

Things already familiar to the other he passed

over sketchily; to fresh facts he gave more minute details.

He spoke of his continued ill-luck, when the men around him were praising work that he could not exhibit, could hardly even sell.

"Though I doubt if any of you knew how often I went hungry to bed," he added. Then seeing the look of pain on Garvie's face, "Not that it was your fault, old man. You would have fed me up like a prize pig every night for the asking, I know."

"I ought to have done it without the asking."

"You did, many a time."

There was an old dealer in second-hand rubbish in a small den not far from Thorpe's studio, and this Jew would occasionally take a canvas of his for a few francs. What became of them Thorpe did not know, for he never saw them afterwards in the dusty windows amongst the old iron and books.

His discouragement had taken the freakish turn, which incipient despair sometimes manifests, and he would lounge in the Louvre or Luxembourg, studying masters old and new, with the idea that by trying to curb his strong originality he might find the path to success.

It was in accordance with this half-joking theory that, on a summer's day excursion, he painted the sketch Sylvia had recognized at the Meudon villa.

"I will give you ten francs for it," said the Jew when he took it to him.

To his protest that the sum hardly covered the cost of paint and canvas, the old man rejoined.

"Twelve, then. Take it or leave it. I can buy a dozen as good any day."

The problem of to-morrow's meals was too imminent for him to hesitate, and the sketch vanished in old Abraham's clutch. A day or two later, Thorpe was forced to swallow his pride and implore credit from Britski for the frame of a picture on which he based high hopes in an American exhibition.

The picture-dealer was quietly inexorable, and seemed to have reason on his side when he spoke of the unpaid frame for last spring's Salon picture.

Thorpe was turning away in a grim silence that veiled a sickening sense of failure, when Britski called after him.

"By-the-bye, old Abraham persuaded me to take, as part of a bad debt, a little sketch he got from you, a vague landscape bit. I have an opening for such things just now, and if you can bring me some more in the same style and they satisfy me. You ought to do Cazin effects well— I will see about letting you have your frame. Only, you must work out its value before you get it. No more credit here—nor I think elsewhere," he added significantly.

It was a glimmer of hope on a desperate situation. If he could get no more frames, all chances seemed closed to him.

He hurried back to his studio, and hastily ransacking his studies, spoils of the past summer, he set to work on them as he had never worked before. In two days, three more small canvases were taken to Britski. Two he chose, rejecting one that was most up-to-date in treatment.

"There is a demand for things of the Barbizon school—stick to that," he said. "Bring me more like these two, and you shall have your frame." The others were painted and brought, and Britski promised the frame.

Leaving the shop with a lightened mind, Thorpe threw a careless glance at the window, where, as usual, the red velvet draperies set off one or two choice paintings. What was his amazement to see, in the central place of honour, his own Ville d'Avray landscape, his careless initials obliterated, and the unmistakable signature of Corot in their place.

This, then, was the reason of the order. This was the demand for the Barbizon school! He had sunk to be one of those forgers of better men's work of whom he had heard, men whose course lay

In the scorn of the Outer Dark

that surrounds the artistic Bohemianism of great cities.

In his first wrathful impulse, Thorpe turned to re-enter the shop, but a sense of pride checked him, making him unable to put this shameful thing into words.

And so he strode away to hide in the solitude of his studio, even the street passers-by seeming to come too near to the raw edges of the wound.

The careless life he had led had tarnished many of his personal ideals, but its corroding fog had had no powder to assail the lofty heights where he had enshrined his art. Those had hitherto remained clear and undimmed. Now, the darkness seemed to have engulfed him and them alike.

It was two days before he mustered courage to return to face the foe.

"See here," he began brusquely," I am not going to do any more more of those 'Barbizon school' things."

"Indeed, and why not?" was the suave reply.

"Because, whatever failure I may be, I am not the forger you seemed to think me when you had the damned cheek to put that thing in your window re-signed as a Corot."

"And I suppose you never dreamt of such a possibility when I took the painting that had no value under your own signature?" sneered Britski. Then with an abrupt change into the voice of an angry slave-driver:

"See here, then. That frame is not delivered to you yet, and it never will be if you turn coward and make any trouble now. If you are fool enough to quarrel with your bread-and-butter, I have a newspaper man or two at my beck and call who will soon have some nice little paragraphs going the rounds, to tell how the disreputable young *rapin,* Rupert Thorpe, tried to take in the high-toned picture-dealer, Monsieur Britski, with clumsy forgeries. Go home now and paint me a Cazin, as you can paint it if you choose."

In a choking mist of helpless wrath, Thorpe walked away, to go down into dark valleys of humiliation. It was in those days that he began to give up meeting Sylvia Dorr. He would have avoided all his comrades if the persistent friendship of Garvie, Frye and Howe had not made this impossible.

He mechanically carried out, with a certain fatal dexterity, the orders he received from Britski. All feeling seemed numbed into quiescence. He had just enough purpose left in him to go on with the Salon picture, begun with such high hope, and to hoard every possible franc towards getting it framed without Britski's knowledge. No shadow of his evil genius, he was resolved, should fall on the one thing into which he put a superstitious hope. It alone could save him from his enemy's clutches. It became his fetish, and when too exhausted to stand any longer before it, brush in hand, he would sit staring at it studying every detail with a view to possible improvement in repainting. Throughout this tragic time, he was not without glimpses of Sylvia, for, knowing so well the routine of her life, he could often watch her from a distance as she came or went. Not too often, though, for the sight would sometimes unman him, forcing him down into the depths where death beckoned to peace.

He had enough stuff in him though to set his teeth and mutter, "It will take more than Britski to drive me out of the world."

The day that Garvie found him at the Taverne du Panthéon, the waters seemed to be near closing over his head. The offered chance of painting Julia Praed's portrait roused him into a fresh struggle for existence, and the meeting with Sylvia acted on him like a saving spell.

If he ever had enough success for his work to become of any value, he said to himself, why should he not be able to buy Britski off with the sacrifice of an occasional picture. Surely it must be to the man's advantage for his work to increase in price.

Once free of him, he would go back to America, and try for portrait painting. These new hopes were dashed to the ground by Britski's curt mandate to drop the portrait, and go away to the country for a week or two.

He rebelled against this order, and, defying Britski, announced his intention of keeping on with the work.

"Very well, in a few days you shall see what power I have to make or mar," was the retort.

He did see, when the refusal of his Salon picture came, a picture for which good judges had predicted a No. 3. He was crushed. It was evident that Britski intended him to remain the poor tool he had become, lost to all his early promise.

He wrote the letters to Julia Praed and to Sylvia, letters which cut him off from his friends, and after posting them went back to hide himself in his studio.

XXIX

HUSKS

THE night that followed was a momentous one for Thorpe, for throughout its sleepless hours it was a toss-up whether or not he would then and there end a life stamped failure.

Some inherent sturdiness of nature prevailed, or perhaps it was his very youthfulness that cast the die. It does not come easy to turn one's back on the world at twenty-five.

Mechanically he began to pack his things as though for a journey. The action in a measure, cleared his brain, and as he worked, a certain purpose evolved itself in his mind. He was not going to forge any more pictures at Britski's orders, and he was not going to sink into one of the more or less disreputable hangers-on of the studios and cafés of the Quarter, who live on borrowed five franc pieces and lie in paupers graves. Neither was he going to be driven out of the world, which besides containing Sylvia Dorr, held so much beauty.

Billows and breeze, mountains and seas,
Mountains of rain and sun.

What was he to do then? The one thing certain was that he must get away from Paris, where Britski blocked every road.

There were other places besides Paris, though. He had not enough money to take him to America, or to make a fresh start among the artist groups of Munich or Venice.

Then the wayfaring instinct of men who had hewn down northern forests, had crossed prairies to make themselves a home, revived in him their descendant. He would go out on foot into the green highways where the solitudes of sun and wind might wash the city stains from his spirit.

He would, for a time at least, leave the craft he had debased, and take up some humbler fashion of earning his bread.

As these vague thoughts took shape, he was scattering the contents of a cupboard used as a lumber-room. Here was the camera, which, one time when cash was more plentiful, he had bought to use for studies of boys bathing.

He had grown skilful in photography, and, but for the expense of materials, might have gone on using it to fix a difficult pose, or a study of drapery. The camera was good, and the whole outfit was lightly made for traveling.

As he looked at it, his own careless words of the day before came back to him, bringing a sardonic grin to his face.

Why not turn traveling photographer, going far from railways, putting up at village-inns, haunting fairs, working south as winter came, according to the fashion of tramps the world over?

At all events, he might in that way keep himself honestly, and hide himself from all who had ever known Rupert Thorpe.

In the blind alley to which he had come, even this opening seemed tempting. No sooner was the idea entertained than it was acted on.

In the sunny April days, Thorpe was tramping the pleasant vineyard country of Champagne, his face turned eastward. He had taken the train as far as Troyes, so as to get well beyond the suburbs of Paris, and plunged into the heart of rural life, keeping clear of anything larger than a village.

The adventures, good and bad that he encountered, would make a story in themselves. At first, he tramped in bitterness of spirit, caring little where he went or what happened to him.

But the outdoor life and exercise, the isolation among those who bore hard work and scant food, and utter absence of comfort and pleasure with the stoicism of habit, often with cheerfulness, acted gradually as a tonic, and in a fortnight he had acquired the armour of a new philosophy of life.

In his worst time, he had lost even the artist's power of vision, but now as he went his way, the world once more became to him a possible series of great pictures, of studies to be thought out with loving care, and his fingers itched to be at work again.

With the restored activity of his mind, he realized that he had made but a poor fight of it against Britski; that he had been a fool to let himself be driven out without asking advice from any friend. Surely, it must be possible with so unscrupulous a man to find the weak point in which a counter attack might be made.

He was daily drawing nearer to the regions where the Moselle winds through the lower slopes of the Vosges mountains, and the villages began to have a less purely French aspect.

"Monsieur is going to Epinal?" said the innkeeper as they smoked their evening pipes together on a bench before the door.

"Epinal!" What associations made the name sound familiar? He had certainly never been nearer the place than he was now.

A tall, blonde-haired woman in a blue cotton dress, passed along the road, and as she went supplied the missing link of memory.

It was Marie Krugg, the silversmith's wife at Neuilly, of whom the woman reminded him, and it was she who had told him that she came from Epinal.

He had met this queer couple when, late one evening, he had gone on some half-furtive errand to Britski. He had been struck by their sullen shyness as of untrained animals astray in city streets, and following them out, had begun to talk to them.

His casual fashion won their confidence, and

he paid them more than one visit at Neuilly, and even gave some hints in drawing to the husband, who apparently, half-idiotic in all the affairs of daily life, was little short of a genius in his craft. Marie, who seemed the leading spirit, asked him questions which revealed a fear of Britski, and a desire to be back again in her own little town whence the dealer had tempted them. At first, Thorpe supposed that the work done for Britski was merely a matter of repairing old metal work, but one day he saw on the silversmith's bench, a porringer that was a gem of workmanship.

"Hello," he said, taking it up, "this doesn't need repairs, surely? It's fifteenth century, isn't it?"

The man shook his head solemnly.

"It is new. I made it," he said in his usual monosyllabic fashion.

"You! But it is pure *cinque-cento*. Where did you get the design?"

"He gave it to me, and I copied it," was all the answer.

It was that day that Marie Krugg, coming in from her marketing, broke out into frightened sobs over the enmity of the neighbours.

"They think us German spies," she said; "a little more and they will treat us as such. I don't care what any one pays for work that may end us in prison. Next week I shall take my man and we will go back to Epinal. I am frightened here. Perhaps you may pass by there some day, Monsieur, and will come and see us in the Rue de la Vielle Tourelle."

This was the last time Thorpe had seen them, and now, as he idly wondered what had become of them, it suddenly dawned upon him that if he could only find these people, here was his avenging weapon ready to his grasp. He knew that they had been working for Britski, whom he believed they feared and hated. He also knew that they looked on him as a friend, and so would probably tell him anything he wanted to know.

What a fool he had been not to think of them before.

Now, the question was, were they still in Paris, or had they returned to their home? He was only a few hours distance from Epinal and he would go there first, and make enquiries; if that proved fruitless he would return to Paris by train. He had been lucky of late in his visits to prosperous farms where the young folks wanted their pictures taken, and he had enough money for the journey, third class. That day a mail cart took him to Epinal, nestling against the slope of the Vosges with its ruined castle still keeping watch above.

The friendly driver pointed out to him as they jolted over the stones, the direction in which lay the Rue de la Vielle Tourelle and he was soon exploring that quiet street that skirted the great blind wall of a turreted convent.

Down by the river, was the modern stir of

factory and warehouses, up here among churches and schools reigned an ecclesiastical stillness.

Ah, here was a tobacconist's where news is always to be found, for those who do not smoke yet buy postage stamps.

"August Krugg? He who did the silverwork for the priest? Yes, indeed, he and his wife had come back from Paris, where they said the people were wicked and thought them spies. No doubt, August was a German from beyond Strasbourg, but Marie had been born in sight of Epinal, out there across the river, and had learnt her work of repairing church embroideries from the nuns up at the convent. Their house? Yes, they lived above the little shop where holy things were sold, rosaries and candles for the church.

"We are pious folk up here, Monsieur," the man ended with a fat laugh, "all save me, who would not have got this tobacco-shop from the government if I were."

The little shop with its window-full of ecclesiastical odds and ends was soon found, and above it, in a neat flat were the Kruggs.

Marie was, as usual, standing before her frame where an old church banner was undergoing repairs, and a regular tinkling beat from the back room told that her husband was at his trade.

Her welcome was warm.

"August," she cried, "here is the gentleman who was good to us in Paris."

August appeared, in his long white blouse,

quite able to speak French when it suited his humour.

Their tale was soon told. Marie had got an idea that Britski was a Jew, and that she would peril her soul by traffic with him. Coming across a priest from her own Lorraine, she had told him of her fears; of the secrecy as to their work on which Britski insisted; of the costly objects which her husband was making from the models and drawings supplied to him, objects which were taken after dark to the shop, and never exhibited in the galleries. "Things that had strange figures on them instead of the saints," she said.

The priest had given her the good advice that such secrecy implying fraud, the sooner she and her husband gave up the work and went home, the better. They went together to tell Britski that they must leave Paris, but brought down on their heads an avalanche of wrath in which he declared that if they made any difficulties he would have August arrested on the charge of selling him modern work for old. "And he will be put in prison until he is an old man, and will have to sit idle in the dark all day," he ended.

The terrified pair submitted, and beat a hasty retreat.

Again Marie sought the friendly priest for counsel, but he was out of town for a few days, and they dared not wait.

Hastily packing their few belongings, they left Paris, only breathing freely when once more under the wing of their church patrons at Epinal.

"And August is making a beautiful monstrance for the cathedral at Nancy. The cathedral! fancy then, monsieur!" Marie added proudly.

Her face had lost its sullen gloom and she looked young and pretty.

A canary sang in the window above a row of plants, and there was an air of peaceful happiness over the little household.

Thorpe felt his heart swell with sympathy for these simple folk. With all their simplicity, they had been more adroit than he, in freeing themselves from the spider's web. Now, to impress them with the dangers they had escaped, and to get at what incriminating facts they could supply him with.

"You were right," he said shaking his head solemnly. "He is a Jew and a bad man into the bargain. Those things that August made, he was selling to rich men at a hundred times the price he paid you. But people have found him out, and he may be put in prison himself before long. If you had stayed he would have tried to cast the blame on you."

"Holy Virgin!" Marie cried as she crossed herself.

"You said that I was your friend in Paris," Thorpe went on, "and if you can help me to any proof against this rascal, you will be doing me a great kindness, for he harmed me as much as he said he would harm you. He has driven me away from my work, and I cannot go back to my friends or to the pretty girl who loves me—" Marie clasped her hands in an ecstasy of sentimental sympathy—"until I can prove what tricks he has played."

He paused, and husband and wife looked at each other. "The drawings! Fetch them, then, August."

Then Thorpe heard how every drawing and working plan supplied by Britski had to be returned on completion of the order. With the cunning that often accompanies a slow intellect, August had made minute tracings of each design before surrendering it, and had carefully saved the papers. These papers, Thorpe unrolled with an interest that was almost painful. They might mean so much to him.

Absorbed as he was in his own aspect of the affair, his trained eye took in with delight the beauty of design.

Here, amongst others, was a patera chased with reliefs that seemed to portray the contest between Bacchus and Hercules. It was bordered with medallions evidently representing Roman emperors.

A second piece, a large dish, was embossed with scenes from the story of the abduction of Briseis and her restoration to Achilles.

"And you made these things—you?" he asked in amazement, of the placid-faced workman.

327

"I did them all—in silver," was the proud reply. Then, understanding Thorpe's incredulous stare, he added, "I could not have done them if I had not worked for years in the studio of Schwartz, the great bronze-maker."

In all, August seemed to have produced about eight or ten of these works of art for Britski.

"The last one he hurried me with, and when I took it to him he bade me carry it into a room, and there were all my beauties being packed away in cases. And the name painted on each case was the same. I remembered it, and Marie wrote it down. Here it is."

Thorpe's head was swimming with his own success, as he read the address to a

Maison Guillou,
Lorient,
Department of Morbihan.
To be forwarded by sea.

He would have been puzzled enough at this costly stuff, fit only for state museums or a millionaire's collection, being sent to such a remote corner of France, if he had not heard Mr. Praed talk by the hour, during his studio visit, of the wonderful Breton chateau with its still intact ancestral plenishings, which Britski had discovered for him.

Now it was all plain enough. The man had actually had the impudence to stuff some old house with rubbish to be palmed off on Mr. Praed as genuine. He had gone too far, and delivered himself over into the hands of his enemy.

With grim triumph, Thorpe reviewed the situation. He knew that Garvie was interested in the Praeds and would be willing to make an effort, if only for the daughter's sake, to free the father from the humiliating position of a dupe.

Garvie had been his friend too—so, indeed, had the Praeds—but perhaps he had disgusted them all by his unreliability. Perhaps Garvie might refuse to believe his story.

Well, if it came to facing his former friend's contempt, he would take his punishment manfully.

There was nothing he dreaded like being branded before those who had made his world, comrades, older men who had praised his work, as one who had debased his art, but if that too must come, it must. All his heart was set on the defeat of Britski, on winning back to the honest standing he had lost.

He would make his way to Paris and find Garvie, and consult him as to the best means to cow Britski into harmlessness.

If in so doing he were to be of service to the Praeds, all the better, for he had kept a warm memory of father's and daughter's kindness.

And so it was with spirit eager for the fray that he persuaded the Kruggs to entrust the drawings to him, and prepared to start for Paris.

Then came a reverse of fortune that checked him with its renewal of ill luck. In his last day's journey he had lost one of his cherished gold pieces that made travel by train a possibility.

It was a knock-down blow, and for an hour or so he paced the river bank in sombre mood. But his new purpose was not to be readily abandoned. If he might not go by train, he would start afoot. With luck he might earn enough to pay his railway fare for the latter part of the way.

It was done. Sometimes on foot, sometimes getting a day's drive; once or twice, going a bit of the way by train.

He often slept in barns, now and then under the stars. He spent not a sou more on food than was needed, but at last, gaunt and travel-worn, he reached the bourne of Garvie's studio.

"I never dared think what I would do if you were still *là bas*, for you are the only man I felt I could ask for some cash to go on with," he ended. "And now tell me," with a painful fixity of stare, "do you think that I can ever take my place as an honest man among you all again?"

Through Garvie's mind flitted a jumble of old-Sunday school lessons, "the ninety-and-nine which needed no repentance," "the sheep which was lost," but such phrases would have sounded incongruous to them both and he could only stammer:

"My dear fellow—don't be morbid—you're all right."

Poor as the words were, they served their turn, for the other muttered hoarsely:

"I knew you would not go back on me. And I do not mind you knowing, but if Britski gets

cornered and brings it all out, it will be hard to
have all the other fellows talking of it, and Sylvia,
though I would tell her if ever I saw her again—"

You will see her soon enough," Garvie interrupted, "for in my opinion, the best thing we can
do is to start right away for Trêmalo, and tell Mr.
Praed the whole story. Between you and me, we
ought to convince him that he must shake off this
scum that have fastened on them. You do not
know the service you are doing me in enabling
me to get Miss Praed out of this unpleasant position," he added, more gravely.

He had struck the right note, and Thorpe
brightened to it.

"And what is more, you don't need to ask cash
from anyone," Garvie went on, "for you have
only to cross the gardens to Howe's diggings
where you will find a millonaire sitting on the
doorstep begging to be allowed to buy your 'St.
John's Eve.' "

"Do not fool me, there's a good chap," Thorpe
pleaded, paling under his tan.

"It is truth, I tell you."

Thorpe shook his head.

"It does me good to hear that someone wants
the thing I nearly broke my heart over, but I
could not sell it now, you know."

"Why not?"

"It would not be fair, when my name may be
in all the papers any day."

"It is not going to be. I will see to that. But come, you are dropping with sleep. We can settle the rest to-morrow."

XXX

THE FATTED CALF

THORPE slept on the studio sofa saying, "Lord, it's a bed of down compared to my late average. And then—I remember a picture in a Pilgrim's Progress I used to look at on Sundays when I was a kid. There was a big, fat bundle rolling off *Christian's* back, while he danced a sort of religious Highland fling. Well, I feel just like that. I will sleep as only a tramp can sleep."

He was as good as his word, and Garvie had to shake him into wakefulness the next morning, for there was much to be attended to, if they were to leave town that night. With the awakening came matutinal doubts, doubts whether he was fully armed to attack Britski.

"Do you feel sure those drawings are proof positive enough to convince old Praed against his will?" Thorpe asked as they sat over their coffee. "For if they do not, he will be ramping round like the American eagle on the warpath. If, after all, there should not turn out to be any silver amongst the stuff Britski has put in the chateau, it strikes me that our case may fall through."

But Garvie was steadfast in his opinion. "I

am utterly and totally sure that no sane man can
help believing us. Let alone your and my iden-
tification of Virginie, and those photos I told you
of, I am certain the silver that Krugg made is
there and will be our proof. All along, I have
been puzzled as to Britski's reason for making
such an outlay, and running such risks for so
small an affair as the mere selling of that amount
of furniture would be to him. Now, if that stuff
they shewed me was merely used as a screen to
the real venture, it explains everything, everything, that is, except how he persuaded Mr.
Praed to keep from talking about the silver. He
must be asking a fortune for work like that."

"Still, you do not know that it is there?"
Thorpe persisted.

"Where else could it be? We know that it
was sent to Lorient, the nearest seaport. But,
anyway, to satisfy you, I will wire Miss Dorr
and find out for certain. I meant to let her know
that you have turned up safe and sound."

Casual as was the suggestion, it made Thorpe
wince with new sensitiveness.

"Why should she care where I am?" he muttered.

Seeing that it was not a time to mince matters,
Garvie spoke out, "Why she should I can not
say, but that she does I will vouch my soul for.
Heavens and earth, you idiot, when you get such
a woman to care as she has cared, to wait and
watch for news, to refuse to believe anything

against you, to persist that you were wronged—
well, I can only say that you are a pretty lucky
fellow."

"God knows I am!" Thorpe said, low and
tense, standing at the window, his back turned to
the other.

For a moment there was a surcharged silence,
then Garvie went on briskly, "I will give you a
bit of advice: If that millionaire of Howe's ma-
terializes, you take the money for your picture,
get married, and go and make a fresh start at
home."

Still Thorpe stood staring out at the opposite
houses. At last he spoke in the hard, brief
words of deep feeling:

"How can I think of accepting any man's
money for a picture of mine, or of asking Sylvia
Dorr to take my name, before I know that it is
safe from Britski's malice?"

Garvie saw that it was no use to urge him
further.

"Thinking about it can do no harm," he retorted lightly. "Meantime, we will send that
wire."

He had taken up a pencil when Thorpe interrupted: "Look here. Do not think me too
cranky to live, but I'd rather you did not wire.
I'd like just to go to her—" He stopped, and
then went on in a more ordinary voice. "After
all, I am certain you are right, and that the silver
is there, sure enough. And if the story I have

to tell does not convince any sane man—well, then, he is not sane, and must be locked up."

Garvie laughed and yielded the point, though he would have dearly liked to open up communication with the Trêmalo garrison.

His forbearance was rewarded by the postman's advent with a letter from Sylvia, telling of her arrival, and adding a few words about Julia that, while not betraying confidences, yet brought an eager light to Garvie's eyes. She was lonely and downcast, missed him; welcome news to any lover.

A rapturous shout from Garvie startled Thorpe.

"The silver's there, sure enough, and Britski is at our mercy. Just listen," and he read out the account Julia had given her friend of her visit to Rosbraz.

"Mr. Praed *must* prosecute now," Thorpe commented vindictively.

"I am afraid his wisest plan will be to hush it up," Garvie regretted.

Sylvia went on to tell of Mr. Praed's intention of buying Rosbraz, and ended with a strong caution as to his growing infatuation and the need of haste in any exposure. "I should not be surprised to hear any day now of his marriage," she said.

"Thank goodness, it is not so simple a matter to get married in France as it is in America," Garvie added.

Thorpe only reached out his hand for the letter, as though hungry to touch it.

Garvie now made ready to go out and attend to some necessary business, while Thorpe stayed indoors, out of reach of chance encounters. Garvie was to go to Howe's studio and get a trunk that Thorpe had left there.

"Afraid you will have a long day of it," he said.

Thorpe looked up from a blissful contemplation of Sylvia's letter.

"Oh, I shall enjoy the novelty of indoor life, I guess. If I might paint—" he added, with a wistful glance towards his friend's easel.

"Paint all you like, of course. You will find pochards and canvases behind the screen," Garvie answered, pretending not to see how Thorpe's hands shook with eagerness as he took up palette and brushes.

He found Howe in his studio, and at first had a little difficulty in quenching his eagerness to sell Thorpe's picture. As soon, however, as Howe saw that there was something not to be told, he waxed discreet, and took no interest in the destination of the trunk. The friendships of young men are the only ones unaffected by reservations.

"If you should come across Thorpe," he said at parting, "do get him to let me sell his picture. It is a pity to miss such a chance."

"It is all that," Garvie agreed. "I am off to Trêmalo tonight, and I may see him there."

"Off again? Why, you have only just come back. There must be a strong attraction down there to keep you from running the successful man business in town. Why, you will never be a lion if you do not let people hear you roaring round a bit."

"Oh, I will roar round all right, afterwards," was all Garvie answered.

That afternoon an appointment with a friend took him to the Salon.

One of the first people he saw was Miss Oakes in the stiff splendour of her Sunday dress, absorbed in study of the pictures as expounded by David Frye. Noting their evident pleasure in each other's society, Garvie checked his first impulse to join them.

"The old woman-hater," he chuckled, and turned in another direction. After all, it would have been difficult to talk to them without telling of Thorpe's return, and that was best kept secret for the present.

The next familiar face he spied in the crowd was Mrs. Mallock's. The expensive cosmetics lavished on that face were powerless to conceal her haggardness of anxiety. It twitched the corners of her mouth, it lurked in her furtive eyes. There was a queer flash of terror in those eyes as they met Garvie's. Then, without any sign of recognition she was sidling away into the crowd.

"The woman's frightened of me. All the more reason I should tackle her," he determined with a sudden inspiration.

A man can always make his way through a crowd quicker than can a woman. He has no skirts to be trampled on, no laces to catch on opposing objects. Mrs. Mallock made the fatal error of leaving the throng, and slipping into a deserted room devoted to architectural drawings.

Here Garvie cornered her, and seeing flight useless, she turned at bay with the ghastly semblance of a smile.

"Mr. Garvie! Why I thought that you were still in Brittany with our friends, the Praeds."

"I suppose that was why you sent Miss Praed those interesting photographs," he said grimly.

The poor woman gave an undisguised jump.

"Photographs?" she quavered. "I—I do not remember sending any photographs."

"Not of Mademoiselle Virginie Lapierre?"

"Oh, those!" with a strained giggle. "That was just a little joke of mine. Do you not even allow photographs of your precious model, Mr. Garvie?"

What a poor attempt at skittish mischief it was that Garvie answered sternly, "I do not allow anyone to misrepresent me to Miss Praed without repenting it."

Mrs. Mallock must have been in a state of arrant cowardice for she ceased to show fight at once, and metaphorically crawled on all fours.

"My goodness, Mr. Garvie. I am sure I never meant to misrepresent you to anybody. Why should I? Those photos were Britski's, and when I got hold of them I just thought it would upset some of his fine schemes if I sent them to dear Julia. Indeed, that was all. He had treated me so meanly, me who had taken the Praeds to him and to Marcelle, and who only wanted the usual little commission. A poor widow must live somehow, Mr. Garvie."

"I am not sure that I see the necessity," he commented. "And so you and Britski have quarreled over the prey, have you?"

"He has treated me abominably," she whimpered, carefully wiping away a genuine tear of spite.

"All the better for you, perhaps, if it comes to arrests for fraud. Then you are not in this pretty castle in Spain business, eh?"

She was wailing openly now.

"Oh, Mr. Garvie! Arrests for fraud! That wicked, wicked man! To think that I, with my social position to maintain, should ever have got mixed up with him! Indeed, indeed, I knew nothing about the affair until I found those photographs in his—in his room, and then I guessed. You believe me, do you not?"

Her hand was clutching his arm, and Garvie looked down at her in contemptuous pity for so invertebrate a thing.

"Strange to say, I do," he said reflectively.

"Though I do not know that it is much better to have tried to bargain Miss Praed off to that wretched little Faubourg rat. I know his unsavory record. Luckily for you, you did not succeed. Now, look here. If I let you off scot free, will you tell me all you can?"

"Indeed, indeed, I will," she gasped.

Garvie had bethought himself that the thoroughly scared woman might prove a useful source of information to leave behind him in Paris.

"Well, then, when did you last see Britski?" he asked.

"Did not you know he had gone?"

"Gone?" the word epitomized a whole commination service of wrath and dismay.

"At least, they say at the shop that he is out of town for a day or two; but there is a disorganized air about everything, and Marcelle is invisible. It is given out at her place that she is ill and ordered complete quiet."

"You know that she is his wife?"

A vicious sniff told that Mrs. Mallock was reviving.

"I know that she is called his wife, but whether he ever married her is another matter. If her hold on him was secure, she would hardly be so madly jealous as she always is. I believe that he has gone off with some other woman, and left her in the lurch. Madame Comerie is as mysterious as a great fat, white sphinx."

Without enquiring into the habits of such a

creature, Garvie meditated. The uncertainty as to
Britski's whereabouts hastened his desire to get
to the Praeds and find what was going on; in
other words, how Julia was faring.

He had little time to waste on this woman, yet
he would make what use of her he could.

"See here," he began, "if I promise to leave
you out of this row will you undertake to keep a
sharp lookout here, and wire me at Trêmalo if
there is any move among these precious people?"

"Oh, I shall be on the watch night and day, I
assure you. I will do my very best, dear Mr.
Garvie. And you will tell that sweet Julia, won't
you—"

"Do not make any mistake," he interrupted.
"If I let you off with a warning, it does not mean
that you are ever going to get within reach of
Miss Praed again—that is, if I can help it. Now,
go home, and take your lesson to heart, and try
not to be a disgrace to your country. Good day!"

With this admonition, he turned and left her.
Mrs. Mallock glared after him, a picture of baffled spite.

"You beast!" she muttered. "I may give you a
scratch in the dark yet. But it might have been
worse. After this, I cannot be too careful. Perhaps I had better try London for a change. There
are sure to be people I know about there at this
time of year."

Garvie made his way out as quickly as possible.
The knowledge that Britski was not in Paris filled

him with vague alarms. He was all impatience to be back in Trêmalo near Julia.

He found Thorpe blissfully absorbed in the study of a great bunch of pink peonies, that stood in an earthen jar.

"Back already?" he said stretching himself. "Jove, I have been having a regular picnic. The smell of the blessed paint fairly hypnotizes one."

Something in the restrained eagerness of Garvie's face checked him.

"Well?" he asked.

"Britski is not in Paris!"

"Where is he, then?" came the quick demand.

"Do not know. Wish I did. Anyway, we are starting in two hours, and shall reach them tomorrow morning. If he is there—" he paused, and neither filled the blank.

"Come over to Clairons' to dinner. Your shewing up can not do any harm now," Garvie said practically.

XXXI

JULIA'S LONE HAND

DETERMINED not to acknowledge, even to herself, her many misgivings, her forlornness, Julia, on Garvie's departure from Trêmalo, took refuge in perversity. She told herself that as she could no longer trust this false friend, it behooved her to act in all things against the advice he had given her.

Following this theory she planned an attack on her father with the photographs.

"He must know that the ridiculous creature could not be a lady," she assured herself, forgeting that to Gabriel Praed this hardly presented the obstacle it did to her. Garvie's absence strained the situation between father and daughter in throwing them more together. Mr. Praed, while in one way relieved to be free from the observation of a man of the world, was bitterly disappointed that the hoped for engagement seemed to have gone up in smoke.

Julia's marriage would have been his best excuse for following her example. It had come to that now, and he was seriously thinking of asking this girl who for him epitomized old-world romance, to become his wife.

344

"She's a delicate, aristocratic young thing to take a rough old lumberman like me," the poor man said to himself, wistfully. "But I'll see that there isn't a pretty thing she doesn't have if she wants it. Old Gabriel Praed's money's good enough to make a great lady of her."

These amorous visions did not save him from the discomfort he endured in Julia's society. Sheepishly surly with her, he justified himself with the plea that her ill temper had driven Garvie away. "Just the same nasty, tricky ways as she tried on my poor, meek, Mam'selle that day. But I'll shew her that I don't mean to stand any nonsense."

For all these valorous resolves, his good heart was apt to go back on him, and revert to the old habit of affection, if he saw his girl looking the least bit less of her buoyant self than usual.

To avoid this, he took after-dinner refuge in the billiard-room, dreary enough to him with the noisy French chatter of the bagmen.

A man with a troubled conscience toward his womenfolk scents a scene from afar, and goes to much inconvenience to dodge it. But Julia in her way, was equally determined.

A chilly, rainy day had followed the early fine weather, and her indoor discomfort was evident, and further irritated her father.

"Why don't you get Mary Jane to rig up a sitting-room for you? There's lots of them studio rooms empty," he said as he stood at her door,

watching her struggles with a fire of damp wood.
The fierce sea-wind rattled the window and drove
the smoke out into the room.

Julia's red golf coat was the only spot of
brightness.

Abandoning the fire to its fate, she stood up
and confronted him with a look in her face that
made him consider a retreat to the masculine security of the billiard-room.

Her words did not match the resolution in her
eyes, for they were cheery and casual. "Oh that
is hardly worth while for the short time we are
to be here now. I suppose we will be off by the
end of this week? If we don't hurry we may be
too late for Venice, and that would be such a
pity."

"I thought you'd soon be tired of it," was the
brusque retort. "There's nothing as I know to
prevent you're being off to-morrow if you like."

"Oh, I might as well wait for you. I hate
travelling alone," she said, resolutely ignoring
the belligerence of his tone.

"Well, then, you may just have to wait longer
than you bargain for. You see, it's this way;"—
in his sudden determination he made an unguard-
ed step forward into the room, and a gust
slammed to the door behind him. He knew that
he was delivered into her hands.

"I've been a-thinking of it over, and I've made
up my mind to buy that castle down there, and
keep it just as it is—"

"To buy Rosbraz! Why, whatever would you do with it. We should never want to come and live there," she cried in dismay.

"That's as may be; anyway, I've made an offer to Mam'selle for it, and she has to pass it on to her lawyer people in Paris, and I never heard of a lawyer yet who was in a hurry about anything. I mean to see it out, and as those rooms in Paris are, so to say, eating their heads off in the stable, I think you'd better go back and look after them."

"If I get angry with him now, it is all over forever," was the restraining thought that curbed Julia into patience. All the fiercer burnt her wrath with those who had taken such an advantage of his simplicity.

"I could kill that girl," she inwardly raged, as she tried to think of the most convincing answer.

"It would be so lonely going back by myself," she said gently.

He was not to be propitiated.

"You came by yourself," he retorted.

"Yes, but that was coming to you."

"Well, stay if you like, but don't try to set yourself against what I want, for I warn you that I wont stand it," he blustered.

Her hands were toying with the envelope that held the photos, and the problem of shewing them was troubling her brain. She would venture it, though making no accusation.

"It is only, father, that I am anxious. Such

a strange thing—someone sent me these pictures. I do not know what they mean."

With a steady hand she held them out, so that he could see the two marked "as chatelaine" and "as A. G.'s model."

With a growl her father seized them from her, and scanned them eagerly, shuffling them in his hands like a pack of cards. The veins in his face swelled, and Julia saw a look that reminded her of a dreadful day in her childhood when he had faced alone an angry mob of miners who had come to threaten him.

"Some damn fool has got hold of a picture or two of Mam'selle," he muttered half to himself, then turning on her, "and they've thought as you were another fool that they could play with, up and down like a concertina. But don't you be fool enough to play with *me*, that's all. I'll take care of these pictures. They're no concern of yours. Look out you don't make 'em so!"

With this he turned on his heel and went, slamming the door behind him.

A gust shook the window, and sent an answering puff of smoke into the room. Julia looked from door to hearth and her mood was distinctly dangerous.

Fortunately her active nature sent her forth to brave the storm, in struggling with which she recovered her powers of endurance. That evening she wrote the letter asking Sylvia to come to

Trêmalo, though pride prevented her saying how sorely she needed a friend.

The next day she set resolutely to work to get through the time in as cheerful a fashion as possible. Taking possession of Marie Jeanne's two-wheeled dog-cart and smart dappled pony, she drove about the country in solitude, save for the presence on the back seat of Michel, the stable-boy.

She thus explored the neighborhood, basking for hours on the sands at Raguenez to watch the Bay of Biscay breakers roll in, wandering over the rocky cliffs at the river's mouth, venturing into the worst by-roads in search of some fourteenth century chapel or *calvaire,* some Druidic dolman or menhir that Marie Jeanne had told her of. In this fashion she took defeat and flourished on it.

All the same, when in a few days Sylvia's telegram came, she shed some tears of sheer relief. It was only then that she realized the full extent of her recent isolation.

In her present humour nothing could have so softened her as the thought that here was someone who, tired and unhappy, needed rest and comforting, needed the beauty of woods and seas as balm to her spirit.

"I shall take her for a whole long day by the sea. How different she will look after that," she planned with renewed spirits.

The next afternoon she started betimes on her

long drive to Bannalec station. "If she were to arrive first, she would think herself dropped down at the very tail end of creation," she reflected.

She was waiting on the platform when the train deposited Sylvia and her trunk. "Oh, how brown and outdoor you do look!" the latter exclaimed as they met.

"And what a poor, bleached indoors creature you seem. But we'll soon change that," was Julia's retort.

Through the lovely country, peaceful under the level evening sunshine, the friends drove in a temporary content that, for the time, veiled their more sombre mutual problems.

"What does your father say to my coming?" Sylvia asked presently.

Julia laughed harshly.

"To tell you the truth I think he looks on it as a re-enforcement of the enemy. Poor father you'll find him so changed. When I see the harm that creature has done him it almost makes me believe in the tales of witchcraft the people here tell. I assure you, it's not too pleasant a state of affairs here. It was a real act of friendship your coming. I don't know what I should have done if you hadn't."

"That was what Mr. Garvie said—"

"Mr. Garvie?" Julia interrupted, "then you've seen him?"

"Oh, yes, we met at the bank, and he asked me to drive up to the Bois as he wanted to have a long talk. He was so kind," she added with a little sigh as her thoughts went back to her own affairs.

"Get along, Sargent," Julia said, waving her whip over the pony. Then:

"And he wanted you to come here?"

"Why yes, he hardly gave me time to pack my trunk, he wanted to get me off so fast. He seemed so worried about you, and said he never would have left Trêmalo, but to try and find means in Paris of showing your father how he was being cheated."

This was said in the most matter of fact fashion, and Julia kept her eyes fixed ahead as she asked briefly:

"Did he tell you how horrid I had been to him?"

"He told me that some of these people had tried to set you against him, but if he thought you horrid he'd hardly be in such a hurry to get back here as soon as he can, would he?"

"You're a dear," was Julia's irrelevant comment.

XXXII

RE-ENFORCEMENTS

JULIA was mistaken as to her father's welcome of Sylvia. True, he had received the news of her coming with marked grumpiness, but as they drove to the door, in the clear, yellow twilight, he greeted them with the nearest approach to heartiness that Julia had seen for days.

"Thought you were a better whip than that, Miss Julie, not to get here under the hour. Here's Mary Jane trying to save a fresh salmon hot and good for you, the which I did my best to tell her can't be done. Salmon's not going to be kept waiting for nobody. Come along in, Miss Sylvia, and we'll try if the good lady hasn't got some fizzy stuff as will put a bit of colour into them cheeks of yours."

This was surprising enough, but the reason for it was revealed two mornings later when Sylvia, sitting at the door waiting for Julia to start on a ramble, was joined by Mr. Praed.

She had already noticed a change for the worse in manners and looks. The simple heartiness that was not without its own rough dignity was replaced by variations between a forced jocularity and fits of sullen brooding, which were apt to end in outbursts of anger. It was plain to be seen that he was a man ashamed of what he was about to do, while, all the same, resolved on doing it.

"Bit of change this from Paris, Miss Sylvia," he began, with a comprehensive wave of the hand towards the quiet Place.

"Yes, indeed, and a very welcome change too. Big cities are apt to get on one's nerves in spring-time," Sylvia agreed.

"Exactly so. And you look as though it wasn't before you needed it—fond of travelling, eh?" and Mr. Praed glanced sharply at her from under his beetling brows.

"I used to enjoy it once," she answered, with the feeling that he was leading up to some pre-determined topic.

"Been to Italy and Venice and all those places, I expect?"

Whether Mr. Praed thought Venice was not in Italy, Sylvia did not enquire.

"I have been a good deal in Florence and Ven-ice. It would be lovely there now."

"Eh, would it? Not too hot, eh? And I suppose you speak the language and can find your way round those parts easily?"

"Can he be going to offer to take me as a lady-courier on his honeymoon?" Sylvia marvelled, as she answered, "Oh, yes, I speak Italian well enough to get along. It is all very easy."

Her answers seemed to please Mr. Praed, who visibly brightened.

"Well, then, my dear young lady, see here," he said, one arm on the back of the bench. "I've got an idea in my head as I want to talk over. What say if you and my girl were to start off and take a little tour round them Italian cities you mention. I've been promising Julie that trip, but now I've got things to look after and can't go, and she's a sort of fretting and ain't happy here."

"No, Julia is not happy here," Sylvia put in firmly, in spite of an inward tremour, but even this much assertion seemed to irritate her listener.

"Lord knows why she shouldn't be," he growled, "but girls is queer. Anyway, she's taken fancies into her head, as perhaps a change might get out again. Seems to me that you and she might enjoy yourselves together." A wistfulness came into his voice, as though he were remembering the recent time when he would have enjoyed himself with them, and Sylvia felt a genuine pity for the man. "And seeing as money aint any object, I don't see why you shouldn't have a good time, all expenses paid. Perhaps," he added doubtfully, "when Julie comes back, she'll have got over her silly fancies against that poor Mam'selle down at the castle. I guess she's told you about it, the way girls tell each other things."

He peered at Sylvia as though he were really anxious to get at Julia's point of view.

With a sudden resolve the girl took her courage in both hands, and spoke out desperately:

"Mr. Praed, you have always been kind to me, and I know that you mean to be kind now. Do let me try and help you a little bit in return. If Julia is unhappy surely you must see that it is because she cannot bear to be estranged from you, cannot bear to see you imposed upon in your goodness of heart—no, please, listen to me for just a moment—" She hurried on as he shewed signs of restiveness—"I know Paris better than you do. I have had bitter reason to know that Britski is an unscrupulous imposter, with his ready tools everywhere. He is cheating you now. He has filled this chateau with worthless stuff—"

She could get no further. Mr. Praed stood before her, trouble and anger struggling in his face, as he growled out:

"Look here, what's the good of talking like that? If you're trying to prove as that furniture's false, what are you going to make of Mam'selle, I'd like to know."

Sylvia would not give way before his wrath. "Dear Mr. Praed," she urged with a catching of her breath, "I know you won't like it, but I must tell you that she is a girl that Britski sent down from Paris. Mr. Garvie knows her—"

Here the storm broke.

"Garvie go to hell! I thought better of you than that you'd come making yourself the tool of Julia's jealousies, and that fellow Garvie's creeping round to slander honest folks at her bidding. Want my money, do they? Well, they needn't be too sure of getting it. I may have some one to care for me too, as I'll spend it on. I thought better of you, I say, Miss Sylvia. You and Julia can do what you like, go or stay, but as long as you're here in this house, I sha'n't be. I'll go over to the hotel at Concarneau. It won't take me much longer to get to the castle from there, and that's all I care about now. You tell Julia, with the compliments of Gabriel Praed, that he never was known to give in to any one as tried to bluff him, and won't now. She'll find she'll have to swallow the dose, sooner or later. Here, where's that Mary Jane? I want my bill!"

The torrent of his wrath rolled off into the house, and his victim stood gasping as if from the effects of a shower-bath.

"Sylvia! Sylvia! Come up here!" sounded a low call from above, and looking up, she saw Julia's face peering over the window-ledge, framed in dark, disordered hair.

Lightly she ran up stairs and into her friend's room. Julia stood near the window, her hair hanging around her shoulders, a forgotten comb grasped in her hand. There were tears on her face, and a sob caught her breath as she gasped:

"Oh, he can't be really going, can he?"

She had evidently heard all, and Sylvia only nodded.

"Where is he? Oh, I mustn't let poor father go away like that! I must go and find him," and she flung down the comb and began to twist her hair into a heavy knot.

But her friend laid a restraining grasp on her arm.

"It is no use, just now," she said. "He would only get more angry, and say something you could never forget. You heard how he refused to listen to me."

Julia wrung her hands wildly.

"Oh, I'll promise to put up with his 'Mam'selle,' I'll promise anything rather than have him quarrel with me! You don't know all we've been to each other, ever since mother died when I was a little child, the youngest of them all."

But Sylvia had her arm around her now, and protested:

"The more he has been to you, the braver you must be for him now. If, from cowardice, you yield about this wretched girl, you help him to wreck the rest of his life. Think what she is, a model from the Quarter, a creature of Britski's. You can't guess what such things mean, but, in a way, I know."

"Yes, I can. I've seen the women in mining camps," Julia answered, half absently. She was staring out the open widow with the look of one listening.

"What's that?" she said sharply, as a burr and whiz sounded from the Place. The warning toot of a horn left no doubt, and the two girls rushed to the window in time to see Mr. Praed's back as the auto rushed down the Place towards the bridge.

He had been as good as his word, and had gone off to Concarneau without further leave-taking. Then Julia broke down and cried as she had not cried since her school days. The preparation of her father's estrangement had not softened the blow. It was home, and family, and all the sweet dependencies of childhood that were lost to her. But it was her father for whom she grieved more than for herself. If he married this girl, what would become of him when, before long, she revealed herself in her true colours? She dared not think of the lonely, shamed old age that lay ahead of him. Her brothers, she knew, would make less allowance for his folly than she did. He would inevitably quarrel with them, and so be completely cut off from his own family.

"Poor father! Poor father!" she sobbed, as she lay huddled on the bed, utterly abandoned to her grief.

For a time, Sylvia let her mourn unchecked, then as the sobs lessened, she began to talk to her and presently coaxed her to come down to the hotel garden, a high-walled, untidy, terraced place by the river, where they could talk undisturbed.

Julia languidly let her friend do as she would,

and it was not until they were established under the willow trees opposite an island where a mill droned sleepily to the river's babbling, that Sylvia made her first suggestion.

"Do you not think it would be a good idea if I were to go up to the post-office and send a wire to Mr. Garvie telling him what has happened? If he has succeeded in finding out anything, he should act at once."

Her words galvanized Julia into sudden energy, though of the stormy kind.

"You think that I am going to ask Mr. Garvie to help me, after the way I treated him?" she protested. "I really believe I would sooner embrace a whole armful of 'Mam'selles' with their 'damns' and 'devils'—so there."

"But if it was I who telegraphed?" Sylvia urged.

"He would know it was the same thing. If I am lonely and unhappy, it is just what I deserve. Promise me you won't, Sylvia," and with the words, tears seemed imminent.

Her friend looked at her with a mixture of penitence and mischief.

"I wonder if you will be very angry," she began, "when you hear that I wrote to Mr. Garvie the night I came. I never thought you'd mind."

"What did you say?" came the eager question.

"Oh, well, I told him about the journey, and meeting you, and how you looked—" she paused, but there came no sign of wrath, "and I said I thought there should not be any time lost in converting your father to common sense—and, oh yes, I repeated the story you told me about the silver. I thought it might help him find out something. I hope that did not matter, did it?"

"No, I don't think it mattered," Julia said quietly, "but all the same, don't let us send any telegram. I am going to think things out, and act for myself now."

To this Sylvia made no objection, and Julia sat silently watching the golden-brown ripples against a rock, as though reading from the open book of Fate.

Presently she looked up and spoke out her thoughts:

"I have decided to go and see that girl myself," she began.

"Oh, Julia!"

"Wait a moment. I have it all planned out. You see, father does not think it is proper to go there before half-past ten or so—he told me so. Said it was not French manners. Well, if I got up early, I could be there by nine o'clock, easy; walking by the shore, I mean. I do not want to drive and risk meeting him on the road."

"But if they won't let you in!" Sylvia urged breathlessly, seizing the first objection that offered.

"I'll get in somehow or other."

"But is it safe? These people may be desperate. You do not know who is in the place."

Julia laughed.

"I'll take a revolver. And when I've got in, I'll offer this girl a settled income for life, or a lump sum down, whichever she likes best—I can do it, I've got the money all right—if she will go off and never let father know where she is. She can't really want to marry him, you know. Perhaps there is some younger man, an artist, or something she'd rather have—" Here Julia blushed finely, and Sylvia gave an amused laugh.

Recovering herself, the former went on energetically: "If it takes all I've got, I should far rather work for my living than have this happen."

Here her inveterate buoyancy asserted itself, and she added: "I think I should go to Dawson City, and start a boarding-house. I'd make a fortune in no time. What fun it would be."

"If you really go—to Rosbraz I mean, not to the Klondyke—you must take me with you," Sylvia said.

The scheme seemed wild and dubious, but she felt that Julia had a right to try it if she chose.

Her friend looked doubtful.

"I'm afraid it might be too long a walk for you. I'm used to scrambling about the country, you know, and then I'm as strong as a horse."

"Oh, I'm a better walker than you think," Sylvia insisted, and Julia yielded, glad at heart not to go alone.

XXXIII

THE SIEGE OF THE CASTLE

THE May morning dawned over the country as a new, shining gift from Heaven. The first red sun rays scattered the river mists that veiled the Rosbraz walls, and drew long, level lines through the chestnut avenues.

When high enough to reach the courtyard, they found no lazily untidy girl lounging on the steps over her breakfast. Instead, there was Mère Suzanne, her parchment face, haggard under her black silk handkerchief, as she tugged at the heavy bundles she was dragging down to the landing.

With a stony stare, Virginie stood watching her, as though the work symbolized salvage from life's wreck.

"Here, then," the old woman panted, "lend a hand with this stuff. Britski won't thank you if, after his orders to bring the silver with us, you turn up empty handed."

At the same hour, Julia and Sylvia had finished their early coffee and gone out into the dewy, gleaming meadows, where every spring blossom seemed to be lifting its head to rejoice in existence.

Julia's face lacked its usual bright colour, and was drawn as though from a troubled night, but as they left the houses, she looked round on the still beauty and drew a deep breath of relief.

"It's a day that reminds one of *Pippa Passes*," Sylvia said, and then she quoted the lines ending:

> The morning's dew-pearled,
> God's in his Heaven,
> All's right with the world.

"Oh, don't!" Julia said with a little shiver. "All this glory seems to make wickedness and suffering such false notes in creation. I hate to think of that wretched girl I am going to see."

"Then do not," her friend put in with a detaining touch on her arm. "Look at those blue-bells instead," and they loitered a moment in the meadow-path to gaze down a slope that seemed to have caught a quivering line of blue from the sky overhead.

As they went on their way, Sylvia returned to the subject.

"I think that you, like me, are a bit sorry at heart for that girl. How can we tell what her life has been?"

But Julia interrupted vigorously.

"No, indeed, I am not sorry for her. Just think of the harm she has done, and may still do. If she had caused you as many wretched hours as she has me—" she paused, apparently following out her own thoughts.

Presently she went on in more subdued tones;

"If I could only be sure of seeing the last of her, forever, I believe I should be just as glad that the poor wretch did not come to any harm. I have so much, and she so little."

On they went, up on to the bare hillsides, down into green valleys where little fern-fringed brooks sang their way to the river.

Once or twice Julia looked at her watch, but forbore to urge Sylvia into haste, remembering that her feet were more used to the smoothness of town pavements than to these granite foot-paths.

It was later than she had expected though, when, rounding the last cove, they saw the mea-dows and chestnut avenues of Rosbraz, and be-yond them the chateau.

Sylvia shivered nervously. "How grim it does look. Every hobgoblin and wicked giant of my childish nightmares is somewhere in there, I am certain."

Julia laughed. She never quite followed the freaks of her friend's imagination.

"As long as father has not got there first, I do not mind the hobgoblins," she said.

They went on in silence under the flickering light and shade of the long chestnut leaves danc-ing to a southerly breeze, and now there was no more talking or laughing.

"Look!" whispered Julia, with a grasp on the other's arm, and they saw the witchlike figure of Mère Suzanne scuttling down the path like a black rabbit, a bundle grasped in her arms.

"Perhaps that is the fairy godmother," Sylvia jested under her breath.

"Do not let her see us!"

They skirted the landward side of the chateau, to reach the courtyard.

"Look!" again came from Julia, and this time it was an ordinary enough thing that so excited her. Two bicycles leant against the wall by the entrance.

"One is Mr. Garvie's. He left it in Trêmalo. I saw it in the hall, yesterday. And I know the other too; I hired it from Lorient when he was here. Who can have used them?"

Her face was all aglow with the undefined expectancy which Sylvia put into words.

"Mr. Garvie must have arrived on the morning train after we left, and got here ahead of us. He easily could, you know."

"But the other?"

It was Sylvia's turn for a wide-eyed hope, a hope that deepened and brightened into a full glory over her face, as they held their breath to listen to voices inside.

"It is Rupert Thorpe," she murmured to herself, her voice sweet as a half-awakened child's, then turning to Julia.

"They have come together. They must have got proofs against Britski," she triumphed.

365

"Come!" was all Julia said. Her eyes had answered the rest.

It was a strange picture that met them as they paused in the gateless entrance to the courtyard.

On the house-steps stood Virginie, facing Garvie and Thorpe who seemed to have just come upon her as she was running out, a small but weighty bundle in her arms. She wore the same demure mourning dress in which Julia had seen her before, but now the demureness did not extend to her hair, which swirled around her face in all its old, untidy splendour.

With haggard eyes she glared down at the two men.

It was Thorpe who was speaking and there was an almost pitiless ring of exultation in his voice as he greeted the girl.

"So, Virginie, we find you breaking up camp, eh? Going back to Paris, perhaps? Will you pose for me as a noble Brèton lady carrying off her silver before the sacking of the castle by freebooters? Heavy, isn't it?"

The girl bleached to a more deadly pallor, as she flashed out. *"Canaille!* If you two have followed those American girls to Trêmalo, why can't you leave me in peace? Does Monsieur Garvie think that the doll-faced daughter will have no money left to give him if I keep the old *bonhomme* under my thumb much longer? Ah, he is well there, look you. And the poor girl.

The one who smiles and sighs at Britski for her orders—"

Here Thorpe's voice broke in, clear and trenchant, as a danger-signal, "See here, Virginie. We have had about enough of this commination service, thank you. Just set down that bit of family plate you are clasping to your heart, and tell us quietly where you are going, and where Britski is picnicing to-day, there's a good girl."

His surface jesting and under grimness evidently puzzled and alarmed the model, and she sent a quick glance of inquiry towards Garvie who remained determinedly silent. He had promised Thorpe the first innings.

"Where can he be, save in Paris? How should I know what he does to-day?" she parried, her fierceness turning into sullenness.

"You know well enough he is not in Paris, anyway," Thorpe retorted, then with a sudden flash of insight, "Jove. I believe we've caught you in the very act of making off to join him on his way to one of those foreign haunts of respectability, such as Tangiers or Buenos Ayres, and that he is waiting round the corner for you now. So the little game is up, eh?"

The two listening girls began to understand the meaning of Thorpe's fluency. He was holding her there captive in the hope that if Britski were anywhere in the neighbourhood, he might suddenly appear in search of her.

That Virginie realized this, could be seen by

the desperate glances she cast from one side to another. The two girls had pressed on until they stood in the partial shelter of the round pigeon-tower, relic of feudal days.

Julia caught the wild-cat flash of her strained eyes, and was sure she had seen them, though she gave no present sign of it.

"I don't know what you are talking about, I tell you. The white wine of Nantes is strong, and you must have taken it early to be so *toqué,*" she said in attempted scorn.

Thorpe's answer shewed a contemptuous pity.

"You had better own up. In a way, Virginie, I am sorry for you. You know Garvie and I have always treated you fairly—"

"Fairly," came the shrill cry. "Was there ever a scoff or *blague* that you failed to sharpen on me? And he over there, who is afraid to speak one word for himself—" Again Julia met her eyes and knew that the words were flung at her—"how does he relish having his American *fiancée* know what my name was in the Quarter? 'Garvie's Theodora,' 'Garvie's redhaired model.' That's a bit different from Iseult de Rostrênan, eh?"

At the last wild words, an oath that was half a growl of wrath and half a cry of pain, rang out from the gateway, causing them all to look around and see Mr. Praed standing there listening. There was a certain dignity on his set face and rigid figure as he stood, intent on the girl to the ignoring of all else. After that first oath had been ground out, he made no sign, until Virginie pausing, he came slowly forward.

And now these two seemed only conscious of each other, the incongruous two had been so strangely brought into contact.

Julia's first impulse had been to run to her father, but Sylvia caught her hand and checked her, whispering, "He will mind it more afterwards, if he thinks you heard."

Instinctively Thorpe and Garvie fell back, and left Mr. Praed standing there alone.

For a moment there was a weighty silence, and then he began in deliberate tones, "Look here, Mam'selle, you just say that over again, will you, that about your being known in the Quarter as Garvie's model? I don't want to make any mistake about it, this time."

Shrill and clear came the prolonged whistle of a steam craft, almost unknown sound in these waters.

Each one listening started and stirred in an answer to it, as though it were separately a summons, a challenge, a defiance. The sullen despair in Virginie's face changed into wild recklessness.

"What is that to you, old imbecile?" she shrilled. "Ah, I was a charming *Mlle. Nitouche,* wasn't I? Well, you've got the chateau and the collection, and paid for them, but you haven't got *me. 'Adieu,* Papa Praed."

369

An airy wave of her hand, and she had slammed the great oak door and they heard the bolts grinding to. There would be no taking such a fortress by storm in a hurry.

"Is there any other door?"

It was Thorpe who spoke, and Garvie answered, "There may be. I only know of the one leading on to the chapel terrace, up there."

As he spoke he pointed beyond the pigeon-house to a tumble-down, ivy-grown wall, terraced to the height of the chateau's first floor, above which some old shrubs and plants clustered around a tiny grey Gothic chapel. This was the garden where the dames of Rosbraz had taken the air in troublous days.

Every eye was fixed on it as the sinuous black figure appeared there. She turned and looked down at them with a laugh, crying: "I wasn't a circus girl for nothing."

With one hand she caught at a branch of the old mulberry tree that overhung the landing, while her other still grasped the bundle, and swung herself down out of sight. Those watching caught their breath, though Garvie, who was most familiar with the place knew that, save for her woman's clothing it was a simple enough feat, as a big boulder rose beneath the tree.

"The landing! We may catch her there," Thorpe shouted, and had turned to rush down when he was checked by an iron grip on his shoulder.

"No you won't! You let her go." Mr. Praed growled.

"But don't you understand? It was some of the silver she had in her arms," he insisted, maddened to feel his proofs against Britski slipping out of reach. But Mr. Praed held firm.

"I understand, fast enough. It's none of your business. The stuff's mine, and I paid for it. *Let her go.*"

Dropping his hold on Thorpe, Mr. Praed turned and strode towards the landing, the two men following. From their corner by the pigeon-house the girls could see it all.

The tide was brimming high, and a little way from the shore lay a steam-launch, spic and span with white paint and shining brass work. On the deck crouched a dark bundle which represented Mère Suzanne, and near her stood Britski staring intently towards the landing. One hand, Garvie noticed was hidden in his pocket. "He's got a revolver," he said to himself.

The sound of oars in the water, and they saw Virginie, still poising herself after her leap from the boulder below the mulberry tree into a dinghy which a sailor boy was rowing out toward the launch.

The boat was light and skimmed over the water with a flashing from wet oars. In a minute or two they saw it pass round to the other side of the launch, where Britski ran to meet them. Garvie searched with his eyes, the curves

of the river and the opposite shore for signs of
life. Yes, there were some of the coastguards
fishing not far out. They would, he knew, have
no scruples in raising the hue and cry against
those whom they thought "Jew spies."

He strode up to Mr. Praed and said, "You
know that Drilski, who has cheated and robbed
you, is there, making off with his booty?"

"Yes. What of that?"

"You see those men fishing? They are from
the coastguard station opposite. I can easily hail
them, and they might get word to Lorient or
Concarneau—"

"What for?"

"The launch might be followed or intercepted.
It cannot be going far."

Then Mr. Praed turned on him.

"When I said 'let her go,' young man, I meant
it. I've been a fool, and I've paid for it. That's
all about it. There, they're off," as the launch,
already headed down stream, sped out of sight
round the nearest point.

He drew a deep breath, as though many illus-
ions had gone with them. "Now I'm going back
to the Concarneau hotel. You can come and see
me there this afternoon, if you like. Guess we'll
have some things to settle, anyway. Tell my
daughter she'll see me in a day or two."

"Julie!"—

For Julia was coming down the bank towards

him, the tears wet on her face, where a great tenderness shone.

"Father!" she said with a new timidity.

She had not looked at Garvie or greeted him, though every inch of her was conscious of the relief of his presence.

Mr. Praed waved her aside as he passed on. "Yes, Julie, it's all right. I'm just going off for a bit by myself. You go and talk to Mr. Garvie. He'll tell you all about it."

And so he went to "drink his bitter beer alone."

XXXIV

THE PRIMROSE PATH

STANDING on the bank in the simple navy blue dress she had worn the day she and Garvie parted, her hair hanging down in a long, thick braid, her wet eyes wistfully following her father, the magnificent Julia looked like the most delightful of penitent school-girls.

"Julia! I've come back to make friends! Aren't you going to give me any welcome?"

Her mouth still drooped at the corners as she murmured, "I'm ashamed to. I was so horrid."

A tender laugh greeted this, and then the gates of Eden swung open for yet another pair entering in to the blessed heritage of their youth.

Meanwhile Thorpe had caught sight of a certain slim, grey figure hovering in the shelter of the pigeon-house, and forgetting his baffled vengeance, had reached its side, receiving pardon for all his weaknesses in the glory that transfigured the delicate, worn face.

"At last," was all he could stammer as he held the thin hands in his.

But words came later in plenty, and his tale was told to a love that, like the God who created it, understood all and forgave all.

It was nearly an hour before the two couples turned their backs on the deserted chateau and started on their homeward way.

In the after years there were four people who remembered that morning walk through the Breton woods and meadows as a vision of the primrose path of joy, a vision to be recalled for comforting on days of disillusionment, in the grimness of winter city streets.

With sight of the village house-tops, the affairs of every-day life began to resume their reign, and before they reached the Place, Thorpe had even confessed to a fine hunger.

"Where did you breakfast?" Julia asked. The two couples had formed into a group for the better facing of the hotel.

"Marie Jeanne gave us a glass of beer, and some bread and cheese. How you bolted it, Garvie, and what an age ago it seems."

"You see," Garvie explained, "we were a bit nervous, when we heard your father had gone off, and we didn't know where Britski might be. It was rather rash, your going to the chateau," he added, with a look that told his pride in her venture.

"So Sylvia said," Julia laughed, "but I had this," and she shewed a smart little revolver.

"And Britski had its pair," Garvie commented.

Marie Jeanne who always rose to the occasion, had ready for them a festive luncheon that would not have disgraced a Paris chef.

There were pink shrimps and big red lobsters, and she herself had cooked the three dishes which have caused her name to be gratefully remembered in three continents.

There was a mighty bowl of classic *bouilleabaise,* redolent of garlic and saffron and red peppero; there were cutlets *en papillottes,* and last came an *omelette au rhum* borne in by Marie Jeanne herself with the blue flames leaping around it. At this they drank her health in white wine of Nantes, and her brief and apposite reply brought a laugh from the men, and a smiling blush to the girls' faces.

Now and then Garvie saw Julia's eyes grow pensive as she remembered how dark these hours, so bright for her, were to her father, but a low word from him brought back the light to her face —she could not help being happy.

"I suppose I mustn't come with you," she said wistfully, as Garvie ordered the dog cart for the drive to Concarneau.

It was a great temptation to the newly acknowledged lover, but he shook his head.

"I think it is better to do just as he said. There may be a chance of his coming back with me," he said, though he really did not think so. "And then, it might not be so easy to discuss you in your presence," he added with a smile.

"Me?" and then she remembered that it was her future that was to be settled by these two men.

Garvie took with him a bundle of letters and telegrams which had been accumulating during the last two days.

Meantime, with a blessed sense of relief from unshared cares, Julia slept away the afternoon hours like a tired child, while down in the garden by the river, Sylvia and Thorpe planned a happy future at home in Boston, when Sylvia's book should be brought out, and Thorpe would go in for portrait painting.

They did not yet know of the letter from a lawyer, even then on its way across the Atlantic, announcing the death, of an old lady cousin of Sylvia's, and a substantial legacy that was to make their start in life so much easier.

It was after dinner when Garvie returned, looking somewhat thoughtful.

"Come for a stroll," he said to Julia, and of one accord they turned towards the quay and the pine-crowned knoll.

"There is no doubt that it has been a hard blow to him," Garvie said, as they sat there above the river. "But if I'm not mistaken I took him his cure in those telegrams."

"Why, what were they?" she asked curiously.

"They told of trouble in mining stock, a slump in the market that he should have had his eye on. If he had been in touch with things it would have been all right, but as it is he may have heavy losses. Do not be frightened dearest," he reassured her, "if he does lose somthing, it's go-

377

ing to do him good all the same. As soon as he took the thing in, he braced right up and said: 'Ah, and so they can't do without the old man after all. It's time he was back there to pull them through. Gabriel Praed may have made a fool of himself when he got among these foreigners, but we'll show them he's not in his dotage yet. Next Saturday's boat for home—that's the ticket for me.'"

"Home!" Julia echoed, without the old note of gladness on the word, "then I shall have to—"

"No, you are not going," Garvie interrupted. "At least not unless you want a honeymoon among your mountains. We can go wherever you like. It is settled that we are to be married in Paris the day before your father sails. We return there at once, but perhaps you and I may soon be back here, for your father means to give you Rosbraz as a wedding present. How would you like to make a country home there? Could the chestnut woods and the heaths ever take the place of your mountains?"

"They could, if you were there," she answered softly. "But would you really like it? Could you paint there?"

"No better place in the world for painting. You have seen a Brèton spring, but wait till you see a Brèton autumn, when the bracken and the chestnut leaves are golden bronze and the heather is abloom. I have been feeling that I must get away from Paris, and all its studio talk, and work in solitude for awhile—and *this* solitude! You shall see the work I can do when I paint the genuine chatelaine of Rosbraz," and he pressed the hand that lay in his.

"But father?" Julia asked presently. "Do you think he expects me to live here? It seems like deserting him," and she sighed gently.

" 'Tell her not to be worrying about me being lonely,' he said 'I've got my hands full of work as just suits me, in straightening out this snarl. Guess I'll have been up as far as the Klondyke before I'm settled down ready to entertain her next summer at home.' I really think he is quite happy about you," Garvie added tenderly, "You know he always had a fancy for 'old man Garvie's son.' "

"That isn't strange," Julia asserted with more of her old gaiety.

And so, next day father and daughter met at the station, the awkwardness of the meeting lessened by the bustle of their start.

A little taciturn at first, Mr. Praed was soon talking away about his new plans, and Julia saw that Garvie was right and that nothing could have so well roused him as this summons to fresh activities.

On reaching Paris they found the art world greatly stirred over Britski's disappearance, but to Garvie's relief Mr. Praed's name never appeared in connection with it.

Madame Marcelle became bankrupt and the

Hotel Cleveland changed hands. Mother and daughter were recognized a year or so later in a South American city, in apparent prosperity.

Virginie Lapierre, her origin, her connection with Britski, remained a mystery.

THE END.